. . . And didn't Dale look like a young sun-goddess. Didn't she haunt me with her magical beauty. Didn't she seem to know a coronation was due her, and didn't she do all that she could to bring it on.

She let herself in that Sunday morning and woke me as she sat on my bed.

She was bursting with adolescence and her new sexuality. Her cheeks were fiery red and her lips looked stained as if with some kind of berry. Her eyes were hardly open she was feeling so much desire. The flesh of her body seemed to want to burst from her clothes and her roundness was even rounder with sensuality. I could hear her breathing short deep breaths as if she were strangling from all she felt.

She leaned down to me and I smelled her clean hair. She must have been lying on the grass outside because it smelled like a newly mowed lawn. Her breath was hot as the sun. Her breasts, above my hands, were so round in their red plaid shirt, so close . . .

Old Dyke Tales

Also by Lee Lynch
TOOTHPICK HOUSE
THE SWASHBUCKLER
HOME IN YOUR HANDS
DUSTY'S QUEEN OF HEARTS DINER

Old Dyke Tales

by

Lee Lynch

THE NAIAD PRESS INC.

1988

Printed in the United States of America
First Edition
Second Printing, March 1988

Cover design by Tee A. Corinne
Typeset by Sandi Stancil

Acknowledgements
"The LoPresto Travelling Magic Show" and "Oranges Out of Season" first appeared in *Sinister Wisdom*. "At a Bar, In the Morning" and "The Coat" appeared originally in *Common Lives/Lesbian Lives*.

Library of Congress Cataloging in Publication Data

Lynch, Lee, 1945–
 Old dyke tales.

 1. Lesbianism—Fiction. I. Title.
PS3562.Y4255O4 1984 813'.54 84-3439
ISBN 0-930044-51-7

I thank Debbie Pascale for her unfailing love and support and her editorial suggestions; Tee Corinne for naming this collection, for titling the story *The Abrupt Edge*, and for her constancy; Katherine Forrest for sharing her knowledge and great editorial skill; Donna McBride, Caroline Overman, Carol Seajay, Joan Nestle, Judy Sloan, Judy Rosenberg, Debbie Johnson, Harriet Desmoines, Katherine Nicholson, Michelle Cliff, Adrienne Rich and the Common Lives/Lesbian Lives Collective for their encouraging response to these stories.

for
Barbara Grier
whose commitment to
lesbian literature
has kept me working
in the face of
all my fears and discouragement,
when I too might have disappeared
into the silent legion

CONTENTS

FRUITSTAND I
Oranges Out of Season

My mother would give me an orange, as big to me then as an orange summer moon is now, and a little green lime which I'd name Baby, and I'd use them to set up housekeeping under this row of wooden shelving. One side of the fruitstand was the bedroom, another the living room and another the kitchen. This front area here was the yard. The orange was Mama.

Oh, I know it sounds silly, Curly, but that's why I say I been in this business almost half a century. You think I'm kidding? By the time I was five I worked after school, after *kindergarten*, dragging out bags of trash or empty crates. My father would give me a nickel for the afternoon. One day I asked for five pennies instead of a nickel for the gumball machine at Izzy's, the ice cream shop over there, across the street, see? Between the cleaners and the bakery. And he started me off waiting on customers right then, making change.

Oh, my family's been here a long time, Curly. Long before I took over and started hiring lazy babydykes like you. I pay you to help me and all you want is to hear stories about this place, the neighborhood. You know, people say all the time things are so different, but how do they say it?

1

The more things change, the more they stay the same, am I right? Yeah, the kids still come by, like I did, from the Sister school, in plaid pleated skirts and little white blouses. Can you believe I was ever that little? Um-hum, till I was about thirteen I was a regular shrimp like you. Then by the time I'm seventeen I'm five foot-eight. Never did gain the weight to go with it.

Look up there, middle of that next block, that's where I learned to shoot baskets. *Now* if I was seventeen and five-eight I'd probably get a scholarship to one of them Catholic girls' colleges snapping up the girl basketball players. So I'm teaching the little ones how to get snapped up. Yeah, I coach a team. Ten, eleven-year olds. Call themselves the New York Nukes. I know, I know, it's a crappy name. Don't even sound like a girls' team, but they voted for it. Give 'em more spunk, anyhow — can't beat the deadliest team in Queens. Am I right?

Oh, I got the fruitstand from my dad. Yeah, he died when I was twenty. I'm supposed to look just like him now my hair's gray. I stoop like him. From lifting all these crates *you* should be heaving. My mother died not much after that. I had to come in and help. If I hadn't, my mother would've killed herself trying to pick up the fruit at Hunt's Point four o'clock in the morning, then set up, run the store till six at night. She wouldn't have hung on the ten years she did. I was only supposed to be helping her. But, shit, she was *sixty*! She couldn't handle it. Yeah, I was born real late. She had seven before me. Practice makes perfect, you know! What — I'm not perfect? You're fired! How do you like that? Contradicting the boss. Here, let's at least fix up these pears. Poked half to death from these fussy housewives. Wait, that one's a mess, can't sell it, chuck it.

No, we were all girls. None of us was *expected* to help out here. I just liked it. Loved it, as a matter of fact. They sent me to business college after St. Andrews and I learned bookkeeping, so I worked a year in the city.

No, she must work for a different company. She'd be up on the next block if she works for them. Yeah, I loved it too. But it wasn't home, if you know what I mean. I wanted to work here. But my father, he wasn't ready to retire. "What would I do?" he always asked when Ma mentioned it. Oh, and complaining he didn't have a son to take over the business. I *told* him I'd take it, but he thought I was going to be like my sisters and be a full-time mother. Can you believe it? Every damn one of them, housewives on Long Island.

What are *you* laughing at — you that I picked up from the gutter! Seven straight sisters and then me? You're right, it *is* funny. And they're all real short! A bunch of cackling midget hens! Stop it, stop it, Curly, you're making me cry I'm laughing so hard. There, see, you dropped a pear — and here comes Mrs. Gonzalez. The rush is going to start, wait and see.

★ ★ ★

That wasn't bad, really it wasn't, Curly. For your first day. Sometimes it's so slow I think I'm going bankrupt, then all of a sudden we get twice as many and I don't know how I'm going to handle it. That's why you're here, for all the good you're doing me. Did you see that big blonde with the short hair? Reminded me of Sophie, my old partner. No, no, I'm not going to tell you about her till we get some work done around here.

What's to do? Lazy Brooklyn dyke. They didn't teach you to work over there? No wonder the Dodgers moved out. They were embarrassed to be from Brooklyn. Only kidding. I got nothing against Brooklyn. Just glad I was born in Queens. Come on, start hauling that fruit out from under the stands. No, no, the apples first. Here, put the green ones here, they got to pass them to get the eating apples, then they'll think of making pies. That's called merchandising. Sophie taught me that. Right side up, you backwards Brooklynite!

No, she was almost a real partner. Fought her off tooth and nail. She'd say, "Henrietta . . ." I was named for my father. They figured I was the last chance for a son. And Sophie always called me that when she was going to lecture

3

me. Anyways, she'd say, "Henrietta, you need vegetables in here. And to run your vegetables you need a partner." And I'd run her out of the store, even though she was working for me by then. This is where I met her, too, I tell you that?

The delicious next, the red delicious. Or should we go green, yellow, red? No, use the contrast. Put up the red delicious. Then the yellow. Here comes the milkman. Sophie's the one got me to put in the milk and bread, too. Thank goodness. I put it in a whole year before Nicky, who runs the vegetable stand two doors down, came. The ladies got in the habit of buying here and Nicky had to give those items up after six months. Didn't Sophie gloat then.

Oh, she was gay all right. Sophie was, but I wasn't. Well, okay, maybe I was, but I was the last to know it. When you were *nine*? Impossible. Now Sophie, maybe *she* could have come out that early. She was something else. I didn't know she was gay at first, but I knew she was real special.

First time I saw her my heart kind of heated up, you know how it is? What am I asking you? You're too young to know anything, you just *think* you know it all, smart aleck. Shut up, maybe you'll learn something. This is what I get, hiring a seventeen-year old dropout. What are you sitting on the orange crate for? You can't do no work if you fall and break your ass. That thing won't hold you. As a matter of fact, I'm putting you on a diet starting now. When Kathy brings lunch around I'm telling her to lighten up on yours. Yes, Kathy that I was with at the bar. She always brings lunch. Before her lunch rush at the diner. Over on Roosevelt Avenue, right across from where you got off the subway. She's the cook there. Good cook. That's why I married her. Only kidding. Twenty-three years we been together. Well, you better believe it, because it's true. And that's something else I have Sophie to thank for. Learning to work hard at loving.

Anyway, I'd look up from this table of fruit we used to have right here, parallel to the front — it was all open then. I'd sit behind it to wait on customers. The scale was there, and paper, the books, knives. It was my "office," but there was fruit displayed on it too, whatever was out of season, to catch the customers' eyes.

That was my father's idea. He'd always call one thing out of season, even if he couldn't get anything that week that was really out of season. He thought the ladies would splurge on something special. And it worked.

That week, I was using navel oranges. They're never really out of season if they grow in the right climate with the right care. But they were sure out of season for this neck of the woods. I'd cleaned off every one of them and they was sitting there shining — rough, bright orange balls, a surprise at Christmas time. And I'm leaning down behind them, doing the books or something. It was a slow time of day and I look up through this orange kind of glow from being surrounded by the oranges and working on them and all and there's this short-haired blonde, almost tall as me, with big gold hoop earrings. She was . . . misty looking, is the only way I can say it, with this orange haze around her and this real *physical* look about her. She looked like the word *sensuous* sounds. With these full lips like you'd have to kiss. And blue eyes, hungry looking, behind these almost matching blue glass frames.

What are you laughing at now, ignoramus? Remember we're talking nineteen fifty-seven, near thirty years ago. People wore glasses like that then. Yes, even lesbians. Sure she was wearing a skirt. Women wore a lot of skirts in those days. Besides, she was visiting her grandmother. Sophie was on Christmas layoff from the factory where she worked. A sewing machine operator. No, it was a lousy job. Hour after hour bent over the machine. One of those heavy industrial ones. Stitching leather. Now, that's a tough job. And getting paid lousy. She'd gotten fired a lot of places, that's why she was working there. But I didn't know that then. So she was shopping for her grandmother who was sick over Christmas. Sophie was, oh, caring. Do anything for you. Shopped here every day of her vacation, bringing her grandmother fresh fruit on her way from the subway.

Well, of course we got to talking. I can feel now the two

5

oranges I picked up and played with while we talked that first day. I was nervous and I juggled them, dropped them and just ran my fingers over them the whole time she was there. The skins were textured, and all the tiny grooves and pits and ridges were smooth and pleasant to find.

I remember my father when I was little used to hawk the fruit on the sidewalk like when he started as a peddler. "Awrengis ow-ta *see*zon," he used to call. They'd think I was crazy if I did that now, but sometimes I wish I could. I guess that's just what they call nostalgia.

Hey, you're goofing off again. And you got me doing it too. Naw, not yet. Kathy won't be here for another hour. What a teenager. You think about nothing but your stomach. *I* been up since three, you know, and ain't eaten since then. Eat some fruit, you're hungry. Careful, gently — don't bruise the other bananas in the bunch, the ladies won't buy them. One big stomach at your age. That's all you ever think of. All right, all right, *al*most all, you dirty little dyke. Am I right?

What did we talk about? That day I guess we talked about the neighborhood. I don't know for sure. Mostly I remember what she looked like and the oranges. Touching them was like touching her. I never thought of that then. I mean, she didn't just come out and say, "I'm gay, come home with me." No, we must have talked about the neighborhood because she'd been visiting her grandmother here all her life. She was a few years older than me, maybe twenty-three, twenty-four. Poor thing, she was from Brooklyn, too, just across the bridge, what's that section called?

What do you mean, what do I have against Brooklyn? I'm teasing you, you ragamuffin deisel-dyke. You're so touchy! Hit me again and I'll make you wait on Mrs. Muller. She's rough, man. Oh, she'll plow right over our stuff, leave a mountain of poked, peeled and smashed fruit and every display *un*displayed. Oh, I think that's what I'll do to you, just to see you apologize to her after *she's* made a mess and bought half a dozen of the eggs we got on special and absolutely nothing else. If she ever bought enough to make it worthwhile you wouldn't mind what a kvetch she is, but she does that to every one of us — Nicky, Frankie the fish man, the butcher. Even poor Nora who runs the florists across the street — on the corner, see? She even manages to paw her flowers and leave them wilting, though Nora doesn't have to put up with her every day.

Now Nora's nice, too. She and me got together a long time ago, after Sophie left and before I met Kathy. But she couldn't handle it. Ran off and got married a couple of months after we broke up, divorced him three kids later and moved back to the neighborhood to get fat. That's her uncle's shop, Nora just runs it. Salt of the earth. She has us over for coffee a lot. She's the kind of person who's only happy single.

You want to know why Sophie left already? I didn't even tell you why she stayed yet. She did come back after that first day, I bet you guessed. Well, anyway, every day we'd talk a little longer and pretty soon she was telling me she was gay. I guess I backed off and got kind of cool because she didn't come by the next day. Or the day after. And then it was Sunday and we were closed.

I took my mother to church on Sundays in those days. Then out to eat. That gave her a thrill. Usually we just went to the diner, but you'd think it was Lindy's or some place the way she got so excited. That's how I got to know Kathy, taking my mother to the diner. That Sunday I took her to a little Italian place, tiny, stuck under the El, it's not there anymore. Trains rumbled your teaspoon. I loved it. Italian places always seem so exciting to me. Romantic. Chianti bottles on the table. Red and white tablecloths. The whole bit. I caught myself being jumpy that day, though. Looking up every time the door opened. I was looking for Sophie in the only romantic place I knew. It scared me, but it made me realize I missed the big blonde queer. That was a funny feeling. Like the time me and my best friend in eighth grade, Ana, from Hungary, held hands during a movie in the school auditorium. *The Man Without a Country*, it was. Don't ask

7

me why. Maybe because she was foreign and feeling like she didn't have a country. But that wasn't what *I* was thinking about. Am I right?

So the next day Sophie comes by again, all bouncy like she never left and I say, "I thought you had to go back to work?"

"Decided not to," she says, just like that.

"How you going to live?" I ask. "Moving in with your grandmother?"

"Maybe," she answers, looking mysterious, almost like she knew what I was thinking in that Italian restaurant. And she takes off.

Well, at the time my mother was still working with me and that day believe it or not she decides to fall. On a banana peel of all things. One of the bananas in that shipment was rotten and slimy and she dropped it when she took it off the bunch, then forgot about it waiting on a customer. She used to wait on the ladies those days and I did your work. So anyway, to make a long story short, she's in the hospital and then home for a long time with a broken hip. You know how older people's bones are. I didn't know then, but she was never going to get better. Pneumonia, you know, and the whole route. Had too damn many kids if you ask me. Not that I'm ungrateful she waited for me.

So Sophie hears this the next day when she comes by. Then around time for the rush, which is coming up now if it don't start snowing any minute — don't it smell like snow? Come here, stick your nose out in the air. Oh, you're chicken, afraid of a little cold. I'll take you down to Hunt's Point some morning with me. That's *cold.* So Sophie shows up at rush time. Just hanging around when I'm going crazy. And I see she's starting to leave. Well, you know I didn't want that to happen.

"You want to help out?" I yell.

She walks over to where my mother's apron is hanging, one of those bibbed white ones like I'm wearing, and starts waiting on customers, talking up a storm, pushing fruit like she owned the place. I'm amazed. After, I asked her did she ever work in a market before. "Sure," she says.

8

"My uncle's got a candy store. I worked at the fountain for years."

"But how do you know enough about fruit to handle this?"

"I made it up," she says, winking.

You know our sales went up like crazy with her there? 'Cause of course she started coming around every day for the rush. Wouldn't take a cent. After about two weeks of this I told her I wouldn't let her go on bringing more money into the store without getting paid. "So make me your partner," she says.

It was so promising. I mean, I said no to the partnership at first, but I knew it was worth a try. Sophie had so much to give. And I think at that point I would have paid her just to stay around. She made me laugh so much. I really had a crush. No, it was more than that. I loved her. As a friend. Real deep. You know plums? The deep purple ones always with a thin cloud over their skins – like royalty in lace? Well, that's how I felt about Sophie. She moved me, you know? Way inside. It was warm just being with her. I felt like we could make anything work, the two of us.

Anyway, to get back to it, she asks me to make her my partner. Her grandmother will even put up money for her. Seems she's been talking to her about it. I don't want to change my father's way of doing things and Nicky, the veggie man up the street, he just opened a few months before and I like him, I don't want to cut him out. But Sophie, she works on me and finally I say to her, okay, wishing, I think, I was giving in to something else, "Okay, bring in a couple of veggies. Just a couple. Maybe potatoes and onions. Something we ain't going to lose our shirts on. And no partnership. Let me see how we do. Anything you bring in extra you get a percentage on. And we'll go on from there."

Well, Sophie went at it like her life depended on it. Later, I found out that it did. She came with me to Hunt's Point every morning whether we needed the potatoes or not. "Just to see how the market's doing," she'd say. Of course, it was only a matter of time before she'd be running over to me with a deal on stringbeans or a deal on squash. You know.

9

Sucking me into it because she knew I couldn't resist the bargains. And it wasn't long either before she brought this little girl into the stand and introduced her to me. "My Sweetie," she called her, though I don't know why when her name was already Cookie. She was about nineteen, scrawny and real femme. Black hair teased up like a pineapple top, eyebrows ripped out and drawn on again in incredible arches, white ghoulish lipstick. Only about five foot. I swear, she looked like a little kid at Halloween dressed up like Snow White's wicked witch or whatever she was. But Sophie, big Sophie who dressed in black, from her pointed ankle-high black boots to her short belted black vinyl jacket, would parade her little Cookie around so proudly. They moved to the neighborhood to make it easier for Sophie to go with me to Hunt's Point.

Well, yeah, Curly, I was jealous and I wasn't jealous. Sophie was so proud of Cookie, but also she was so − butch, like she owned her, you know? I felt real deep about her, but I didn't want to be *owned* by her or by anyone. That's why I wasn't married like my sisters. It was exciting for me to know I'd be with her every day and I guess we kind of, maybe teased each other because it gave us a good feeling, but, you know, I was convinced I wasn't gay because I didn't want to live with Sophie or to take her away from Cookie. I mean, Sophie used to tell me all about these butches fighting over femmes and all that and I knew I wouldn't fit into it. You, you're lucky, with the liberation movement you don't have to be butch or femme and nobody thinks twice about it. Right up till Kathy I tried to be like a man.

What are you laughing at? Sure I was butch. When you're tall and not pretty or nothing, that's what you are. As soon as I came out I went and bought myself a pair of boots just like Sophie's. Only brown. Do you believe that? Right, it *is* kind of sad. But so is the shape these bins are in. Here, you're finished with sweeping. Straighten that fruit out while I get the bookwork started. Oh, and we got to get this money to the bank before it closes. What time is it? That's good, after the rush we'll just get dribs and drabs of customers till suppertime.

10

Hmm? Quiet? I'm not being quiet. Just concentrating on these numbers. Yeah, I can answer a question while I work. What? How come I got no vegetables now? I don't know. I was happy when the store was a fruitstand. I didn't really need a lot more money and after Sophie I had no taste for veggies. I was never really comfortable with them. People mess them up. Pour sauces on them, slather them in butter or sauce. Fruit is a miracle. You might have to peel it or wash it, but when that's done it's ready — perfect and whole for you to taste, juices most likely running down your chin, your eyes closed from the tartness or a groan coming out of your mouth from the sweetness.

Hey — Mrs. Marseglia! Look sharp, Curly, they're starting again. Eh, Mrs. Suarez, look at what we got, your favorites — peaches! Yeah, and nice ones. They're going to cost you, out of season, and still I won't make nothing! But I couldn't resist when I thought of how much you love them. And, lookit, I got this here basket of spoiled ones real cheap for your pies — you like? I thought so. Hey, Curly, walk Mrs. Suarez and her peaches home, will you? She can't carry all this.

★ ★ ★

Yeah, I know she's great, my Kathy. But ain't she a good cook, too? Where else have you worked where you get lasagne for lunch, huh? Now you know why you got to work hard, I want you to earn what you're getting. And speaking of earning it, how'd you like that Mrs. Muller? Boy, didn't Kathy ever laugh when she seen you following Muller around. I'd love to see her in the diner. Kathy says there she's completely different. Thinks she's queen. Orders all sorts of stuff she hardly eats and tips like crazy. Don't even ask for a doggy bag. I can't figure it. Yeah, I think you're right, she must use everything she saves to eat out. Once a week she goes, Tuesday nights. Oh, I could go for a nap now, but we better clean up this mess or we'll never get out of here later. Am I right?

Sophie? Oh, yeah. Here's a broom. You want to know

what happened to her. Ah, I don't even want to tell you. She just disappeared. All of a sudden, no Sophie in the morning. I drove off to Hunt's Point expecting her to come running after me like she had a few times when she overslept. But she didn't. And she never came to the stand. Her veggies wilted. Her potatoes grew eyes — luckily, since mine were wearing out looking for her. Sorry, vegetables make me corny. When her section, which had grown quite a bit from two items, began to smell, I just dumped it, cleaned it out and left it empty. It looked like I felt: abandoned. I'd been up to her and Cookie's place a couple of times for dinner. They were very uncomfortable evenings with Sophie playing the loving husband and tough butch. Anyway, I knew from those visits where she lived and I went up there the first day she was missing.

Cookie was there. She was a mess. "She tried to kill me!" she whined when I asked what happend. "Your good friend did this," she yelled, pointing to a gap in her teeth. "And this." She pointed with her long red nails to her black eyes and bandages. I must have looked as if I didn't believe her because she started screaming, "Get out of my house! Go ask your friend, your good old partner what she did. I didn't do nothing. You tell her that, closet case. Now you can have her all to yourself."

Of course I'd never heard that term and I was scared of all the yelling Cookie was doing at me. I mean, I was only looking for my friend. Anyway, she scared me so much I forgot to ask where to find her and I was too scared and embarrassed to go back. But I was even more desperate to know what had happened.

Luckily, Sophie had mentioned the name of the bar they went to most. I knew it was in the Village and that Sunday I hopped a subway and went down there. I found a phone book and looked the name up and then asked people along the way how to get there. What a little alleyway it was in. I didn't know what I'd find inside, but there were just a few short-haired women sitting around. The place was pretty dingy after being outside on a bright winter afternoon. I ordered a beer. The women ignored me. I mean, I looked

12

just like them. So I asked the bartender, a hard-faced, good-looking woman who wore her hair in a pompador.

"Sophie? You a friend?" She looked at me with a real suspicious look. "We don't want nothing to do with Sophie, do we guys?" she said, walking over to the butches. One of them got off her stool and hitched up her black denims. I felt like I was watching a Western, Curly, I mean it. I remember all their words so good because it was like watching a play in slow motion. This one says, "Who're you?" and lights a cigarette. Then she stands there with it hanging out of her mouth. Finally they told me that Sophie was probably almost across the street from the bar at the Women's House of Detention.

I practically ran out of the bar, really thankful I wasn't gay. You're not laughing this time, Curly, what's the matter, you don't like this story? You're right, it doesn't have a very happy ending for Sophie. I found an entrance and was told that Sophie wasn't there anymore. She'd been "violent" and got shipped to Bellevue. Well, I thought, at least it's just Bellevue, glad it wasn't the big state hospital, Creedmore.

But when I ever got there . . . I hit visiting hours and got directed up to her ward. You've got to go through these heavy doors and all these guards or nurses or whatever they are check you out through thick glass, and by the time I got to the lounge where I had to wait and I first saw the depressed, wandering, bedraggled women, I was ready to crack up myself. I felt sick to know that strong, beautiful Sophie was locked up with them. I wondered, too, why they let her be with all these women if she was supposed to be so violent. I'd persuaded myself it was all some temporary problem already resolved, when I saw why they could trust her.

Sophie was sagging. She shuffled over to me and gave me a brave little smile, looking like she had a mouthful of novacaine. Then she sat as if she was exhausted. Drugs, I thought, finding an explanation for everything, Sophie's on drugs and they're going to get her off! But, no. Sophie was on some powerful drugs on purpose, to keep her calm.

She told me what happened. Cookie was spending too

much time with another butch. Sophie beat her up, didn't even realize how bad. She hung her head and shook it slowly, but didn't seem to have the energy to *feel* bad. Somebody called the cops because it would just cause more trouble to have another butch defend Cookie and they thought she might be hurt too bad for them to handle. The cops locked Sophie up because she had a record. Of beating people up, being in fights. That's why she lost so many jobs, she told me, I guess thinking that I knew more than I did about her. Worse, she'd been beating on Cookie for a few weeks.

"I was good a long time, Hen," she pleaded with me, as if I could make it better. "Ever since we started, you and me. I figured with a hand in a business I could straighten out and fly right. I had a great partner, a great little woman and a great job. I could respect myself, you see? I was like everybody else. Nobody could put me down. I wasn't just a misfit, a queer, no more."

"Then why didn't you keep it up?" I asked her.

"Cookie was making eyes at this chick. I thought she was going to leave me. I was scared it was all going to fall through." Her black clothes, the same ones I guess that she was wearing when she was arrested, looked grey, were wrinkled, and there was blood on them here and there.

"Just 'cause she looked at someone else?"

"I warned her. She talked to her on the phone, she saw her at the bar. I warned her how it would be. She didn't listen to me. She didn't stop. She didn't care."

Sophie cried. I couldn't take it. She was always laughing.

"I can't explain it, Hen. It's my pride. Everybody'd know if she left me. I couldn't face them all. I couldn't face you. I had to show them I could control things. That she wanted me most. She did like me best, you know."

Sophie's crying and talking kept getting louder and a male nurse came to lead her back to her room while another nurse told me that it wasn't good for Sophie to be upset, I'd have to leave. She said there wasn't anything I could do. I left my address and number. I don't know if they didn't give them to her so she wouldn't get upset or if Sophie was too ashamed to get in touch. Anyway, she never did. Hey,

14

you better let go of my hand. There's a customer at the door. You wait on her. I don't want to just now.

That was quick. What did she want, just milk? Yeah, I saw Sophie once more. No, leave the rest of the work for a minute. Why am I telling this whole story to a tough little dyke like you anyway? Because you're so tough? What does tough get you? What it gets you is Sophie. Or a life like hers. She thought being gay meant she was no good. She had to prove herself and she thought it took acting like a man to measure up. It's not hard to see things her way. In this world all we're told is that a dyke is shit. We're all perverts and there's laws against us. Oh, God, what the world does to us. What it did to Sophie. Am I right?

Anyways, Kathy and me went to a bar out on the Island a few years ago to celebrate one of our birthdays or something. We were sitting watching the women dance. I must have seen Sophie out of the corner of my eye without knowing it because I was already thinking of her. I often think about her in the bars anyway, and this time I was wondering if I'd taken her on as a partner whether she would have felt she had more of a stake in it and maybe felt better and not started fighting again. We were sitting watching the women dance — we only dance the slow ones now, being old, you know, kid — and the song stopped, the floor cleared and there she was, standing at the bar in her old pose. The old Sophie stance where she looks like a Texan who just struck oil. I was so glad to see her I told Kathy and started to get up.

Kathy put her hand on my arm and kept watching Sophie. I looked at her too and watched her order and down three shots in a row. Then she picked up a beer chaser. She turned toward us. She was wearing a hokey black leisure suit and boots like the old ones only square-toed with stacked heels. But she looked so washed out. Like a stick person someone had hung a stiff new suit on. I wondered if she was dying of cancer. She looked like her vegetables looked after she left and they started to rot. I looked back at Kathy and decided to get drunk. We were halfway there anyway.

15

But I couldn't stay away. In a little while I went over to the bar, knowing Kathy was there if I needed her. Oh, I'd always wanted to touch Sophie, but now when I reached out to do it I pulled my hand away because she was repulsive to me. But for the sake of what she'd meant to me I stood there till she looked around. The lively clear eyes I'd known were cloudy. They didn't show any light at all. I wondered if I'd made a mistake and this wasn't Sophie. But when I told her who I was she kind of started, patting me on the back in a hearty manner and talking real loud, introducing me to the people at the bar.

I could tell this was the nicest thing that had happened to her in a long time by the way she carried on. It was like she was showing all the people at the bar she really did have a friend and a life beyond them. I wasn't sorry, I didn't regret having come over. It was the least I could give her, the first woman I had loved, the woman who really brought me out, without touching me.

We went back to my table and I introduced her to Kathy. My warm, loving Kathy who told me later that she felt a chill when Sophie pressed her hand. But the night is wavy in my mind, like there's a screen of heat between me and it. I guess that's my emotions, huh Curly? Sorry about you having to get the customers. At least there's not many.

So she sat there and we told her about our life, our great love and how peaceful we feel; and about the neighborhood and the business. She smiled and nodded. She asked questions. But, Curly, she wasn't *there*. I was sure of it, that she hadn't heard a thing we'd said, when we asked her what she'd been doing.

"Well," she said, her lips just big now, kind of slack, not full anymore, "they sure cured me. Cured me of love. I ain't been with a lady for these many years." I couldn't tell if she spoke with bitterness or not. "But I'm still gay," she boasted. "They can't take my gayness away from me. Still spend my time in the bars. Read all the new gay books and magazines. Things have changed. Sometimes I wonder if I've changed. But I don't take no chances. I stay out of trouble. I don't hit nobody no more. 'Cause you know," she warned, trying to look wise, "if you love, you hurt. Ain't no way around that."

I don't remember how Kathy got me out of that bar. My partner. My real sister, not like the hens, Curly. My real big sister. Couldn't I have saved her? Kathy says no, she was too far gone into it even back when we met. I was still looking for myself then. She would've taken me under with her, taught me her ways. Kathy says I should thank my lucky stars I came out my own way. I know she's right.

Hey, are you crying? That's okay, little dyke. I cried too. Sophie's sad, but I figure without her, maybe my life couldn't have been so good as it is. Am I right? It's like everything here in my fruitstand. It all grows, right? Some is sweet, some sour. Life ain't always sweet to us. A lot of it is sour because we don't get much sun. Sophie came along in an ice age, as far as sunlight goes. And she didn't know how to help herself grow. Knowing what she went through, I worked at being different.

Speaking of sun, it's going down. Look, you let those Sister school kids make a mess in the nuts. Shells all over the floor. Better get the broom. Ahhh, I'm stiff. It gets harder to stand up from these crates every day. Clean out the scales, too, will you? Hey — here comes that good looking cook from the diner done for the day!

Hi, Kath, what's cooking? Besides you being tired of that joke? The kid? She'll do fine. Cares about the fruit, real gentle with it. Real gentle.

17

AT A BAR I
The Jersey Dyke

The sun shines again through the big window of the *Cafe Femmes*. It makes a new generation of bottles lined up behind the bar sparkle. Habitually, Sally the bartender leans her tall thin frame over the counter to wipe it with a damp rag. Her blonde hair falls over her forehead brightly, covering blue eyes somehow too wide and clear for such a tiny and normally dim bar.

But in this daylight, before the first customer has rung the cowbells by opening the door, the lingering stale smoke is more obvious. It is a film on the windows, a fuzziness in the air. Sally's nose is more sensitive to it this early. And the pinball machines — even the new space age game — look tawdry in the light.

Sally watches workmen across the street load and unload trucks from the platforms. She reads the backwards lettering of her bar's name on the window, then reads the company names on the trucks, then the name on the building. Every day she looks at this same scene, except Sunday, when the street is deserted. The men sweat and swear and struggle on the loading docks. The trucks wheeze and groan entering and leaving the street.

She could not say why, but Sally finds this all comforting.

19

It is familiar. She has her place in it. She bends to pull a bottle of cold white wine from the crushed ice. She pours some into a wine glass. It's a habit she should probably drop, but. . . . All day she stands behind the bar and waits for what life will bring her. This is her little treat, now and then through the day. At night her lover, Liz, does the same, but she drinks other things: whatever her first customer orders. That is her little game. Sally sees Liz when their shifts overlap so she knows what liquor Liz will smell of when she joins her in their bed after closing up. They see each other on Mondays, too, when the bar is closed. They never drink that day, but try to get away from all this, at least to Central Park, or to the riverside, somewhere open and airy. They blink in the full sun those days, and find all the straight people scurrying about the city very strange. By Tuesday they are glad to return to their bar, to the lesbians, to their accustomed life.

Jenny, the mailwoman, startles Sally as she hits the cowbells with the door. Sometimes she'll talk over the bar for a minute, discussing what happened in the course of the night — news Sally otherwise doesn't get until Liz comes in. But today Jenny has a busy time of it — she explains quickly that Sunday will be Mother's Day.

The workmen across the street knock off, running to the tiny lunch stand down the block or emptying lunch-buckets their wives have prepared. Sally can see them examining this and that in disgust or with pleased smiles and boasting. In a few minutes, her own lunch crowd, dykes who work in the neighborhood factories or offices, come in. She has told them to bring their lunch bags, their subs or pizzas, even if they don't want to drink, and she keeps cold sodas on hand for them. She likes their company. After a while they go back to work, dragging their feet, leaving the smell of pizza behind.

A stray straight man, an artist from one of the lofts, has been drinking beer at the far end of the counter, but he, too, leaves. Good — she was afraid she'd have a drunk on her hands.

The sun is still out as the workmen begin again, but it

no longer shines brightly through the window. At two o'clock no one has been in for an hour. It's one of those afternoons that make Sally wish she ran a bar in Mexico — perhaps she would close for siesta each afternoon. She pours herself another wine and takes it around to one of the tables where she sits now and then to test the feel of the place.

After a while a woman comes in, a stranger. She's almost as tall as Sally, but on the heavy side. She shambles up to the bar, as if depressed. Sally gets up tiredly from her table and takes her wine behind the bar, which she wipes down unnecessarily. The woman asks for a Michelob, in a Jersey accent.

Sally takes stock of her without seeming to while she readies the beer. She wonders if this overgrown sulky child is old enough to drink. Her jeans, plaid shirt, her high school jacket all look loose as if she had recently lost weight. Oddest of all, she doesn't check the mirror as most of the kids do first thing, to make sure they are looking sharp.

Neither speaks, but now and then the newcomer glances from under heavy eyebrows up at Sally as if to see if she is interested.

Sally feels hurt exuding from this woman as if an injured animal has come and fallen at her feet. When she feels the other's pain too acutely in her own body, she carefully wipes down each bottle again to distract herself. Then she works on the books awhile, but she can't concentrate.

Finally, the newcomer, looking down into her beer, says, "My girl killed herself."

Sally, wondering what to say, need not have. The girl took care of the silence.

"Do you mind? It's been two months now and I couldn't tell anybody. Oh, I don't mean nobody knew, they all knew she killed herself, but nobody knew we were, you know, together like we were, because she was so pretty and popular."

She pushed forward her Michelob. "You better give me another one of these. My name is Julie."

"Sally."

Julie held out her hand. Sally could only shake it and go on listening. "We live — lived — in this town in New Jersey.

It's real, real small, but close to Somerville, which is a little bigger. Only by close I mean you have to use a car to get there which I don't have. My folks have one but they use it to go to work in so I got a job after high school in town, at a cleaners. Yeah, I know it's not much waiting on customers, tagging dirty clothes, but they won't hire me any place else. Look at me. I'm fat and they think I'm a guy anyway when I go look for a job. Everybody knows me at the cleaners now, they put up with me. It's our day off, Wednesday, the owner was driving to the city so I got a ride from him. I have to meet him at seven to go back.

"See, I had to tell somebody. I don't know anybody at home I could tell. *She* had friends, lots of them. She was always dancing and laughing and had the lead in the school play, she was a senior this year. Her parents thought she was great. She got accepted at Rutgers too and was going next year. But me, I only have a couple of friends, old ones from high school. You know, from the ugly crowd. We used to ride the schoolbus together, but they're secretaries now, spend all their time trying to get prettier so some man at work'll marry them."

"Do they . . . know?" She felt compelled to ask, if only to stop this rush of words.

"That I'm gay? They might've figured it out by now." She looked self-conscious. "Well, how can I tell them? What if I lose them too?"

Though Julie spoke so quickly that time in the bar seemed to have speeded up, the workers across the street seemed to be slowing as their break approached. Sally could see them lounge more and more frequently against the portals of the loading dock, smoking. She wondered if she'd like the kind of work where kids weren't always spilling their guts out to you.

"How did you get together with this girl?" Sally asked when she saw Julie had fallen silent. She could at least ask a question.

Julie looked up at her in surprise as if she'd never asked herself this. "I guess because I was gay."

22

"You really think you're the only queer in town?"

Julie let out a choked laugh. "I guess we both thought so. Otherwise, why would she come to me? She was so pretty."

"Did she give it all up for you?"

"You mean the dates, the parties, the football games?" Again she looked at Sally in surprise as if this possibility, too, had never occurred to her. "No, man, you got it all wrong. She *had* to have all that stuff. She wasn't the kind *could* give it all up for love. I wouldn't ask her to. That's what I don't understand. She had it all. She had a girl lover *and* she had boyfriends. Everybody loved her and looked up to her. Why would she kill herself?"

Sally didn't have an answer. She looked around the empty *Cafe Femmes* and smiled inwardly. No matter how shabby, it was *hers*. She went over to plug in the pinball machines; she'd forgotten to before lunch. Their lights began to flash.

"If only she'd thought to ask me, we could have made a pact," Julie said.

Sally walked back to the bar, wondering if the girl might join her lover. Perhaps she should refuse to serve her more. Liquor would do her no good. Even now, after two, her speech was a little slurred, as if she wasn't used to drinking. But who was Sally to decide what was good for the girl? Perhaps this was the only way she could let it out of her system before she returned home.

"I got to tell you," Julie said, facing Sally, not looking sulky now, but suddenly almost radiant, "this one day, we went to the shore. She got hold of her folks' car and we drove and drove and drove. Touching, you know, all day. We'd never been able to do that before, never had the privacy of the car for so long.

"Oh, and the sun was shining and we ate fried clams at the beach and drank beer, a little, and walked by the water, along the rocks, holding hands. This was last fall and it was already a little cold, so there was nobody on the beach. We found some rocks we could lean against where it wasn't windy and we smoked cigarettes and held hands and once in a while she would let me kiss her right out there in the open."

Julie sighed. "It was beautiful. I always tried to figure a way we could have a day like that again, when the spring came. But the spring never really came. For her."

Sally looked over, but the girl didn't cry. Probably she was so used to hiding her tears they wouldn't come out anymore. "I feel so . . . kind of empty. You know?" But she wasn't looking at Sally.

"Did you ever come into the city together? To the bars?"

"Us? No. She wouldn't like that. She was a nice girl. We went for walks in the woods. Or hung out in her parents' family room when they were upstairs. We never went anywhere together, except that one time."

"And *you* didn't want to go to college?"

"Me? Sure. I got into Rutgers too, by the skin of my teeth. But I wanted to stick around. I mean, she was really special. Maybe she would've let me go to Rutgers when she did. I guess I was kind of counting on it. But without her there . . . " She began to bite her nails.

She asked for another beer. For the next hour she alternately chewed on her fingernails and drank beer. Sally moved around quietly, getting ready for the evening, asking no more questions — not because she couldn't think of any, but because a bartender soon learns that to express interest sometimes is interpreted as taking some kind of responsibility in another woman's life. She couldn't help *all* the needy kids who came in.

The workmen unloaded their last truck. They were worriedly glancing at their watches, hoping no one would drive in at the last minute and make them work overtime today. She heard the loud slam, finally, of the sliding metal doors closing on the concrete platforms. The men drifted off the street like a fog, echoing goodbyes at one another. Julie kept biting her nails in silence.

Soon the afterwork kids dropped in for drinks on their way home. The light inside the bar was dimmer, even though it was still daylight outside. Late afternoon the dark seemed to close in early, which was good for business, as the kids began to party earlier. Those who had a reason to go home for dinner left. A few returned as they walked their dogs; more, home from uptown, stopped in. Pizza appeared again. There was a constant turnover of kids.

Liz appeared. Shorter than Sally and with slightly darker, slightly longer hair, and glasses, she greeted Sally with her eyes. Sally threw the bar rag at her. Liz laughed, catching it, and threw it back. It didn't take her long to notice Julie, now sitting like a liquor-sodden lump, staring at nothing. Maybe she'd bitten her nails down to the quick.

Abruptly Julie stood up. Bang went her fist on the bar. The glasses rattled. "It's not fair!" If she was trying to shout, her voice was too hoarse. She turned and left the bar, slamming the cowbells angrily.

Liz and some of the kids at the bar looked to Sally. "Her girl killed herself," she explained quietly as she ran the rag over Julie's place.

They shook their heads. There was silence for a while. Then someone played a slow sad song on the jukebox, like a dirge, but when it stopped a fast dance song began and the sound in the bar picked up.

By the time Julie returned, darkness was closer to filling the cavity of the street outside the *Cafe Femmes*. Most of the kids were huddled at the space-age pinball machine watching someone top the highest score. They didn't even notice her. Sally was getting ready to go home. She looked at her watch. So Julie hadn't left with her seven o'clock ride to New Jersey.

She set her up with a clean glass and a Michelob.

Julie's face, when she looked up to thank her for the first time that day, looked different. Maybe she'd finally been crying. No, it was anger. That hadn't been there earlier in the day. Could it be that she had never gotten angry over her girl's death before? Over the unfairness of her situation?

Maybe, Sally nodded to herself as she walked to the door. When you're the only one in town you don't think you have any business being angry. You're out of step, so it's your own fault.

25

She looked back.

"Hey," called Julie, lifting her beer in a toast. "To my girl!" she said.

Sally stood in the doorway. "*L'chaim*," she said, not sure she wanted Julie to hear her.

Julie smiled. A little bit. "To life," she agreed.

AUGUSTA BRENNAN I
The Coat

It's not so bad sometimes, being old. You can rest at last. And I need a rest. I feel so tired it's all I can do to keep up with my memories. They wear me out so.

Since I got sick that's mostly all I do — remember. I sit here in my vinyl convalescent home chair, not at all an easy chair, but one to which I've gotten very attached. Something about getting down to just a few things in your life makes you hang onto every little bit that much more. The day I came out here to the sunroom and that new lady was sitting in my chair, I could have killed her, that's how upset I was. It was *my* chair, *my* corner of the room, *my* patch of sunlight. The next day, she was too sick to sit up, poor soul, so I'm glad I didn't murder her over it. Wonder if they would have put me in jail. Wonder if it would have been much different. How embarrassing, to kill for a bit of sunlight.

It's safe here. Perhaps that's it. Safety in familiarity, when there is no other safety available. When I was working I thought I'd be all taken care of when I retired. How wrong to think a good income in 1950 would be worth anything today. So here I sit, in my tiny corner of the world, a small old lady with sparse short hair, sitting in the sun, remembering and feeling my life as if it were happening today.

And memory is safe too, sometimes. You're pretty darned sure of the outcome. Safer even than the TV at night. I watch it when I'm too tired to remember. That happens more and more and frightens me. I never thought I'd give up so easily and even now, on my best days, I've still got some fight left in me. I filled out an application for the senior citizen housing the other day and made plans to share food with an old lady who's moving out of here soon. One of my greatest pleasures and triumphs is finally not being afraid people will notice all I care about are the women around me. No one expects me to move in with an old man or flirt or dress for men. The men hardly even expect or want it from the patients, but the nurses are a different story. On top of putting up with the demanding, dependent ways that are even more exaggerated in old men, the nurses must bear their coarse humor and repulsive touching. And then go home to their own men for even worse treatment. I don't see how they do it and I wish I could tell them they don't have to.

Not that most of these old ladies around me are any great shakes. But there are a few tough old gals — like I was till I got sick — who aren't about to let a little old age get them down. Do you know how much you must give up when you're old and have no family to take care of you? This is when my memories are not safe ones. Remembering my little apartment, my cat. When you're too sick even to take care of yourself and you're too old for them to expect you to recover enough to ever do so, others have to make decisions for you.

I'm lucky, though. My young friends are kind and help me all they can. They're in a couple, as they say, and live in my apartment building. We had many long talks over tea, Karen and Jean and me, before I got sick. They gave up my apartment for me when I couldn't afford it anymore with the nursing I needed, and took in my cat Mackie for me. I'll see him when I visit them, but I'm afraid that may break my heart almost more than if they'd had him put to sleep. He's old, too: sixteen. The fattest, proudest striped creature in the land. Faithful as can be. And dignified! He never begged like other cats. Just insisted on a partnership. He wouldn't wake me in the mornings as long as I got up early enough to feed him when he needed food. Of course, he decided what time that would be, but then he was the cat and as such had certain prerogatives. And he'd never wake me before six-fifteen. I used to think that was his little compromise, waiting until fifteen minutes after six instead of waking me at just six. I never needed an alarm clock with Mackie. He'd prod my cheek gently with his paw until I sat up and then he'd lead me patiently to the kitchen. I wonder if Karen and Jean let him play the same game with them. I wonder if he'll know me.

The sight of snow outside chills me. That's what's making me think about Mackie. Cold, winter, age, sadness; it all goes together in my mind. But I know it shouldn't. I know there's something good in winter and in age. The snowflakes, taken singly, as they fall, are so lovely. But it's hard to realize that when the winds drive the snow into my window with a vengeance. It feels like an enemy, it makes me draw my blanket tighter around my lap. Makes me think sad thoughts.

Does Mackie feel betrayed? Does he understand it's my old body doing all this to us? Or is he pleased with his new life at sixteen and eager to start anew without the old biddy pawing at him all the time? I haven't had a lover in all the years he's been with me. He's not used to sharing affection with someone else. Where would a lesbian in her eighties find a lover? What other old woman will admit she'd like a lover?

★ ★ ★

I must have dozed off there for a moment. Dreamed I was patting Mackie on my lap in the sun. And I see why now. That *was* a quick snow — the sun's back out. The ground is clear. It might never have snowed the way the kids are going at it out there.

I thought it was crazy to build a convalescent home next to a school. They are noisy going to and from school and at recess, but they don't bother me. A harmless, crazy old lady sitting here day after day watching is hardly noticed. I have

29

a game with a few little girls I've chosen to be lesbians when they grow up. Lovely little lesbians I'd drool over if it wouldn't look as if I was senile. I'm going to will it into them, send some sort of light rays over to protect them from all the socializing going on around them so they'll be strong enough to escape the net of heterosexuality when it's cast over them. I'm going to bring them out right there in their schoolyard.

Oh! How perverted you must think I am! How sinister! Little girls after all are sacred. I couldn't agree more. That's why I'm giving them everything I've got to help them be true to themselves as they really are.

It wasn't too hard choosing them. Some of the girls were too straight already to save. The little ones in their well-starched skirts with curled hair. The ones who, at eight years old, bring their nail polish to the schoolyard and put it on while the other girls are throwing themselves into games. I rejected them because I don't feel strong enough to undo what's been done. I picked some easy ones: the tomboys in their checked shirts with their band-aided knees. The ones who play cowboy, not house, the ones who start the games. If only I could live long enough to see two of them pass by some day holding hands. But even if I do, since I won't be in this place, I'll just have to trust in the fading powers of an old lady lesbian.

The sun is hot. Maybe I can take the afghan off. Who ever thought I'd be sitting like an old lady with an afghan over my knees. It's still got a few of Mackie's hairs on it and I'd cherish it for that even if one of my lovers hadn't made it for me. "Sloppy old cat, always misplacing your coat," I'd tell him. Like that little girl, one of my chosen people, who won't wear her coat when she plays. The teachers have a terrible time with her! The minute she runs out of the school there's her coat, thrown up against the fence under my window. Almost as if she knew I was in this corner watching her and she was asking me to keep an eye on her coat. Her coat and her rebellion, because, of course, the casting off of the coat is really her way of saying, "No! I *won't* be like you, I *won't* play by your rules, I *won't* wear your restrictive clothing, I'll throw it away and be myself!"

I suppose I am beginning to sound a bit senile, but she's my favorite, the strongest contender for the royal dykedom. And she looks like Dale, little Dale, my old landlady's daughter. They're both round and full of energy, with sparkling eyes and ready to yell as loud as the boys, and they have long but wild hair that never stays where their mothers train it to go and glasses that don't slow them down a bit.

But Dale is old now, almost forty. It's hard to think of her like that. I watched her grow from ten through fifteen and she'll always be those ages for me. The five years I lived in that building were so strange. Like a different life from my own. I was between lovers in a town so small the nearest gay bar was 120 miles away, hardly worth the trip unless I was desperate for lesbian companionship. I only made it there three times, if I remember right, in all those years.

The little building I lived in was sort of an apartment building, though it looked more like an oversized private home. I think it was built to house unskilled workers at the town factory. It was L-shaped and had six apartments. I was in the short part of the L in a one-bedroom on the second floor. I worked, of course, at the factory, helping set up their bookkeeping and accounting because the new owners couldn't make head or tail of the family's system of doing things. Then I stayed because they said they needed me to set up the office and train some girls. Then they wanted to expand and needed me more than ever. Well, it was five years before I got out of that country town, though I knew I should have left long before that, before Dale turned fifteen.

If I hadn't gone to the hotel bar for my Sunday dinners and overheard the coarse men's jokes I would have thought the town didn't know what a lesbian was. Who else could Dale turn to but me? She used to follow me around even when she was ten and I had just moved there. A little tomboy who wouldn't stay in and watch how her mother ironed and cooked, she was a lonely kid who spent most of her time with her dog Lassie. I laughed everytime I heard Dale call

31

Lassie because he wasn't a collie, but a tiny, tiny thing with black and white markings and long ears. And with Lassie for a name he was comic. But Dale told me she'd always wanted a collie like Lassie, and when her mother let her have a dog, Lassie it would be.

What a kid Dale was. Taking me on long hikes up into the hills with Lassie, asking me to go fishing with her when her Dad was working weekends. I should have known what it would lead to. All of a sudden one day she was an adolescent. And not a sulky, awkward kid with big feet and a bad attitude. She had been a handsome little woman from the beginning. Still in jeans and plaid shirts and sneakers, she just filled them out better. Instead of going through a pale and listless stage, she got more color in her face than ever and was full of a creative energy which, at 53, I had a hard time keeping up with. And I was still her favorite person.

In my isolation you can imagine what this beauty did to me. I'd come around the corner home from work and oh my, my heart would flip over to see this sleek young woman, one foot up in back of her, arms folded, leaning against the side of the building. She'd bought herself a men's panama hat at the general store and it made her so sexy when she looked at me from under the shade of the brim I could have melted every time.

She was the only game in town, but I knew I couldn't play. As a matter of fact, I tried to stop her from hanging around with me. I was afraid for her. I knew I could leave town anytime, but she was still too young to escape if there was gossip. I suspected that she would move to the nearest city as soon as she learned she wasn't the only lesbian in the world, as I knew she inevitably would. My problem was how soon she learned and what she decided to do about it, as I knew I would be tempted to teach her myself and not just in words.

If only the sun would stay out. It seems to give me energy. I don't want to fall asleep during this memory. It's one of my favorites and if I doze I'll dream about Dale and get mixed up about what's real and what's not. Even now as I watch that little girl out there in the schoolyard I get confused about how Dale looked, because I see Dale in her. Here she comes for her coat, the little tiger. Teacher following her all the way, yelling at her to put it on. Oh, she smiled up at me. I never knew she realized I was watching! Next time I'll be ready with a smile of my own. With a message in it. So she won't see some poor old lady, but a stronger older woman with life in her yet. Someone she might want to be like someday. Just an impression, that's all I want to leave on her brain. Just a hint that she *can* be different, that she doesn't have to be like the rest of them. After that she'll be on her own, do her own growing, as long as she has that assurance around her like a coat that it's okay to grow up your own way.

What comfort, when the sun comes out from behind its cloud. How strong it is, and it's older even than me. Now that I'm not in pain all the time anymore, I'm not as drained. Perhaps I'll get back on my feet yet. How I'd love to go for walks again, even just around the block. Perhaps by spring I can go outside and watch the schoolyard from there. I'd like to be invisible, so that my age wouldn't scare the little girls and they would just feel warm and good and sure when I was around. Does it sound as if I want to be the sun myself? Clothing them in the warm rays it wraps around me? But I do feel like that sometimes as a lesbian: special, lucky, touched by some magic and given some knowledge that brings me a certain majesty and power. I think those new-style lesbians, the feminists, are discovering reasons to feel that way. Karen and Jean bring me books and magazines that the feminists write. My eyes aren't as good as they used to be, but I read what I can. They say such insightful things and dig up such exciting facts from women's history that I know I'm not crazy for having felt blessed since I first came out.

And didn't Dale look like a young sun-goddess back in her little town thirty years ago. Didn't she haunt me with her magical beauty. Didn't she seem to know a coronation was due her, and didn't she do all that she could to bring it on. I'd get home to find she'd let herself into my place with a passkey. I'd allowed the little girl to do that, but was afraid about the young woman doing it, too. Wouldn't she be

33

stretched out on the couch that came with the place, patting the dog and holding a bunch of brown-eyed susans for me. Wouldn't she be poring over my books when I finally decided to leave them out to be sure she heard the word lesbian.

Words, for the first time, became strained between us. I'd had long arguments with myself about Plato and Socrates and whether their love for boys was just an excuse to be dirty old men or whether it was really one of the highest forms of love. I didn't know any better than to judge what I did by what men did. Finally, I left Plato on my coffee table in hopes that Dale would read it and help me decide. And I started packing because I knew, whatever happened, it couldn't go on. I needed a woman to touch too badly. And I needed one I was free to touch and continue touching.

Wasn't the sun strong that day, didn't it beat down on me just as it does now, too bright for me to open my eyes, so I hardly knew then or now whether I'm dreaming or not? She let herself in that Sunday morning and woke me as she sat on my bed. On the second floor I had no near neighbors, and slept with the curtains open for the sun to stream in. I was half-blinded by it as well as by her beauty.

She was bursting with adolescence and her new sexuality. Her cheeks were fiery red and her lips looked stained as if with some kind of berry. Her eyes were hardly open she was feeling so much desire. The flesh of her body seemed to want to burst from her clothes and her roundness was even rounder with sensuality. I could hear her breathing short deep breaths as if she were strangling from all she felt. One of her ears stuck out bright red at the tip from her long hair and I realized she was embarrassed to be coming to me like this as well as frightened. I wanted to comfort her, but oh, the fear in me!

She leaned down to me and I smelled her clean hair. She must have been lying on the grass outside because it smelled like a newly mowed lawn. The sweet little kid kissed me on the forehead and withdrew her lips, leaving her face closer to mine than before. Her breath was as hot as the sun. Her breasts, above my hands, were so round in their red plaid shirt, so close.

I touched them.

Dale closed her eyes and her face filled with such sheer pleasure I didn't move my hands at all, just let them stay around her breasts until she moved her head. She tilted it and opened her eyes. I smiled. She leaned over my face and pressed her lips against mine. Not really kissing me, as if she wasn't sure how to do it. I showed her by opening mine a little and kissing her. She caught on fast and soon we were leaning back from each other, needing air. "Listen," I said, before she started again, "when you're fifty-three you need to go to the bathroom when you wake up in the morning. Will you wait for me?" I asked, knowing her patience knew no bounds this morning.

Closeted in that small bathroom I let myself waver, fear, and finally, brushing my teeth, risk. I'd still leave, I planned, for there was no possibility of a real relationship between us, although I've always wondered about that. . . . But anyway, Dale needed me then. She needed as we all do, someone to give her permission, to show her the way, to open the door. And I wanted to plant a few seeds, too, to keep that door open, to let her know we were doing much more than going to bed together. That the ritual of women making love is one of the most powerful in the world, I knew even then. It shook other people to their roots; she must learn to be careful, to protect herself. It committed women like us to lives unimaginable to most of the world; she must learn to live fully despite any way of life imposed on her by fear. It would open her emotions and mind like no other experience she could have; she must learn to temper her passions so that instead of being destroyed, she would be stronger from them and could use them the rest of her life.

And she was more beautiful in her way than any mature woman I'd ever known. My waning body against her blooming one made her seem magnificent. Her crisp full flesh was an experience my hands had never appreciated when I was fifteen. Her trigger responses kept me more alert and responsive than I'd been in years. The sharp cries that came with orgasm, once she relaxed enough to have them, stirred something almost maternal in me because I was watching a young girl discover a staggering capacity in herself to experience beauty through sensation and I remembered how overwhelming beauty is at that new age. Her orgasms themselves were taut and fast, compared to the rolling sensuality my mellower, looser body felt. She was a little flower blooming in my hands.

★ ★ ★

Look at me. An old lady snoozing in the sun. Nodding away over my memories, hardly knowing if they're real. Or if I'm dreaming. That was a long nap. The school is getting out for lunch. And there goes Dale, dragging her coat behind her. No, not Dale, that new little girl. And this stiff old body's got to heft itself out of its favorite chair, out of the sunlight, for lunch. Nourish itself. I need my strength, after all. There's work to be done. Worlds to be won, as somebody used to say.

Dale moved up to San Francisco to win hers. She still writes me once in a while. I picture her with her graying long hair streaming wildly over a battered denim jacket, her eyes still glittering, but now from a new hunger, a new hurry, to make the world fit for the likes of us. She's one of those San Francisco marchers. It warms me to know I helped put her there, that I knew her first hunger. That I live in her.

THE LOPRESTO TRAVELING MAGIC SHOW

The summer seemed to fade behind the train as the city landscape shrunk to trees and lawns and long, flat beaches. The train ride – that train ride every summer to Aunt Terry's – seemed to let me shrug the heat off my body, shake my brothers and sisters like itchy drops of sweat from my hair, until I could whirl in my head in the new free space I found away from home.

Not that Aunt Terry's trailer was palatial. With her and me and Molly bumping around in the twelve by fifty-two foot tin box, as they called it, there was probably less room than home. But it was different. Maybe because I didn't have to weave through the living room furniture. Or because Terry and Molly didn't have a TV to bump into or have fancy ceramic figures dancing on tiny tables. Nothing was break-able there or so sacred you couldn't knock it over, even the beer. The poor smooth rug was soaked in it so regularly they called it their beer-rug.

It just *felt* bigger at Aunt Terry's when I woke in the morning and squeezed my way in and out of the bathroom, walked the few steps to the front door of the trailer and stepped down, barefoot, to the damp, brown ground. There were no elevators or long flights of stairs to the earth there. Just a small child's step out and down and, of course, many of those years I was so small I'd have to hold two-handed to the metal bar outside the door before I'd feel safely landed. Aunt Terry let me play outside in my pajamas even when I was very young, because she and Molly needed to sleep off the night before in the only closed room there, and they knew I valued my visits with them too much to wander into trouble.

I'd sit for a long while on a milk crate just outside the door watching the strange neighborhood wake up and start its day. The trailer across from Aunt Terry's was a mirror reflection of hers except for the little entranceway the neighbors had built on their door to keep the heat inside in winter. With time the tiny space it created filled with such a jumble of brooms and tools and boots and slickers that I was glad I didn't have to find my way through it quietly in the mornings. But inside, where I had been once, the walls were covered with imitation wood paneling and the furniture fit like pieces in a jigsaw puzzle. The old couple who lived there were handier than Aunt Terry and Molly and you could tell they spent almost no time at Gaffney's, the restaurant and bar next door to the trailer park, which so many residents treated like an extension of their tiny living rooms.

Despite the similarity of the trailers, their proximity, and their numbers, the scene was so different from the city, where I lived, that I used to just watch them all sit there without a pattern and I'd try to make some sense of their placement. At home the apartment buildings lined the blocks side by side, up the street and down the street. At Aunt Terry's some trailers were side by side, some end to end, some jammed between others so that only an end stuck in or peeked out, and a few stood in the middle of an invisible circle which could almost be called a yard and was certainly used as one. When I got older, Janis Joplin's voice would always bring back to me that early morning scene of ragged community living when she sang: *Freedom's just another word for nothing left to lose.* . . . Not because Aunt Terry's trailer park was as desolate a place as it looked. Simply because there were no frills, there was no money thrown about, no airs or unnecessary clutter. The ground bred no

38

grass because it was too well used, the homes carried spots of rust and old, old paint because there was not the money to fix those things until absolutely necessary. There were no patios or gardens because leisure there was either non-existent or spent in the easier comfort of Gaffney's. Yet it was the most comfortable and unthreatening place I have ever been and I wish now as I did then that Twelve Elms Trailer Park could have been my home more than two weeks a year.

Eventually Molly would come to the trailer door and call me back from whichever corner I'd strayed to. Sometimes I'd be visiting with one of the many cats or dogs of the park, sometimes I'd get all the way over to the miniature golf course and driving range out back that was run by the park's owner. On a weekend morning her call might find me half-way out the driving range, gingerly barefoot on that huge expanse of grass, my pajamas wet from rolling in the dew. Once back at the trailer there was Aunt Molly's breakfast for the three of us no matter how much they'd drunk the night before. They always had lemons, and before eating breakfast Aunt Terry would cut one in quarters and bite into its pulp, shaking her head with the rind against her lips like a sunny, yellow smile, eyes tearing above it. "When you're old enough to get hung over, Princess," as she called me, "don't forget your Aunt Terry's cure. If you survive the shock you're ready for a new day!" Then she'd lift her juice mug and toast Molly silently.

Aunt Terry was quite a woman. I sensed it then and I know it now. Those breakfast feasts were a statement: whatever happened to her the night before, she was always very alive come daylight. Of course, I had not shared the night life they led until that trip. I knew they went over to Gaffney's where Molly was a cook. I knew they drank every night as much as my parents drank in a year. I knew they had friends my father would not approve. My parents did not even know that Molly worked nights in a bar or that Aunt Terry had been through several jobs since I'd begun visiting. One of her problems was that she wanted at least one month off every summer. And she took it.

"Two weeks for my Princess," she'd say, "and two for old Mol'." It seemed like a good system to me because I had exclusive rights to Aunt Terry most of the day and did not have to feel bad about Molly, because her two weeks were coming. Besides, though Molly worked long, steady hours at Gaffney's, she worked them at night when Aunt Terry would be there with all their friends.

My parents thought Aunt Terry was the cook and that she worked days in a restaurant that closed down two weeks each summer. They believed that the same way the whole family had believed anything about Aunt Terry since she'd left home. I knew that Nonno LoPresto, my father's and Aunt Terry's father, had kicked her out for some reason, but no one ever talked about it. When Aunt Terry, on a Christmas visit, first asked if they'd like to send one of the kids, me for instance, up to see her that summer, my parents jumped at the idea. To get one kid out of that apartment for almost nothing they would have forgotten anything they'd ever heard about Aunt Terry. Especially since they couldn't believe there was anything "wrong" with someone in their family.

I was seven the first year and twelve the year it all happened; so I knew, or thought I knew, everything and everyone up there pretty well. Terry LoPresto was a feisty, short, skinny Italian daughter who the family said should have been a son. She had muscles on her upper arms and I used to compare mine to hers at the breakfast table with Molly laughing at us and calling us both juvenile delinquents from the Bronx. And I felt as if we were just that, because Aunt Terry acted so young. "Never took any responsibility," my mother said about her when Nonno LoPresto died, and maybe she was right, or maybe Aunt Terry only took the responsibilities she was needed for.

In either case her forty-three years had left her looking a lot more than ten years younger than her brother, my poor, pale, shrunken father who, if he had a muscle sure never let us see it. It was just his choice in life, I know, to get married and strap himself down to supporting six kids on a clerk's salary. It must have shrunken his soul, too, because that showed no resemblance to Aunt Terry's either.

She had an exuberance about her that made her leap around like she was my age. Her tight, wavy hair was as short as she could get it and her clothes, dungarees or chinos with flannel shirts or sweatshirts, required as little care as her hair. She worked hard every year, most of the year, at whatever job she could get. One of my favorite years she worked for the lumber store and got wood and materials free to make a lean-to next to the trailer. She waited until I came up to build it and that was practically all we did those two weeks. I was nine and had never been prouder in my life than when we finished that little storage shed. Aunt Terry called it my room and said she was going to build a special bed in it so they could rent it out to me when I grew up. I knew it wasn't big enough, but it was my dreamhouse all the next year back in the city.

Molly was what people call the motherly type. She was short like Terry and had short grey hair, but hers was straight and cut a little longer so it looked soft and the wind would muss it up. She wore pants all the time, too, but they were different, more like ladies' pants in dark greens and navy blues. She mostly seemed to let Aunt Terry take the initiative in things, but hers was the restraining hand when Aunt Terry started to get into fights, and the comforting hand when one of us was sick. And it was Molly who had initiated my visits. She was the one who believed in keeping up family ties and saw that Aunt Terry had something to give my father's children no one else in the family could offer.

Over the years I met their small, odd circle of friends. Big, slow Bozo told stories of his several years in traveling circuses, but he was a sad person, resigned to the decreased demand for clowns who "wasn't the best," he said. Bozo's best friend was Ed, his next door neighbor. Ed was waiting for his wife to come back and had been waiting since I met him. He introduced new visitors in his trailer to a gold-framed picture of a teased-haired, bleached blonde in a white angora sweater, as if she were his wife in person. Bozo and Ed were both lucky enough to work steady for the town and could only complain that they had to get up too early

41

in the morning. They were on the sanitation crew and bragged of making the town fit to live in.

Minnie and Lester were a retired couple who were "just full of it," as Molly described them. He was the practical joker of the group and big Minnie was the flirt. They always had jokes and cracks to make about everything, and kept the others laughing — the life of the party. The whole group generally gathered, with a few drifters, at Gaffney's every night to down pitchers of beer.

One of my favorite memories is from what must have been the first year I was up there, because I remember Aunt Terry piggy-backing me into the restaurant in my pajamas so I could quickly peck the cheeks of the whole gang before she put me to sleep in the trailer. And I remember falling asleep, alone in the dark as I was, full of a feeling of warmth and security as I pictured them in my mind. They were all in a booth, squeezed together, smiling and laughing, spilling and shouting and smoking, and pleased as they could be that this little child was theirs to love for two weeks. I can still see the wooden booth, dark and carved with initials, the table between them all overflowing with ashtrays and glasses and empty pitchers. They were against an inside wall where the brightest light came from a tiny lamp hung under a dim shade, the shade decorated with horses jumping over hedges and red-suited men riding the horses. It all gave my seven-year-old mind a sense of adventure and excitement and specialness and danger like a fairy tale.

So each summer I left the Bronx with anxiety and anticipation all squeezed together in my stomach. This particular summer was worse because as I stepped on the train I knew I'd just gotten my period for the third time in my life. I found my seat and sat frozen until the train moved out of the station. Then I ran to the bathroom and, going through Harlem, threw up what seemed the sum of all that past horrible year of puberty. I raised my head briefly and saw the long narrow streets of the ghetto, the ripped out walls, the half-smashed windows, the boys roaming in packs, and was sick again.

All that year I had felt prey to the terrors of the city. Vulnerable, now, to men, I had feared them. Unable to compete with those girls on my block who had an aptitude for dressing, walking and talking correctly, I had feared their remarks and my inadequacy, and did not understand why I should be like them. And when my period had come, I was ashamed.

My closest companion that year was the tree outside my window which, stunted, still survived to live surrounded by trash cans in our alleyway. In the summer the smell of garbage rose to our sixth floor windows and smelled as it must have smelled to my tree all the time. Our only release, mine and the tree's, such as it was, came on trash days, at four a.m., when we were tortured by the dragging, scraping sounds of trash collection and the rough, heavy voices of the men who threw the cans back at the tree as if with a vengeance.

The second girl after three boys, I felt like a disdained garbage tree. My femaleness was not special as it had been for my older sister, but had become familiar enough for my brothers to taunt me about it. That older sister, one of the popular girls, scorned my embarrassment and wore her femininity like a flag. For me, the last three months had been colored by hot, painful cramps, and shame. Now here I was, the only one on the train having to face this ordeal, alone and with no preparation.

Like my little garbage tree, though, I adapted, made what repairs I could, and skulked back to my window seat to be lulled, finally, into the familiar release that came to me every year on the train. I was glad to see poor bow-legged Lester at the station, beaming up at me through a window. He had no teeth and his shrunken cheeks were covered with short white bristles. Even on that hot summer day he wore the navy blue watch cap I'd never seen him without, but Minnie had pressed his black chinos until they were shiny, and his bony wrists were a welcome support as they emerged from his sweatshirt and his hands swung me, suitcase and all, off the steps almost before the train could stop.

43

Lester drove a cab to supplement his Social Security, and he sped me in it as I sat importantly in the front seat, gaining a little confidence, to Twelve Elms. He tried to give me the year's news in the ten minute ride along the blessedly familiar Post Road, and by the time we arrived I didn't even cry when I confessed to Molly what my needs were.

She smiled and nodded and sent me into their tiny bedroom to change while she rustled through her things to find the right supplies. Then we sat at the pull-down kitchen table and Molly told me what she had gone through at my age. When Aunt Terry arrived after shopping I was laughing and telling Molly how I wished I could transplant my garbage tree to Twelve Elms where I knew it could grow better.

Aunt Terry gave me an affectionate punch on the arm and yelled for lunch. Molly got up to fix it while Aunt Terry and I walked around the park, Aunt Terry showing me all the small changes since last year, the new important people, the new drifters. We got to the edge of Twelve Elms and Aunt Terry pointed to some activity at the far end of the driving range.

"Carnival coming in," she told me.

"Here?" I asked, excited.

"Sure is. That's why we changed the week you were coming, to give you a surprise. The owner's having trouble making anything off of this golf thing, so he's renting it out to the church people. Going to be a big one, too, by the looks of it. Bozo's taking his vacation now. Going to be a clown the whole weekend."

I was too excited about it all to answer, but Aunt Terry looked over at me, then leaned over and gave me a hug, a rare thing for her to do. I could feel she was as excited as I. A carnival in our own back yard!

When the trucks began arriving sporadically that night I could hear them as I writhed on my cot, fighting the cramps as Molly had told me to, by relaxing. Images of the city came to me in my sleep, but I woke and was comforted in the knowledge that the trucks brought carnival people, not garbage men. I imagined people pitching tents, setting up a gypsy-like camp, rolling the rides into place. I learned better

44

the next morning when I ran to the driving range and saw not dozens, but maybe five or six unadorned tractor trailers motionless on the field. I felt foolish for a moment about my childish excitement, and disappointed until I saw that, while this scene might not have the magic of my fantasy, it was much more important to be able to watch the setting up.

By Thursday morning, the early morning driving range looked different. Where usually the grass shone bright green through its moisture, that day it was trampled down in the few spots not covered with carnival equipment. The tractor trailers had been driven into a circle as in a wagon train, and their cabs driven off to rest on another part of the range. The circle was open on one end where an admission booth had been half-assembled. Cautiously, remembering stories of circus-gypsy kidnappings, I walked between two of the tractors and stood just inside the circle. Overnight a merry-go-round and other rides had appeared in the center of the circle and as I stood silent and observant their stillness revealed them to me: I could see the machinery by which they ran and the grease and stains of their traveling, and their careless use. I saw those vehicles of adventure as if they were naked, out of costume, without the motion which gave them their magic. Around them the tractors stood closed, the seams of their flaps exposed to outline the counters hawkers would later lean over, trying to entice the crowds to their games and prizes.

When I turned back to the trailer park it looked like another sleeping carnival. Crazily, it now was shoddy, used-looking, sad and disappointing. The sun broke out and lit up two pots of red tulips outside a trailer and I realized it was a cloudy day. I wondered if the carnival could start if it rained. I decided it didn't matter anyway and walked through the trailers feeling very alone and sad, as if I had lost something. In a book I knew this would be called growing pains, but it did not satisfy me to define my feelings. I wanted everything to be exciting again. I wished I were back in the Bronx with my tree, dreaming of a better place. I wished there were tulips everywhere. I wished the gypsies *would* come and take me. Then, kicking a cinderblock planter painted a garish purple, I reminded myself there were no gypsies either, just workmen I could by now hear revving trucks and slamming things behind me.

As I approached Aunt Terry's trailer she was just stepping down from the door, pulling a long black robe around her shoulders. She saw me and grinned shyly. "I got picked."

"For what?"

"To be the vampire!" she answered, swinging the robe across her face and leaping at me.

I couldn't help but laugh. "What vampire?"

"I'm only kidding, Princess. They want a magician, the people who are planning this. And theirs disappeared. I don't blame him. I wish I knew how," she sighed.

"But you can't be a magician," I protested, remembering the few awkward tricks Aunt Terry had amused me with on rainy days. "You can't do any real tricks."

"That's what *I* said, Princess. But no. Your Aunt Terry is the sucker."

We both sat on milkcrates gazing toward the carnival site. It did not look as stark from that distance, with the ferris wheel poking over the trucks and another ride's rockets looking poised to take off. "Besides," Aunt Terry explained, "they told me it's not *what* you do so much as *how* you do it. Look." She pulled a deck of cards out of her shirt pocket as she talked about how she had been railroaded into the job, and how she'd been practicing a few tricks that she learned a long time ago from an old friend when she lived around the country before she met Molly. As she talked I realized first, that I knew nothing of Aunt Terry's life before Molly except family stories and knew not many of them; and second, that she had performed two card tricks in front of me before I even noticed.

"That's magic!" I said and then got embarrassed as she winked at me. "I mean, I know it's supposed to be, but you really did it!"

"That's why I got picked. 'Cause I can make it look like magic. I don't know how, but that's really the only thing I ever learned to do good enough I was proud of it. Not that I can make money at it, but I can do it."

46

"I bet you *could* make money. I bet you're really good," I remember saying in my childish faith that Aunt Terry could do anything.

"Maybe, but the only way they let ladies practice magic is in a long-sleeved gown with gobs of makeup. That's what Dusty was like — my friend who taught me what I know. But she played second to a man magician and that's as far as she could go. Not for me, Princess."

Of course I had never really thought of magic or any other profession as realistically as Aunt Terry had, so I accepted what she said without too much thought while wondering about the romantic figure of Dusty and how Aunt Terry had ever met someone like that. It wasn't until we'd gone in for the early breakfast Molly had prepared for the practice session (which would last off and on until Saturday with hardly a beer in between) that I realized my sadness and disillusionment had disappeared: I was again looking forward to the carnival.

Now when I think back to that Saturday it's all a whirl of activities I can hardly separate. Molly and Ed and Lester and myself had made a little platform for Aunt Terry with a draped table and a sign that read THE LOPRESTO TRAVELING MAGIC SHOW which we thought was very clever. Aunt Terry was nervous, crumpling empty pack after pack of those short Pall Malls she loved, until Molly made her have a drink over Aunt Terry's protests that it would ruin her reflexes. There was an excited spirit of cooperation among everyone in the group except Bozo, who kept pulling people out to help him rehearse his clowning. Once Aunt Terry had started her shows, the two days quickly became for me images of her black-robed figure surrounded by children, and of Bozo cavorting through the crowds in swirls of reds and yellows and blues — a huge, striped tornado.

We'd all been to the carnival as customers Thursday and Friday nights when Aunt Terry and Bozo were not performing, so we'd had our fill of cotton candy and rides. Molly and I were free Saturday and Sunday to run back and forth between Aunt Terry and the wandering clowns (Ed and Lester had finally volunteered to clown with Bozo) and our

47

trailer. We carried cold drinks and bandaids and supplies for Minnie to repair makeup when the heat of the day rolled it off the men's faces. Aunt Terry needed very little attention and just kept playing magician to crowd after crowd of kids and adults. She simply stood there in her cape, her black jeans, a shiny red shirt we'd found at Goodwill and, of course, a high black hat that fit perfectly over her short hair. As I remember her now, she was a perfect magician. She seemed tall and imposing to me over all those little kids' heads, and composed and graceful on her little stage. Even the show she did Saturday night was a success, despite the older, rougher crowd. There was just something about her — I guess you'd call it her own magic — that kept them fascinated. Even when one particularly obnoxious man demanded a rabbit out of a hat, she pulled it off when Lester supplied a stuffed rabbit he'd won for Minnie at one of the prize booths. The crowd roared, and Aunt Terry, for those two days and forever after in my mind, became a real magician.

When it was all over Sunday night the bar was already closed so everyone piled into Aunt Terry and Molly's trailer. They were so exhausted one beer was all most of them could down to celebrate the show, and they spent the next day resting, slowly falling from the weekend high of activity. But we got a little restless toward the end of the day, so Aunt Terry decided to take Molly and me to the movies to thank us for our help.

She borrowed Ed's old Bonneville to go to the drive-in where a Katherine Hepburn show was playing. Aunt Terry was so impressed with Katherine Hepburn that she didn't pay any attention to what movie we would see; it wasn't until we got there that we learned it would be *Suddenly Last Summer*. It was the first Tennessee Williams film I had ever seen and I sat transfixed by the power of the story and the acting and the more painful scenes. I did look away finally so as not to see the sand alive with baby turtles and their destruction by hungry creatures otherwise so innocent and beautiful. I sat between Molly and Aunt Terry, noticed their frequent looks over my head, but I didn't understand so much of the film they needn't have worried that they had been wrong to take me.

As we drove out of the theatre lot on our way to take Molly to work at Gaffney's I climbed into the back seat. I felt unsettled, as if I was about to get my period again. I didn't feel like crying, but I couldn't talk either. I felt as if I were on the edge of something, as if Tennessee Williams had been speaking to me, as if he'd wanted to tell me something that had to do with all the puzzling I was doing. Cramps, the garbage men hurting my helpless tree, growing pains, the carnival's secret machinery; excitement, the handsome magician; fear, the handsome man in the film — so many images hurtling around the small space of my mind.

"That was a pretty weird movie, huh Princess?" Aunt Terry finally asked over the front seat.

I must have mumbled something; I saw Aunt Terry glance again at Molly. "I just don't understand!" I wanted to yell as I worked hard to figure it out.

I thought it might be the cannibalism that was upsetting me, but I knew it wasn't just that. It had something to do with the handsome man, sometimes not like a man; at least, not like Bozo or my father. I remember feeling the sensuality of the film, the sexuality that surrounded the beautiful, magical figure. It was wrong, something that he was doing was wrong. More wrong than the murderous young boys or the birds. But he was *beautiful.* The boys just wanted part of that beauty. No, they *hated* it, wanted to destroy it. I didn't hate it. I never wanted him hurt. I wished I could erase that destructive scene. And the scene with the turtles. Oh, what if the children had turned on Aunt Terry, I thought sleepily as I drifted into fantasy in the back seat. I remember shuddering as the cool of the night came in through the windows. Briefly I strayed into a more comforting vision of Molly rocking me while I cried.

"Listen, after that, Princess, I think maybe you don't want to be alone. What do you think, Mol? Want to take the kid to work?"

I came back to the world quickly and sat up straight. Scared, but hoping Molly would think it was a good idea.

49

"Sure," she answered. If a cop chances by, you scoot in and be hanging around Mol. Okay by you?"

"Yes!" I answered enthusiastically.

"But don't you tell your father or that will be the end of your summer camp."

"I don't tell him nothing," I answered truthfully.

The scene as we arrived at the bar will be with me forever, like the night I was carried over there in my pajamas. Minnie and Lester were at the table with Bozo and Ed. They made a ring of the night's long-necked beer bottles and pitchers which Aunt Terry and Molly surveyed with a look of mock awe. Ed ducked his head and smoothed his flat, unwashed brown hair in embarrassment as he slid further into the booth to make room. It didn't help much, as Ed was as short as Aunt Terry and Molly and as stout as both of them together. Next to Ed was Minnie, whose red, shiny face got misty at the sight of me, her "adopted daughter."

"In her cups," Lester explained, as he moved from his side of the booth to sit next to Minnie. Minnie smiled and squeezed toward Ed, her pink beads pulling over one of the bottles on the way. "Ooo!" she cried as the beer fell into her lap. She sat very still, staring at the small puddle that had formed in the slack of her skirt where it hung between her heavy legs. When Lester jumped to avoid the spill, Aunt Terry hauled Minnie out of the booth as if by habit, and took her off toward the bathroom, Molly in tow. "Take care of Princess, guys," Molly called. "We'll be out in a jiff."

Bozo, playing the gentleman, had risen and guided me into the booth, sliding in after me. He was huge and red-faced and smelled bad, but I associated him with the wonderful clown of the carnival and beamed at him.

"It's the little Princess, is it?" He smiled across at Ed, leaning his heavy arm across my shoulders. "Well, what do you think, Ed? Ain't she turning out grand? Who'd of thought old Terry'd have a good looker in the family?"

Ed looked embarrassed again, smoothed down his hair till it stuck out straight over both ears, and took a long gulp of beer.

"What do you mean?" Molly challenged Bozo jokingly as she returned to the table and sat next to Lester. "Nothing wrong with Terry *you* could complain about."

"Ah, only kiddin'," he answered, lowering his head and squeezing me to him. "It's just that," and he turned to look at me, his warm breath smelling garbagy, full of garlic and beer, "well, a guy like me don't spend too much time with pretty young girls, you know, Princess?"

"Hey, Boz," Ed suggested, as he cracked all his knuckles, "leave the poor kid alone, you're strangling her there."

"Oh, sorry, Princess," he said, and I thought he meant it, the poor big guy not knowing how to play anything but rough. He slid his hand, which I remember thinking was as big as a beer pitcher, across my shoulders and onto the edge of the table. As they began to talk of other things I felt bad that I had shuddered again like I had when I was thinking about the movie. Bozo had meant no harm. The motion of the turtles writhing in the sand under the shadow of the approaching birds flashed irrationally across my mind, making me writhe. I felt overwhelmed by Bozo's big, dumb, helpless bulk leaning over me and did not want to be sitting next to him any longer. I wanted to be stepping out of the trailer in my pajamas onto the cool, damp dirt in the early morning.

He put his hand on my thigh and I jumped and looked up and there, like magic, was Aunt Terry glaring at Bozo, asking what he was doing.

"Nothing, Terry. Just keeping the kid company until you got back."

"Move it on out," Aunt Terry ordered, motioning with her head for him to get up.

"Pull up a chair, Terry. Let me stay with the Princess a little longer," he whined good-naturedly.

I just stared at Aunt Terry, scared that she didn't want Bozo there either or want him to touch me, for he was just a little drunk and too friendly. I was scared because Aunt Terry was scared too. And I was wishing I was not there, but scared to say that. Knowing somehow it would be bad for Aunt Terry if I said it or if I removed Bozo's hand.

"Get your hands off her, Bozo," Aunt Terry said quietly.

And flashing again through my mind was the beautiful man attacked by the children. And also flashing across my mind perfectly clearly, unsaid: Aunt Terry it's okay, he's just jealous you're the magician and he's only a clown.

I have to stop here, I always have to stop here and picture the terrified, panicked little kid I was, not even knowing the source of my terror. I was perched on a precipice. I feel myself falling, crazy with fear, but every sense open to the revelation I sought. I was being violated on the one side by that big paw, not knowing that that was the source of my pain, and I was being summoned by a magician from the other, not knowing what she offered to me or refused for me.

And Bozo asked slowly, "Why, Terry, do you want her for yourself? Do you want her to be queer like you?"

I was paralyzed. We all were. Innocence had turned into malevolence. Comradery, into jealousy. Stupidity into cunning. Aunt Terry looked as if a harmless beast had turned to attack her. Molly for once could not help. Ed looked back and forth between Aunt Terry and Bozo and his face showed horror.

Then I sprang, it seems in retrospect, straight up, walked as hard as I could over Bozo's two huge legs, and leaped out beside Aunt Terry.

Molly reached over, smiling in a strained way, and patted Bozo's arm, saying, "Always clowning, ain't you, Bozo? Can't leave a night alone without some clowning, can he Ed?"

Ed's face relaxed, "Hey, Boz, you drink enough yet? Gloria," he yelled to the waitress, "get us another round!" His voice made us all aware that the rumble from the other tables went on, that our moment of wrath and truth could, indeed, have been a joke, had lasted no longer than a jest, could be made as insignificant as a simple magic trick.

Minnie weaved back from the bathroom. "Taking the Princess home, Ter?" she asked. "God, we could get arrested for lettin' her breathe the same air as us, we're so polluted."

"Yeah. Yeah, Minnie, guess I will," Aunt Terry finally

answered. "I guess it's time. If I don't come back, Mol', I'll see you at the trailer."

"Okay, Terry. Looks like I just have to help clean up tonight," Molly answered as Gloria arrived with the round, pushing between Aunt Terry and me and the table. Aunt Terry took my hand as if I were a little girl still and turned me toward the door — then suddenly pulled away from me. "Let's go, Princess," she said, pushing my shoulder roughly as she went ahead of me to lead the way.

She waited for me on the stoop outside, looking along the empty road. I pushed the door shut behind me and felt the cool, smokeless night air on my face and I realized I had a huge relieved smile waiting in the taut muscles of my face. Aunt Terry turned away from the road and hesitated as I joined her. I put my hand in hers as we stepped off the stoop onto the hard, cold ground. She looked at me with a great hurt question pulling all her features out of whack. I let that big waiting smile spill all over my face. The tension made me feel every inch of its slow spread, and I watched it spread beyond me all over my Aunt Terry's fine gay face.

PLEASURE PARK

I was young, I was alone. It was summer and hot in the smothering still way of the city. I'd moved here for a job now two weeks old. I hadn't met any lesbians and couldn't find a bar. Loneliness was beginning, by the second weekend, not in any recognizable form, but as an urge for a holiday, a change, some excitement.

During the week I walked to the office for exercise, but today I decided to board a bus for adventure. I remembered a bus I'd passed on my way to work whose sign, Pleasure Park Loop, had intrigued me. The city roused itself around me as I walked its streets at a leisurely pace, noting details ordinarily obscured by my morning dash. A bakery beckoned me, though the mock wedding cake in the window was frosted with dust. I bought two sweet rolls and a carton of milk from a short-haired woman who probably wasn't gay, and I moved on to the bus, munching.

At eight-thirty Pleasure Park Loop was just pulling in empty as I got downtown. Two older women shambled up the steps in front of me, one leaning on a cane, the other holding onto her. I passed them and went to the back of the bus where I opened a window. For the first time in days I felt the air moving as the bus started in the direction of the lake. Finishing my breakfast, I sank back on the seat relaxed and filled with anticipation. This was just what I needed, I told myself.

The bus seemed to ring the center of the city, passing from neighborhood to neighborhood searching for passengers I imagined still in bed, satisfied to hide from the heat. There was one block full of tasteful jewelry stores whose owners were setting out bracelets, necklaces and rings which sparkled like circles of dew in their early morning showcases. No one got on the bus there. Then several streets with churches led into a neighborhood of mothers pulling clotheslines full of white sheets across their yards from second story windows. In neighborhoods like this we picked up a few kids with fishing poles, young couples with beach blankets and bags of chips and beer. It felt more as if I was on a holiday trip.

The neighborhoods changed then, becoming increasingly well-groomed and less interesting as we approached the lake. Then, with the water, came row on row of summer cottages. Obviously the working people from the inner-city neighborhoods had beat the rich to this part of the lake. I wondered if this district was Pleasure Park and considered whether I wanted to walk in its forced holiday atmosphere. I did not. Smug assumptions of moral superiority were crowded into its sandy yards, alongside the barbecues and swing sets of a group of people alien and sometimes frightening to me.

When the bus stopped, the kids and young couples got off, but the older women did not. I held a slim hope that Pleasure Park, with the promise of its name, was still ahead of me. We rode on for a while and just as I began to suspect the old ladies had come only for the breeze of the ride, the bus took an unexpected turn into thick woods. It seemed only to be a turnaround, but the two struggled out of their seats and off the bus. I picked up my backpack and descended the back door steps.

The women slowly followed an overgrown, obviously unused road. I noticed they looked at me a few times furtively, out of what I thought was their timid world of old age. I stood wondering where I had got myself to. There were weeds coming up through the road and sunken trolley tracks. I began to walk and saw through the trees huge plots of white cement, also cracked by weeds, to either side of me. Was this, then, Pleasure Park? A vestigial trolley stop, a ruined memory?

It was, and I was fascinated by it. The sun was on a course to her peak unimpeded by cloud or fog. Below her a couple of acres of the white cement warmed themselves, preparing for a later brightness to rival the sun's. A few wooden structures were all that was left of the park. They, too, were white, or had been so long ago that now the cement was brighter, stronger looking than their paint, and they looked like what they had become: remnants of a civilization which could no longer enjoy this simple pleasure park. And the structures, what had been their function, once so important they were built to last right into a time beyond themsleves?

One, I guessed, had been a carousel, its long gone wooden horses poised as if for escape under wooden columns and an inverted bowl of a roof. There the old ladies seemed to have gravitated. What must have been an indoor arcade lay beyond that. I explored this further, leaving the old ones to what I imagined were memories of husbands. In the arcade I stepped cautiously, unsure of the safety of the boards which showed signs of weakness and rot. Vandals had been there, leaving large-lettered obscenities over the discolored places where the mechanical fortune teller, the flashing pinball machines, the fast board games must have been. They had built fires on the open space once used for dancing. Counters lined the walls, empty of their sugary carnival feasts. There were empty windows with fixtures for shutters or awnings, and gaping openings where doors had been. I felt the vibrations of pleasure-seeking crowds in the ruined grey boards under my feet. The sun crept across the wood toward me and I fled out a back exit to the deck that ringed the arcade.

On this side of the park small replicas of the carousel's shelter, rides once, were scattered. I peered into the shadows they cast. There was also a band shell. The people must have thronged here to lift their spirits in the summer heat and, in the stillness of crowds past, I imagined benches of them fanning themselves. The music would swell from silvery cool instruments like a storm of pleasure. Then, with a sigh and hot applause, everyone would return to what they were, a town come to forget the heat and monotony of their lives, to lose the kids for a while, to remind themselves of the lost romance that had led them to their marriages.

And here, I thought, were two of them. The old women had finished their perusal of the carousel's ghost and had wandered off toward the woods. There must be paths through the trees which shared their memories. Eventually they returned, slower and tired-looking, glancing shyly toward me and toward the bench I now occupied, the only one in shade.

"How do," the taller of the two said once she'd rested. The shorter one still had her eyes closed and patted her forehead now and then with the kind of hanky given to third grade teachers at the end of the year.

"Hi!" I answered, all open and friendly. I must have looked like a puppy, I was so eager to hear about the worlds of Pleasure Park. Their world, I hoped. I never suspected it was a hope they'd once shared.

"Never seen you here before," she said. She had a shy smile, and thin white hair all awry from the bus ride. Her glasses had slipped down her nose in the heat. She wouldn't meet my eyes.

"I just moved to town. Graduated from State last month. I never heard of Pleasure Park and wanted to see what it was."

"What it was . . . ." She nodded. Then she looked sadly toward her friend whose face mirrored her expression.

"Wasn't never much more," the other almost whispered. Her hair was thin and white too, cut just a little longer. She wore a sleeveless blouse and, surprisingly, bermuda shorts. I realized the taller woman was in white pants. How out of place, I thought, on women of their age. "Would you like some lemonade?" I asked, pulling out the thermos I'd packed in my bag.

Their old eyes lit up in gratitude. "Didn't expect it to be so hot out here," lanky said. "Usually get a breeze off the lake. This will go down good about now." She further rolled up the short sleeves of her loose checked blouse in such an

58

unladylike way I could have sworn she was a dyke.

"I packed a lunch, but it's too hot to stay long enough to eat. Drink all you like," I said as I poured a cup for them.

Lanky took it in her shaky, spotted hands and passed it to the other. "Em," she said, "this will perk you up."

"Ice cold," Em sighed after a tiny taste.

The other took it back and had a small taste herself. "I wish we had something to offer you."

"No need. I've got everything I want. You finish that, now. There's as much left in here if I want it."

So they drank with obvious relish. And stopped halfway through the cup. "I'm Madge McCormack," lanky said, reaching to shake my hand while Emily held the cup. "My friend Emily."

Did I imagine she hesitated around the word friend? "Curly Singer," I said.

"Jewish," Emily nodded approvingly.

"I'm glad to meet you both. Do you come out here often?"

"We don't come out much any more," Madge said. "It's a big trip for us now. Em's niece used to drive us once in a while, but she moved downstate to live in a 'real city,' as she says." Madge looked as if she wanted to wink.

"She thinks it's silly anyway," Emily added, "still to be wandering around this ghost town."

I looked puzzled.

"For years we came out here looking for the ring," Madge explained. "The ring we lost here first time we came out after we moved in together. It got to be a habit."

She searched my eyes, looking away quickly then. I left off wondering and began to conjecture. Were there really lesbians *this* old?

"We thought we should keep doing things together even after we shared a house. Why should we stop going out just because we were in our thirties and unmarried?" she asked angrily. "We were paying off the house, but back then the trolley ride was only a nickle. We'd buy some popcorn, listen to the free concert and sit across on the beach. Didn't take much to make us happy then, did it, Em?" she asked her

59

with a twinkle in her eye.

"Not much, Madge," Em answered, patting the hand that held the cane.

"Who used to come here?" I asked, trying to make an opening for them to tell me there were women like themselves here.

"Why all kinds," Emily said. Then she looked briefly at Madge. "Almost," she finished lamely.

Madge took up the narrative. "It would be packed on a Saturday night. That's when we would come mostly. Looking for something, some excitement after the long week of housekeeping and working."

"We were both working. Couldn't make ends meet otherwise," Emily explained, almost apologizing. "But Madge went out and worked twice as long hours as me at the factory. I was only a secretary and kept up the house. That was my overtime!" She laughed affectionately toward Madge.

"Between me being so tired and little Em being so cooped up, we figured we deserved a night out."

"If we came on a Sunday, we could rent a boat for fifty cents and go around the lake. We got a little privacy then," Em explained, again casting that affectionate gaze at Madge. Then she sighed. "I've always thought what a shame it was we didn't lose the ring in the lake. Then we wouldn't have had a hope of finding it."

"Maybe she doesn't want to hear about the ring," Madge said.

"Of course I do." Something about their story appealed to me as much as Pleasure Park itself. I needed to get at the core of both to satisfy myself now.

Madge and Emily looked at each other in a resigned way as if deciding to take a risk and share an intimate secret with me. I couldn't believe two women this old could be sending me the same signals my contemporaries do when they're about to spill the beans.

"I gave her a ring," Madge almost whispered. "You know why, I think."

I smiled in a little sideways way I learned in the city and stretched out my red pinky ring to them. Their wrinkled

60

faces smoothed right out they smiled back so hard and Em dug her elbow into Madge, saying, "I told you so!" She peered at me. "I never knew a Jewish girl who was one of us."

I squirmed a little, afraid their ignorance might be prejudice, but they just seemed glad to add yet another kind of person to their slight collection of "one of us."

Madge explained further, finally meeting my gaze, "Em wearing a ring like other people made what we were seem all right to us, not something to be laughed at or to get us arrested."

Emily began to tell the story. "It was the Fourth of July and we'd spent the day at my brother's picnic, but by the end of the day we wanted to be off on our own. There were so many of *them* and only two of us. It would be the same at the Park, but we could hope to see more of us and we could be by ourselves more in a strange crowd, if you know what I mean. By the time we got here it was twilight. All day it'd been almost as hot as today and there wasn't a breeze stirring then either. The midway was full, but it was hushed. Folks were moving slow, their kids whining, and a lot of them were sitting down at dinner on the benches or in the grass. Back then, they hadn't poured all this cement. That came later when there were more money makers than space and they tried to make room for them all. Seedy was what it got to be then. But that was a long time later.

"We weren't here long when the dark, which had been sneaking into the sky for a while, came on. All of a sudden you realized the darn sun had gone and it took its heat with it. The crowd picked up in the cool and Madge and me hopped up onto the carousel like we'd dropped a dead weight. Under the pretty colored lights, the breeze felt like a waterfall of stars landing on us as we went round and round, all full of ourselves, feeling our new love."

The old ones smiled shyly at each other, as if embarrassed about the passion they shared. I was beginning to look forward to old age. It was going to be, contrary to what the straight world predicted, a happy time.

"Then we got off," Madge said, handing the cup of

lemonade to Emily. "We walked around a while longer and started to cross over to the beach where the fireworks were starting. Em noticed her ring wasn't on her finger."

"I wasn't used to it yet and I'd lost weight since Madge and me got together. Worrying about how we were, what people would think." She looked to me for understanding and got it. "I'd meant to tape it up, but hadn't got around to it yet. There were so many new things to get used to. Like being loved." And she looked that special way again at Madge. "So I'd got in the habit of feeling for it now and then, and when it wasn't there, my heart fell to my feet. I'll never forget that feeling. Like the carousel had stopped turning forever, the lights had gone out and the world stood still. My precious circle of gold was lost!"

I was afraid she would cry, she was so moved, and I offered a refill of their lemonade.

"Not yet, dear, we have plenty," Emily managed to say before she went on. "The rest of the evening till they closed up we spent not on a holiday, but searching for that shiny speck of gold in the confusion of the moving carousel."

"When we couldn't find it we came back the next day," Madge continued, "and under the hot sun searched every horse, every seat, every crack and cranny on the platform. We questioned the fellows who worked here. They said they hadn't seen it and we had to believe them. They were mostly local boys we didn't think would spoil our happiness for a few dollars, though we heard the snickering that went on behind our backs and wondered."

"I thought the world had ended," Emily said. "As if our marriage," she looked shyly toward me as she used the word, "was jinxed because of my carelessness. As if what I was, what we were, would ruin everything no matter how much we pretended to be like everyone else."

"And I felt like a poor specimen of a husband who couldn't find it for her, nor even afford to buy her a replacement. I, too, feared they were right after all. We couldn't ride the carousel with the rest of the crowd. We couldn't have a real marriage."

"Pleasure Park went on around us and the day went by.

We could hear the laughing, the excited screams, the romancing, the buying, the selling. All of life went on and my world had stopped dead in its tracks. We didn't even have anyone to tell of our tragedy because we'd have to explain the ring. It was the first time I really felt how outside of life we were, how much we would be alone in every way."

"Then one of the boys suggested if it got into some of the machinery of the carousel it might have got ground down to nothing by now. We were so hot and discouraged we gave up and stopped for a lemonade. It was Curly's lemonade that brought it back so clear, don't you think?"

"Could be, Madge. But that doesn't mean we gave in altogether. No, we'd come up almost as often as at first, always with one eye to the ground. Took the edge off our fun, always to be looking for that little ring, that missing piece of us, and later we did stop coming. Pleasure Park wasn't meant for people like us any more than rings were. But Madge bought me a little ring at the five and dime because I still longed for one."

"A ring that tarnished easy and had to be polished all the time. It wasn't like the real thing."

"Around about then we met two girls like us. For once we were not alone. We started coming out here with them — what else was there for the likes of us to do? And we told them the story. They began to look for the ring, too. One day they did find a ring, a man's ring, but they turned it in and somebody claimed it that same day. Soon after that the girls stopped getting along together and one moved to a bigger city while the other eventually married a man. Besides, by that time they were pouring cement over the open spaces out here. It wasn't as pretty as it had been, and we thought, though we hardly ever spoke of it anymore, that my ring was probably under one of those rough patches they set down to squeeze money from the park."

Madge winked at me again, as if we had a special understanding. "Progress, you know."

The sun was getting higher and marched boldly across the white ground toward us. They finished their cup of lemonade and would take no more. "What a pleasant rest," they told

63

each other, Madge checking her big watch to plan their departure. "Bus won't be around again for another forty-five minutes," she said. "No use walking over to the stop yet. There's no shade there."

"Did you never find it then?" I asked, wanting more of their story. The white park blazed around us like a desert around an oasis. Our tiny pool of shade would soon be gone.

"Well, the next thing that happened," Madge said, "is that I read in the paper where the park was to be torn down. Gangs and motorcycle clubs were disturbing people and tearing the park down faster than it could be repaired. And those boys had enjoyed the park so much as youngsters, is what I don't understand." She shook her head regretfully. "That was a shock, let me tell you. All those happy families we envied were now destroying the park."

"A part of us seemed to be going with it, even if we never did really belong there."

"We didn't have much excitement in those years before I retired. We'd found a bar in a bigger city not too far away and we'd go look at you pretty young things."

I could imagine Madge sizing us up from a benign corner of a bar.

"Or we'd go up to the restaurant on our street for Saturday dinner, but if you went there too early you were in the middle of families full of squealing young children, and if you went too late, all the young dating couples were there. And we saw family at the holidays. We met no more like us around here and felt nothing of the kind of giddiness coming to Pleasure Park used to bring us when we were kids. It was a dull, even life and I guess we both felt kind of cheated, but we stuck together rather than go looking for what we couldn't have together, with somebody else."

Madge paused to wipe her brow with a handkerchief. The flirtatious twinkle was gone from her tired face. The sun was about to touch me where I sat at the end of the bench. Madge said, "When I read about Pleasure Park being torn down, seemed like we could lie down and wait to die."

Emily nodded. "You were depressed for a long time, dear. Right into our retirement. Then one day I got the idea that if we were ever to find my long lost ring, we might find it when they were taking everything down."

"Sure. It was a great idea. They were taking apart the carousel. Aw, I knew there was no point getting that old ring back. It wouldn't bring us back anything, but the idea was exciting to me who had been sad for so long, who led the kind of life I did. It was excitement enough to make my days new, to make me want to go on. My life was ahead of me again," Madge said, her eyes once more stirring to life.

"We came out here the day they were to start," Emily said, excited. "We explained our story to the workmen who joined right in, helpful as all get out. We were too old to make them suspicious anymore, we thought."

"Probably thought we were a couple of crazy old spinsters, but what the heck, we said, maybe we'll find it and if we did it'd be a kind of triumph after all those years." She looked up at the sun. "Whew," she said, "it's a hot one. What do you say, Em, shall we make a last round?" Emily nodded and rose carefully. "Would you like to join us?"

"Sure would," I replied, hot for the ending now. "What happened when they took it all down?"

We started toward the carousel shell and its small pool of shade. "It was heart-breaking," old Emily answered. "Like watching them murder some gentle harmless old beast. But we stayed. Came back day after day till it was all down."

Madge took up the story again. "Got to know the boys real well, and we'd bring them cold sodas, fruit for all their trouble. The carousel was last. Took them all of a fall day to pack it up. It was going to be sold for antiques. Very careful and slow they worked on the carousel. We followed every one of those horses to their crates and watched them cover up their fine, faded old bodies. And we poked our fingers in every grimy machine part.

"We stood back at the end of the day, exhausted, ringless, watching the workmen pack up their tools. It was gone, the Park we knew. Night was coming on sooner with summer past. Most of the workmen were gone."

We had left the carousel and edged toward the woods. Madge stopped in the shade of the trees. "Right about here, wasn't it, Em?"

Em, smiling wistfully, nodded.

"One of the younger workmen stepped out of the woods holding something in the palm of his hand. He asked if it was what we'd been looking for."

Madge was looking at her hand as if it held something. "I reached out and took it from him. Under the trees it seemed like night had fallen, but to me that gold circle glittered like the sun was shining. It looked good as new, not a scratch on it. I asked Em if the initials inside matched the ones we'd had put in."

"I was in shock, I think," Emily said. "But the tears started by themselves when I saw my initials."

"Where was it, how had he found it, I wanted to know. The boy looked like he hadn't even been born when we lost the ring. He looked sheepishly at us, asking us not to blame him. His father had brought it home back when he worked on the carousel as a youth."

Clenching her wrinkled hands into fists, Madge went on. "*Thief*! I wanted to shout and I wanted to strike the son of the boy who ran the very machine we loved. The carousel, the toy of the crowd, one of the few things we felt we could share with everybody else!"

She shook her head. "He didn't try to excuse his father, but told us the man had a 'mean streak for queers.' The boy was so decent he apologized for the word he was raised to use. He said his father would tell queer jokes and show off the ring. He'd kept it to teach us a lesson, to teach us we couldn't be married like normal people. We were too grieved to say anything, but I kept thinking, *And we believed him! We thought just like he wanted us to!*

"The boy started to go. He explained that he didn't like what his father had done. When he saw how we still searched for the ring, still felt we needed it, he wanted to give it to us."

Madge shrugged, her face sad as any I've ever seen. "I managed to thank him, and the boy took off muttering this was just one of the things his father had done that he was trying to fix."

The three of us stood beneath the trees now. There was a distant rumble and we all looked toward where the bus would come in.

"We'd better get over to the bus stop," Emily said and took Madge's arm. The story had taken a lot out of Madge. "Thank you so much for the drink, Curly." She reached up and mussed my curls.

"Thanks for telling me your story," I said, heavy with sadness.

"We haven't many to tell it to," Madge said, reviving a little as she leaned like a long-legged bird to peck my cheek. "Come pay us a call some day. We're in the book."

"Yes," I said quietly as I watched them venture out from the umbrella of the woods, like two ghosts weighed down by their burdens of life.

I, too, stepped into the sunlight, to take a last look at Pleasure Park before crossing to the lake. The white columns and wooden platforms glared at me across the wasteland of cracking cement. Green weeds were proving their strength through it, perhaps could destroy it. I'd learned what Pleasure Park was and wouldn't need to come back there. Unless to tell someone else the story, to show them the empty shells.

AT A BAR II
In the Morning

Sunrays fell like cobwebs through the dusty bar window. The small room held several round formica-topped tables between the short counter and the window. On one side of the door to the backroom stood a shining new juke box whose flashing lights made it look like a visitor from the future. On the other side of the door, garishly painted women in bathing suits posed on an old pinball machine. Sally the bartender, skinny as a bar rail and tall, with a cap of short blonde hair, leaned over the bar on her elbows to stare past the flaking window sign. She smiled slightly to see Gabby's short, bobbing figure beyond it.

"Hah!" breathed Gabby as she pushed through the door, sounding the cowbells that hung there to warn Sally of customers.

"Hah yourself, Junior."

Gabby protested indignantly, fists on her broad hips. "What's the matter with you, that you got to call me Junior every morning now, Sal? I'll be forty like you next year." She took off a wool plaid jacket and climbed onto a stool, shaking her sweatshirt away from her body and her green work pants. "Got hot out there. I'm sweating like a pig."

Sally smiled at her. "You just looked like a Junior,

69

coming past that window. Like a little kid, coming home to Dad."

"After my night on the town?"

"Where'd you go last night, Gab?"

"Here," Gabby sighed, looking bored.

"What'd you do?"

"What I'd like to do more of right now, Sal."

"Ten a.m. fix coming up. You know, by the time your unemployment runs out you're going to be a real lush."

"Why the hell not?" challenged Gabby, downing a shot and picking up her short glass of beer. "Hair of the dog, like they say."

Sally ran her rag over the top of the bar, picking up nothing but the foam from Gabby's beer.

"Nobody in yet?" Gabby asked.

"You're first, as usual."

"Come on, Sal. Meg's usually here before me."

"Sometimes," Sally disagreed, stretching her long body in boredom.

"You working all day?"

"Somebody's got to keep you high."

"Thank goodness for that. Couldn't stand it otherwise."

"Can't you get into the CETA program?"

"And do what, clean the streets? I'm not ready for that, no matter what they think."

"It'd keep you out of here a few hours a day."

Gabby's face closed. "Lay off me about that. It's my life."

"Sure, sure. I just don't want you to end up like Meg."

"I won't. I'll get a job. I'll get a girl. I'll get a decent place. I just need a vacation."

"From everything?"

"Didn't you ever just feel so damn tired you couldn't lift your head off the pillow in the morning if it didn't hurt so much? I'll get my energy back soon, Sal. I've always got it back before. I'm just tired of falling in love, then breaking up. Finding a job, then getting canned. Fixing up a nice apartment, then losing it when I lose my girl and my job. You can talk. You got this place here."

70

"Which me and Liz worked damn hard for."

"At least you knew what the hell you wanted. Not everybody can be a bartender or run a business."

"Nobody's asking you to."

"Let me have another set up."

"I hope nothing happened to Meg. She cadged more drinks than usual last night. I couldn't shut her off soon enough."

"What could happen to an old rummy like that?"

"What happens to all the other old rummies on the street? You think she can't get sick or hurt just because she's a dyke?"

"No. Maybe. You think she's like the guys on the Bowery?"

"One step away, Gab, that's all."

"No. I can't believe that."

They fell silent. The mailwoman, Jenny, pushed through the door and sounded the cowbells again. "Sounds like I'm down on the farm, Sally. How are you today? Gab? Where's Meg?"

"Don't know, we were just talking about that. You see her around, tell her to drop in, okay? Want a shot?"

"Love it, honey, but that's all I got to do is get caught smelling of it. I'll take a raincheck again?"

"Sure, sure, anytime," Sally said, sorting through her mail. "We'll see you later, right?"

"Could be — it's Thursday!" The door slammed on the dim room.

Gabby rose, taking her beer, and wandered to the pinball machine. "Friday's a bad day to look for a job too, you know?"

"Any day's bad for you from what I see."

"Really, Sal. Friday the bosses are looking to sail their boats, not start someone new. Especially not someone who looks like me."

"How you look don't matter with the kind of jobs you're looking for."

"It shouldn't." She put a quarter in the machine. "Ain't you got this fixed yet?"

71

"Supposed to come today."

"One stinking ball for a quarter."

"Keeps you on your toes. You got to do real well on that quarter. Here's your other quarters."

"No. Never mind. I'm not in the mood. Too much work." Gabby thought for a minute, then walked to the window. The street was empty. "You know how many damn girls I thought I'd be with forever? Five. Five damn girls. Maybe it's me. When it comes to making it work, I can't do it. Falling in love is fine. I got that down pat. But when it starts being all uphill, all I seem to be able to do is to take off. If they don't leave me first. If only I could keep a job. Or if we could have kids — that would make us work to stay together. Even if we had damn parents who'd get upset if we split, it would help. We come down here and what is there? A bunch of chicks looking to make it with somebody, it don't matter who or who it's going to hurt. And like a damn fool I can't resist them. It's so easy to cheat on your girl. You don't care anyway when you're high. Until she finds out. So why try? What's the sense?"

Sally was dusting the bottles behind the bar. "It's got its good points," she said, thinking of Liz coming home that morning and slipping naked into bed with her.

"And jobs. I'm not smart. I'm not good looking. I can't get a job in an office because I look too much like a dyke to fit in. I can't get a job in a factory for anything but minimum wage because I'm too small, too much a woman, to do men's work. I used to work hard to get ahead in a job, but I didn't have what it took. If I work as fast as I can on piecework all that gets me is a little more money and a sore back. I can't even get hired for a waitress job 'cause of how I look. I tried everything. And I know I'll get something, some damn shit job. But who wants it?"

"So you drink."

"Why the hell not," Gabby said again, returning to her stool. "How about I go across the street and get us hamburgers? Might as well make myself useful somewhere."

"Sounds good to me."

"Tomorrow I got to get my check. Won't be in till

afternoon." Gabby thought aloud. "Wonder were that Meg is."

"Why don't you stop up at her place on your way to get lunch?"

"Where's she live?"

"Around the corner. One thirty-six. Top floor."

"That flea trap?"

"At this point she's lucky to have that. One of her old lovers helps with the rent."

"Wow. I didn't know she was that bad off. I'll never fall that low," Gabby said, shaking her head. "Just give me a beer this time. Then I'll take off. Maybe she'll come in while I drink it. How far up is this top floor anyway?"

"Only five."

"Shit. You know I'm not feeling energetic. That's a long ways up."

They sat watching the window. The sun had moved overhead and the sunlight no longer reached directly inside. The room had become dimmer, the two figures in it shadowy and totally still. Only the bottles shone in the mirror behind them.

"Sally!" Jenny the mailwoman cried as she flung the door open before her. Even the cowbells were shocked and only thudded once against the door.

"Is it Meg?" Sally asked in an apprehensive whisper.

"And is it ever. They found her this morning. She fell down the stairs."

"All the way down from the top?" Gabby asked in horror.

"Down the flight from her floor. Then the bannister collapsed where she landed."

"Is she . . . ?" Sally asked.

"She's not dead. Weak as she is, they said she was still alive." Jenny laughed bitterly. "You can't kill us dykes. You can keep us down, shut us up, make us hide all our lives, but we're damn tough to get rid of. She was asking for a drink when they took her to the hospital."

"A drink," Sally spat. "Sometimes I hate this business."

"Maybe I better go visit her," Gabby mumbled. "See

73

if there's anything she needs."

"Could need a lot."

"Don't we all," Sally said.

"She's at St. Vincent's," Jenny said. "I'll go up when I get off work. You want to go with me, Sal?"

"Definitely. How about that hamburger, Junior? Before you run out that door."

Gabby stopped in her rush to leave. "Sorry, Sal. You're stuck in here, aren't you? I'll bring it right back."

Jenny stared after her. "I haven't seen Gabby move that fast in months."

Smiling, Sally answered, "It's sure nice to see."

Once more the cowbells made their jaunty, raucous sound, as four women and a large pizza crowded through the still open door. "Hi, ladies!" Sally greeted them, setting up glasses for four beers. "So long, Jenny. Come by for me?"

"About four?"

Sally nodded assent on her way to deliver the beers to the women who had assembled around the pizza. "Want some, Sal?" one asked. "I know you don't get a lunch hour."

"Thanks, no," she answered, taking their money. "Gabby's bringing me a hamburger."

"Yeah," another woman said as she tried to stop the mozzarella from stretching further toward her mouth. "Where is she? Where's Meg?"

"Well, Meg's had a fall. But Gabby's on her way now," Sally answered, confidence in her smile.

MARY'S GARDEN

As I looked down the long foyer of her apartment, it was difficult to pick Mrs. O'Broin out from the accumulation of bric-a-brac. I was sure she had a souvenir there from every tenant who had ever moved out or died or parted unknowingly from some treasure. China animals, faded in someone's windows, postured on tiny tables. A bow-legged bulldog doorstop grimaced from among the jumble under a dusty tablecloth. Dull, gold-stemmed lamps lined both sides of the hall in uneven procession to the great desk that severed tenants from Mrs. O'Broin's living quarters. On the desk stood the proudest of the lamps, one with a green glass shade set like an upside-down bowl over the desk's clutter.

"Emmie," she'd say to herself when I went to pay the rent, "where'd you put it now?" Or, she'd say before she found the rent pad or the disassembled Papermate, "That wild creature of a granddaughter of mine's been into the desk for candy and upset everything again!" By that time, I would have had my fill of stumbling on the bits of overlaid carpet and would be backing slowly toward the door, nodding while Mrs. O'Broin's voice continued and her tall white body shrank with distance, becoming, as I closed the door, a dusty, brittle fixture among all the others in the foyer.

My apartment was over hers on the second floor. I had a big window whose top curved over two smaller side windows, and this triad of glass fascinated me and lured me from my desk more than I should have let it. Often, I would watch Mrs. O'Broin on her thin, stiff legs wobble determinedly down the courtyard steps past the splendor of Mary's long shallow gardens. She cared for the gardens herself now that Mary was dead; she would survey their half-wild growth as she passed them on her way to the bruised white car which stood patiently rattling at the end of the walk. "Emmie ain't so young as she used to be," I could hear Mrs. O'Broin explain to herself that summer when my side windows strained for the city breeze. And off she'd go, sailing sluggishly through the hot streets to the grocer who had known her when, according to Mrs. O'Broin, first her husband and then Mary had kept the building shining like a great mansion.

One day of the second summer I lived in Mrs. O'Broin's building, when the air even in my high-ceilinged apartment got too fetid to breathe and the typewriter ink made me nauseous, I decided on a walk to clear my head. I took the elevator down, on the chance it had kept some cool air inside. It passed the lobby and went to the basement.

I have always been deathly afraid of basements and cowered in the corner of the elevator, jumping when Mrs. O'Broin stepped swiftly inside. Her hands were covered with soot and she clasped to her smudged bosom three jars filled with silver coins. It looked as if the jars had been buried under the ashes in the old coal furnace that stood down there, useless, even when Mary was still around to fuel it. Mrs. O'Broin was wearing an old cotton housedress, its faded flowers blue and green on a darker green. It sagged to one side of her body and her hair sagged with it. She looked at me for a moment, a flash of brightness eerily lighting her eyes, and said, "Emmie's done," not like an old lady teasing me about her age as usual, but for that moment as if she were that senile person she played.

"Emmie's done," ran through my head like a buoy's bell in a storm and sent a shudder down my back as cold as the first splash of water the wind raises on the sea. Before the elevator door shut all the way I stepped out of it and walked as briskly as I could without panicking to the basement door. The elevator closed behind me and began to rise before I was outside. Feeling foolish, I wondered if Mrs. O'Broin guessed that she had scared me.

I knew, of course, that it was only being in an elevator and a basement that made me feel so strangely frightened. It was a fear I remembered whole and unchanged from my childhood. Mrs. O'Broin was a pretty strange lady anyway, I assured myself as I struck off down the hill toward the intertwining back streets on the edge of the ghetto. The heat must have gotten to her, I thought, along with the memories that must always be with the widow who stays on. Especially in Mrs. O'Broin's case this would be true, as she had stayed and taken on Mary's work, the work Mary, in turn, had taken over when Mrs. O'Broin threw her husband out. She had told me when Mr. O'Broin went, the landlord had ordered her out, but he let her stay when she told him what a bum her husband had been and how she had done most of the work herself or worked just as hard at getting him to do it. She told him that she'd keep the place up, and after all these years she'd put into it he should give her and her poor daughter and the baby a chance.

So the landlord, in the face of so much adamant womanhood, let her stay, and his visits were so infrequent that he never noticed it was Mary who took over. "My own daughter was like a leech," Mrs. O'Broin said, "never helped out at all."

But Mrs. O'Broin forgave her because almost as soon as her daughter was old enough to be of use she'd had a little girl of her own. Forgave her, that is, except when their screaming fights rose up the dumbwaiter shaft to my apartment. After one of the fights the car, which had lain idle since Mary's departure, was put back into use. And I finally figured out that the daughter had found her purpose in life: she would be her mother's chauffeur. She would not go into the grocery store, nor would she dress and attend mass, but she waited faithfully outside, even for doctor's appointments.

For a little while I walked and lost myself in the heat in the little maze of cobbler shops, pizza parlors and corner groceries, noting the mad, fantastic architecture bred from poverty and high hopes. Grandfathers, gnarled and brown as their stogies, had clawed at the earth, raising the colors of their old lands out of it, hosing down tomato plants so that the greens and dull oranges and finally bright reds would shine without the dust of the city on them. In a yard here and there I saw a chicken or rooster in little havens salvaged from the factories. After a while I got to the edge of the black neighborhood and turned as a stone flew past me and small children began to chant, "White lady, white lady." I walked sadly up the hill toward the long street where I lived. It was much cooler and even going uphill was a relief compared to the swelter of my typewriter. So I reached the top and turned away from my building toward the length of Remington Street and its long hill down.

There she was, almost as if I'd expected her to be there: Mrs. O'Broin in the long black dress hanging below a long grey coat which was too warm for this weather, but was her best coat. A prim black hat like a lacquered crabshell was clinging to her hair. Her tiny grey curls were as limp in the noon sun as the black veil was stiff atop the hat. In her hand a large black patent leather pocketbook on a plastic handle pulled her down to the left, while her slip fell with each step beneath her dress hem to the right. She had no nylons on long, shocking white calves black and blue with bruises. She wore regulation flat practical oxfords, and these were the only sign I could see that Emmie O'Broin might be doing a lot of walking and therefore going farther than St. Andrews Church. Until she passed it. And then I thought she was upset or needy and might be going to see the old priest at the parish house. But no, she passed that too. Her walk set that buoy ringing the words "Emmie's done" in my head again. Was she in trouble?

I stopped my guessing for a while, not really caring, just glad to be out on Remington in the summer. The last winter when I was working nights I had walked the very same mile back from work through knee-deep snow because it was so bad a storm the plows hadn't reached Remington yet. My replacement was late and the plowmen were still sitting there at eight a.m. When I finally got home around nine there was Mrs. O'Broin gingerly shoveling at the front steps. "Heaven help us if someone falls on the steps and sues Mr. Greater-Than-God-Himself and old Emmie didn't shovel."

I reached for the tool to take a turn and she let me. After about five minutes she took it back saying, "I can't just stand by here watching someone else do my work. Give it here and scoot inside where it's warm and dry before you catch your death of cold. If Emmie can't do it then she deserves to be booted out. And I'm afraid my time is coming, so I might as well do it while I can."

I am not one to argue with pride, and being exhausted myself from working and walking, I left her there with her shovel and the daughter suddenly in the doorway. The daughter, in her nightgown, red hair hanging greasily onto her shoulders, shouted for her mother to get inside or she'd have a heart attack and then where would her poor grandchild live.

When I awoke several hours later the snow had not so much stopped as hung suspended over the city as if waiting to fall meanly right smack onto Mrs. O'Broin's swept clean steps and walk. It began to do that as my breakfast smells mingled with everyone else's supper.

And here I was, in the summer heat, still worrying about the old lady as she plugged away down the hill ahead of me. Her walk, on those gangly legs, became more uneven as she went down into the steeper part of the decline. It crossed my mind that she might be tipsy, but I remembered there'd been no scent of liquor in the elevator that morning, nor had I ever seen Mrs. O'Broin like that.

Except the one snow-filled evening.

Then I'd gone to the lobby after my twilight breakfast to see if the mail got through. There stood Mrs. O'Broin on the inside of the double doors watching it snow, holding a small tooth glass of amber stuff she kept twirling in her hands. "Mary's been gone a year," she said. "I guess that means she is dead, though I never even saw her body again.

Twenty years by my side." She looked straight at me accusingly. "Twenty years and they just took her body from me on a night like this on a stretcher through the snow."

I was afraid she would cry right there in the doorway while I watched her. "Are you all right, Mrs. O'Broin?" I asked, worried that the shoveling had hurt her.

"I'll never be all right till I'm at my Mary's side and I don't care who knows it, though I think *you* understand," she said, giving my jeans, sweatshirt and short hair the once-over. "She was the best friend a woman ever had." Mrs. O'Broin turned away from me. "Worked herself to death. Had a back as broad as a man's and was willing to use it. When Mr. O'Broin went she filled his shoes five times over. And never lifted a hand to hurt me. The best thing I ever did was to let her buy my drink that night at Maloney's restaurant. And they took her from me. Back to Springfield to be buried with her family, they said. Well, they didn't want her when she was alive, says I. I loved her in her men's shirttails and out of them."

She swayed a bit and I reached out to steady her, feeling the loose flesh on her upper arm and settling the bony elbow in my palm.

"I only wish I'd known her from the start. Mr. O'Broin wasn't nothing compared. But now I intend to know her through eternity, God willing." She shook her arm free of my support and waved me to the mailboxes. "You can look if you want, Curly, but he never came," she complained. "Our walk was clear and not a soul come up it but yourself this morning. Nor went down it. Once the snow, and worse than this, wouldn't keep folks in. Now it's any excuse to do a bad job or none at all."

She stood there like a tall weathered farmer looking out at the lands she'd worked on all her life, humbly respecting nature's work, proudly surveying her own. I won't say I didn't suspect that Mary had been a lesbian, but lonely as I was and hard as I'd been looking for lesbians in the two years I'd been in town, I'd never suspected Mrs. O'Broin and surly, sooty Mary of being lovers.

I'd left her there to mourn alone, feeling my own lack of

contact with other lesbians come rushing into my heart like a snowdrift, heavy and cold.

As I now walked down the hot hill behind her, I supposed Mrs. O'Broin thought she had deserved a drink that night, on the anniversary of Mary's death and kidnapping by her straight relatives. But otherwise I'd never thought of Mrs. O'Broin hitting the bottle, and I dismissed the thought. I reached the iron spikes that fenced in St. Andrews' and leaned against them as Mrs. O'Broin crossed Remington by the WALK sign and started over the highway. I didn't want to be too conspicuous, but the old woman had piqued my curiosity. Perhaps she was just going downtown to shop. It would be very like her to be after a birthday present for her granddaughter, though she'd usually leave the house for nothing but necessities.

Obviously she had hidden money in the old furnace and got filthy rooting around in there for it. Now she was off to buy a huge green elephant or something else that had caught her granddaughter's eye. I ran my hand along the rusting church spikes to slow myself down as Mrs. O'Broin, at full steam, was painfully slow. On the other side of the bridge over the thruway she stopped for another light and stood very straight at the curb. She looked as if she needed a cane.

I followed her again as she passed the new police station. She stopped for a moment and I thought she would go in, but she hesitated by all the police motorcycles grouped pell-mell in front of the station. She seemed to examine each black-and-white oversized machine before going up to one and touching the white bar between the handles and the seat. I had a vision of her, like a Disney heroine, flinging herself onto one and riding off out of the city free of everything, including her sanity. Perhaps she had been considering it, for as the door of the station opened and two policemen strode out she straightened guiltily and swayed away from the motorcycles, as if to tear herself away from temptation.

Down the hill she continued, her bag swinging heavily one way, all her clothes hanging the other, past the old homes taken over by lawyers, past the shoddy Chinese restaurant, past the welfare hotel to which the daughter threatened to move if Mrs. O'Broin stopped supporting her. The hill was deserted in the noontime heat and there was just myself and Mrs. O'Broin, lurching down it toward Main Street.

There I thought I would see her destination. And again I was wrong. Right on she went, past the dirt-splashed windows of the coin shop, the restaurant supplier, the upholsterer, the corner spa. Across the street she went, picking up speed from somewhere. Her profile was toward me and I could see her mouth working. She was talking to herself — but she always did. I ran down the last of the hill to the corner around which she had disappeared, afraid I'd miss her rushing into a dark doorway, and found her crossing the street diagonally toward the entrance to the railroad station.

I heard the buoy's bell ringing in my mind again, and shivered. The station stood like a great dark fact, its mass spilled down the hill from the city. The sun shone in back of it, making it the blacker. The building itself was set high, level with the tracks over the street. Underneath the station were indoor and outdoor passages so that I could see wall and space, all dark, but with some shadows and lines of light falling into the spaces. Steps went up, half hidden, at either end of the building. There was also a ramp at one end. Many a time I had climbed that ramp myself, lugging what I owned, going on some great journey, but always coming back the other side, where the cab stand was. And now Mrs. O'Broin was disappearing from the sunlight that had followed us, already ascending the black stairs toward the shadow of the building.

This I had never considered. Where could the old woman, never having visitors, never visiting, be off to? She climbed the steel steps, leaning heavily against the rail, her heels clanging dully and slowly on the gratings.

I knew the wooden door at the top of the stairs was heavy and that the drafts of the old station all managed to get caught inside to make getting in or out a struggle for anyone, so, unthinking, I ran up the parallel ramp and beat her to the double door, pulling it open for her. She stepped inside, looking at me and thanking me, but showing no sign of recognition.

82

I felt so involved I almost went to the ticket window with her, but stopped myself in time and sat unconcernedly on an old straight-backed wooden bench, looking at the tall, tall ceiling and its pigeons. Then I was up off the bench cursing myself because I'd never discover where she was going if I sat there like the head mourner.

And I was too late. All I saw was a hand pull rolls of coin inside the window. She had her ticket in hand and was flying, for her, to the stairs that led under the tracks to the northbound side. I took the parallel stairs closer to me from which I could watch her, but there was no mystery. She walked the width of the station and went up the stairs on the other side to stand at the track and wait for her train.

I, feeling foolish again — for what was so strange about an old lady taking a trip — walked away from where she stood under the station's partial roof to the hot sunlight, and bent over the rail that faced the parking lot and the harbor. Nothing was happening in the lot except for the cars baking in the sun. There was a barge in the harbor going slowly, slowly somewhere.

The loudspeaker announced the train for Springfield. Mrs. O'Broin got on it. Springfield, I repeated to myself, where Mary is. The revelation became less dramatic as I realized that somewhere inside myself I'd known all along that that was the only place Mrs. O'Broin wanted to go. And I stood there preventing myself from waving just because it seemed someone should. For all the logic of the thought that surely the old lady was just off on a visit, I knew damn well she wouldn't be back.

The train moved noisily away, shaking the station to its foundations.

All the way back up the hill I felt as if I were climbing a whole side of the city, which, the way the city was built, was almost true. It was a hard climb because I felt as if I was going home to an empty house. I couldn't shake the feeling and I couldn't deny it so I just kept walking up the same way we'd walked down.

Had she gone to mourn Mary, to join her? What, in her overburdened old mind, did she want from her lover's grave

83

in Springfield, from that sleeping mound? Would she call across the space of death to her lover and reach her, pushed to it because she found no comfort from this life and no one but me, a dyke stranger, with whom to share her grief?

I looked now across the thruway at my three windows over Mary's ruined gardens and felt alone, desolate. "Emmie's gone," I said, the echo of her voice in my mind. The hillside was now a sad chasm in my life. I resolved to start gardening myself. First there would be a transplant to a place where I'd have something more than Emmie had. Some place where lesbians were. I dreamed, as I trudged up the hillside, of founding a City of Dykes with a museum like Emmie's foyer to house bits and pieces of our lives and a great park called Mary's Garden. Suddenly, I *was* the head mourner, mourning Emmie O'Broin and Mary and a way of life, a solitary confinement we all suffered as lesbians.

THE AWAKENING

Sun splashed against the porch screen as summer breezes lifted the leaves and branches of the wide old tree outside. Every afternoon Momma sat sleepily on the large, thickly cushioned rocker with her two daughters on either side of her, Lillian stiffly on the edge of her straight-back chair, darting forward at each sound in the street, while Nan rose more slowly to witness and judge Lillian's observations.

"There she goes now," Lillian exclaimed, her index finger a stiff extension of the thin hard line of her body. "I told you so. Can't spend a day without him. Like a drug addict. Has to see him up at the corner every day or she thinks he won't come to see her at night." She finished sarcastically, "A lot she'd be missing if he didn't."

Nan raised her limp, heavy form off the flowered cushion of her rocking chair, looked at the figure hurrying through the schoolyard across the street, and sat again, exhaling like an inflated pillow whose plug has been pulled. She shook her head and chuckled. "Can't get enough of him, can she, Momma?"

Momma, her short white hair neat under its matching net said, "Tsk, tsk," and smiled with pleasure.

"Momma always appreciates a good joke, don't you, Momma?" Nan asked approvingly.

"But this is no joking matter," Lillian protested, and snapped her cigarette case open. "Not at all, not at all," she repeated, tapping a cigarette against the arm of her chair. She jabbed the cigarette between her lips before she continued. "The neighbors are all up in arms! Madge Daugherty with her poor sick mother is beside herself with what goes on there weekends. She doesn't want her two girls to get the wrong ideas, you know. That's an impressionable age, the early teens, I well remember."

Nan and Momma looked away as one from the retreating figure in the schoolyard and looked defensively toward Lillian. "Nothing *we* did, I hope," Nan giggled.

"Certainly not," Lillian snapped past the cigarette that jumped on her lower lip as she talked. "Shut up, Alexander," she called suddenly to a caged blue canary which had begun to sing from the corner of the porch. She adjusted the gauzy pink scarf that surrounded her pin curls.

"None of those goings on in *our* family," Momma asserted.

Nan shifted her weight more comfortably and pulled her dress down over her knees. "If it was just one, I'd understand better. But it seems like a new one every year."

"Doesn't it, though?"

"And she had a perfectly good husband."

"Drove him away, they say."

"Needs a lot of men."

"Do you think so?" Nan asked thoughtfully, finishing with her dress and picking up a *Reader's Digest* to fan herself. "Do you think it's her body that needs them? Or just her mind?"

Alexander sang again, briefly, until Lillian glared at him. "It's all in her head, of course," she replied, stabbing the ashtray with her blackened cigarette butt. "No one *needs* that much you know what," she ended in a hiss.

"I guess she thinks she's no good unless a man wants her. Otherwise why would she need them all?"

"Nanette, that worthless bird my boys never clean, what makes it sing? There's something in her. She was brought up just as good as us. Her poor mother would be mortified."

"Devil made her do it," Momma chortled slyly, rubbing the few stiff white hairs on her chin.

Lillian darted forward. "Let me pluck those for you, Momma," she demanded, examining them.

Momma waved her away with a fleshy pink hand. "Don't be bothering me, you," she admonished. "God put them there for a reason."

"God maybe has a reason for her to carry on like that," Nan suggested.

"Who, Momma?" Lillian wanted to know. "Who?"

"That little trifle we're talking about. Maybe we need women like that to keep the men amused so the rest of us can have some peace." Nan let her head drop to the back of her chair. Her hair was bleach-blonde and thin, wisps of it escaping the pink curlers around which it was rolled. "Always touching and poking. They can't think of anything else, it seems."

"Except betting away the money," Lillian added.

"The horses," Momma said, rocking and nodding. "The horses and the drink."

"Speaking of the drink, there goes poor old Frank."

"Poor old Frank," Momma echoed.

Lillian craned her neck to see Frank stumble down the street. "Disgusting," she said as she stared at the disheveled figure. "To think you were his girl once."

"That was before I even met Ned, Lily. I never did intend to marry that old drunk."

"There but for the grace of God go I," Momma nodded to herself. The daughters nodded vigorously in agreement while the bird began a new chorus. Lillian turned to chide him — until her eye was caught by the man's cautious approach to a tree in a secluded corner of the schoolyard. "Oh, no," she whispered in horror.

"What?" Nan asked, excitedly pulling herself forward to the screen. "He's not, is he Lily?"

Lily glanced threateningly at Nan, shushing her and pointing her chin at Momma who was absorbed in straightening the doilies under her forearms and repinning them. Nan and Lillian sat back slightly in their chairs, but kept their eyes on the man.

"What is it?" Momma asked, alert.

"Nothing you want to see, Momma," Lillian answered evasively. "There, it's over, you can look now." She lowered her voice. "He relieved himself over in the schoolyard."

"Do you believe it?" Nan asked and suddenly began to laugh nervously. "Momma could have seen! If school was in session the little girls . . . !"

"Never mind the girls, they'll have to put up with that kind of thing all too soon when they're married. But what an example to the boys! *My* boys."

"They'll be like that soon enough anyway," Nan observed.

"Not *my* boys. If I ever catch them doing a thing like that, I'll skin them alive. My boys will not be rummies like old Frank or lose their paychecks as soon as they get them. You'll see."

"Glad I only have the little girl. I don't have to beat any of that piggishness out of her."

"Well, mine won't grow up piggy. You can mark my words."

"All alike they are," Momma said, shaking her head. "They're all alike, every last one of them."

Nan smiled and lifted her chin while Lillian sat stiffly furious and looked down the street. "I'm raising my two boys to make their wives happy. They'll be different. I don't care what anybody says," Lillian complained, tears in her voice.

"Look, look!" Nan cried proudly, spotting something before Lillian did. "It's the honeymooners," she giggled, "fighting again." A man and woman walked together down the street, glaring straight ahead, not touching.

"Fighting this early in the morning. My, my," Lillian whispered loudly, distracted from her mother's criticism and ready to return to her post. "Why she puts up with him, I'll never know."

"They say it's for the kids."

"All six of them," Lillian sneered.

"Once with him should have been enough, I'd think." Nan looked slyly at Lillian over Momma's head.

"She can't possibly get any pleasure from it," Lillian concluded.

"It's hard enough with a man who doesn't hit you."

They craned forward again to hear as the couple passed under the porch. "The language!" Lillian breathed, outraged. "To his own wife!"

"Words *I've* never heard before." Nan winked at Lillian who did not spare her a glance.

"Shhh," Lillian admonished. "They're fighting about him going to work. He's telling *her* to go to work if she needs more money," she whispered.

Nan clucked. "The *nerve.* Why, that's all men are good for is bringing home the bacon."

"And their troubles."

"Not a drop of good in any of them," Momma added, leaning heavily on the arms of the chair as she struggled up. Her stockings were rolled around thick ankles and spilled over low black shoes. The dark flowered housedress had bunched behind her girdle and the silky material eluded her stiff fingers as she tried to grab and pull it into place.

"Here, Momma," Lillian offered as she rose and jack-knifed behind her mother to help her.

"Here," said Nan, simultaneously flailing for a hold on the dress from her chair. "Why you still wear these girdles *I* don't know. You're old enough to relax."

Momma winked. "Maybe the boyfriend will come by today."

"Boyfriend my foot," Lillian ridiculed her.

"What would you do with a boyfriend, Momma?" Nan wanted to know.

Lillian stood in the doorway calling after her. "Where are you going? Use my bathroom down here. Don't walk up all those stairs to your place." She went back on the porch muttering to Nan, "Embarrassed, I suppose, to use anybody's but her own."

"Do you blame her? After all those years living with

Poppa? She finally has a little privacy. A bathroom all her own. A bed all her own. An apartment all her own except when you can't stand it down here and go up to her. You must spend half your life up there."

Lillian relaxed and sat down after she heard her mother finish climbing the stairs. "Thank goodness I have it. My little refuge. When he," she lowered her voice, looking around the porch, "when *he* starts the drinking you don't know *what* he'll do. He doesn't bother the boys. *They've* started protecting *me*, young as they are. But there's nowhere else I can go. Last night, Nan, he smashed my fresh baked pie on the floor. Ruined it. Then when I cleaned it up he wanted to you know what."

"I don't understand them, I just don't."

"Don't tell Momma."

"No, no, I never do. I don't want her hearing about my fool of a man either. I'm sick of the horses. He found my refrigerator money yesterday. The money I've been saving for a new one. I think Sheila deserves something better than mushy ice cream, poor little girl."

"To the betting parlor?"

Nan laughed. "Where else? Right down to old man Reilly's cigar store. But I couldn't say anything, you know. He won."

"Did he now?"

"He's buying the refrigerator *and* school clothes for Sheila. Taking her shopping himself," Nan boasted.

"Trying to win her favor after all the meanness."

"He doesn't fool her, though."

"Good for her."

"She says she doesn't want new clothes," she whispered. "No plaid skirts like all the little girls are wearing, no little patent leather shoes. I must admit, I don't understand the child, Lily. All she wants is another pair of those flannel lined jeans like we got her last year out in the country when we visited his folks."

"Do you suppose it's a stage?"

"*I* don't remember any stages like that when I was eight. Do you?"

90

"No. Momma always dressed us in the prettiest little white starched dresses no matter how little there was, didn't you Momma?" Nan asked as her mother stepped onto the porch. She leaned over to smooth the afghan on Momma's chair.

"He did his best, poor soul," Momma said as she sighed into her seat. "Did his very best." Her eyes twinkled. "Wonder what his worst could've been." She chuckled.

The daughters laughed loudly. "Momma, you're a scream," Nan heaved, recovering from her laughter.

"He was your father, though. You must respect him. Respect the dead."

Lillian straightened indignantly. "After how he treated you?"

"He couldn't help it. He had a hard time of it."

"He didn't have to take it out on you, though, Momma."

"Who else did he have?"

Nan shook her head. "No one, I suppose. Poor Poppa. He should have been rich. Being poor drove him to drink."

"Like it drives some men to gamble." Lily looked significantly at Nan.

"Or to hit their wives."

"It all comes of trying to raise a family and keep a home together."

"Forgive and forget," Momma advised.

"Still," Lily mused, "sometimes I wonder if we'd be better off without them."

"Don't be ridiculous," Nan scorned her. "Of course not. How could you raise two boys alone? How could I take care of Sheila right?"

Lillian stubbed out another cigarette. "And our lovely flats."

"My nice new refrigerator." Nan beamed.

"Grin and bear it," they agreed in unison when Momma started to say it again.

"Would you like some lemonade?" Lillian asked.

"Sounds delicious," Nan said. "If it's not too much trouble. And I can bring out those lovely fresh cupcakes Sheila picked out on the way over."

91

"Won't take me but a jif. No, Nan, now sit and rest your old bones, I'll bring it out."

"You'll need help carrying it," Nan insisted, righting herself on her short wide legs. "No more argument. I'm helping."

As the sisters went into the house, Lillian quickly and purposefully, Nan following slowly, Sheila at last let herself open her eyes. From the porch cot where they had instructed her to nap while they visited, she gazed at her Grandmomma's back. She never could sleep through their talk, though they always thought she did. She wondered what Grandpoppa had done to Grandmomma. Was it just the same old stuff her father and uncle did to her mother and aunt? She hoped it wasn't worse. Quietly, she sat and looked up at Alexander the canary. He blinked at her. She winked at him. "Why do they live with men?" she whispered to Alexander. He blinked again and flapped his blue wings. "*I* ain't going to, bird. You can bet your sweet tailfeathers on it."

Momma turned her slow bulk toward Sheila. "Awake, rascal?" she asked.

"Um-huh," Sheila answered, pretending to rub sleep from her eyes and stretching noisily.

"Cupcakes coming. And lemonade," Momma offered warmly, opening her arms. Sheila blundered over to her, still feigning sleepiness. She walked between her Grandmomma's open legs and let herself be enfolded by fleshy arms, against a soft breast. Sheila sighed. She had no intention of leaving Grandmomma's arms. Ever.

AUGUSTA BRENNAN II
The Tracks

Well, I made it, thought Augusta Brennan, sighing peacefully as she slumped against the white doily on the back of her easy chair. She had never believed she'd survive a convalescent home, but here she was, settled in her new flat, her old cat Mackie heavily hauling himself into a leap for her lap. They sat, the housekeeping done for the moment.

The morning sun shone on her self-cut, shaggy white hair, often a bit dirty from the difficulty of positioning herself in the sink to wash it. Some thought or other brought a quick smile to her face that deepened the lines and wrinkles around her inquisitive eyes, and a flush which never disappeared, only increased from exertion or excitement. Her stout body looked as if it had grown padding from every blow life had dealt it.

"You didn't think I'd come back, did you, old boy?" she asked Mackie. "Didn't think the old girl would make it," and she chuckled aloud. After sixteen years she knew just how to stroke him behind the ears, and Mackie purred loudly and proudly in her lap. Thank goodness for Karen and Jean, she thought. If her young friends hadn't taken Mackie in it might not have been worthwhile getting better.

Then she would never have known her beloved one-of-a-kind home.

Built between railroad tracks and a street, this row of narrow houses was all some enterprising builder could squeeze in. Gussie had feared at first there wouldn't be room to turn around in, but the girls had reassured her and took charge of getting her furniture out of storage. Besides, the flat cost so little.

She surveyed it above the contented cat. The shape reminded her of water wings, those old inflated rubber things she'd taken to the beach for swimming when she was young. The two swollen sides were connected by the narrow neck of a foyer, closet and front door.

Inside there was a bath and bedroom on one side of the neck, and on the other a sitting room and kitchenette. In these rooms she had made her home, the sun playing on the colors of her favorite possessions like musical notes in a song about her life. It shone on her bright afghan, on some small braided rugs she had admired at an auction and the girls had later given her, on her mother's faded quilt which still lay warm and soft and enormous across her daybed. The first floor of the little stone house by the railroad tracks felt homey now. She puttered about in it just like an old lady, she told herself. The hot summer sun felt better than the weak winter rays in the convalescent home when she'd sat wrapped up in the same afghan, watching the little girls play in the schoolyard, remembering and remembering. Now she hardly had time to remember. It seemed to take an awful lot of housekeeping, this little place.

A one-car train rumbled by. It must be ten o'clock, she thought, time to go across the street to the market. Nan, her next door neighbor, was coming to lunch.

She sometimes felt she was always feeding guests. Between the shopping, the preparation of food, the event itself and resting up afterwards, a whole day would be gone. A whole day in her dwindling number of days, she sighed. Once, her days had been so plentiful she would squander them, wishing them to be over if work was boring or if she had something painful to live through. No more: she hoarded every minute. And the trains reminded her of how fast her days slipped away. Most old folks, she thought, would be bothered by the regular racket of the trains, but she'd grown up next to tracks used much more than these, long before cars took over.

She and Nan talked a lot about how they hated cars. Neither had ever driven the dangerous machines which flung themselves across the country, getting everyone where they didn't need to be faster than they needed to get there. Karen and Jean spoke of how the automobile and trucking industries had used their power and riches to weaken the rail system, just as she saw cars weakening the old ways of life. Now the sound of the trains was like the lowing of the last buffalo on the western plains. Trains were yet another idea men had rejected to make more money.

Gussie closed her eyes in the sun. She was beginning to think like the girls. Next thing she knew she'd be marching with them. She imagined marching down the railroad tracks in the sun.

Mackie purred louder when she switched to his other ear. She'd kept living by the tracks whenever she could in her life. Now each time a train went by her thoughts drifted forward to her disappearing time, and backwards to the full years she'd had. And here was the start of the 10:21 freight train. It would be a long time rumbling by. She'd better get ready to go out.

Mackie leapt down as she rose. The cat strolled to a window where, between trains, birds gathered to peck at the crumbs she put on the sill. The train ran on and on. She moved to the window where she kept her knickknacks. She'd tried to hang a shelf for them, but the old fingers were too stiff and useless for this task, holding a hammer an awkward exercise that produced cracks and gashes, nothing useful. The girls would help. Meanwhile most of the knick-knacks fit on this windowsill, leaving the other sills free for Mackie to lounge on.

She had arranged everything as symmetrically as she could: plants in twin white ceramic pots, new cuttings in old shot glasses, a miniature framed portrait of a cat, a little watering can, a green glass vase and bowl sparkling in the sun, and several little figures bought in Five and Tens across the country. From outside, she sometimes thought, the accumulation must look like an old lady's treasures, fit for nothing when she died but to be thrown away. But to her, this window was a joy, full of suggestions of memories, of thriving living things, of color. The way all the objects crowded on the windowsill gave her a sense of a life which had always seemed to be bursting at the seams with travel, women, love. And loss — poor years too, times when life had been difficult to take, but, as a cutting might not make it, or as a young plant that had been pruned yet grew on, so her life continued with its bustling shoots and blossoms around the cuts and failures.

The blossoming of women in the night as trains sped by. So very many lovely women, lovely nights. But the thought of women reminded her of Nan and she'd best get to the store or Nan would be left standing on the doorstep waiting for her lunch. She went to the closet in the neck of the house, drew a light coat over herself, picked her black purse off the doilied table, and went out the door, locking it carefully behind her.

Earlier in her hurried life her surroundings had often been a blur, but now she walked slowly, sat long hours, and was learning the art of looking, of appreciating what she saw. She was grateful she still had her sight. She held onto the rough grey stone of the house as she made her way down its steps, then turned toward the store. She passed Nan's house and peered up at the windows, but her neighbor wasn't looking out. Nan owned her narrow little home and had lived there for over forty years with her husband. She had no worries but where the tax money would come from and she fretted that to death, annoying Gussie at times with it. Gussie told her to take in a boarder.

"Some old coot I'd have to take care of?" Nan had replied crossly. "I can't barely take care of myself. I'm seventy-seven now you know!"

She passed the travel agency perched on the railway line. She often stopped to read the posters in the window

96

on her days of leisure, when no one was coming to lunch. A couple of big old rooming houses came next where the tracks veered farther from the road. Then the little luncheonette where she and Nan went now and then. At the corner where she crossed to the store, she admired the old fire station, made out of red stone, whose painted towers and cool dark musty smell made her heart race almost as fast as when she'd been a little girl. How she had wanted to be a fireman when she grew up!

Aside from the scenery, her trip to the store was uneventful. She carried the luncheon meat, quart of milk and small jar of mayonnaise in a net shopping bag. The sun was always a little higher in the sky on the way back, and she was always a little tireder than when she'd gone out. A cup of tea, a little rest and she'd be fine when Nan came.

But she still felt depleted after her brief rest and absent-mindedly made the lunch, cutting crusts off the white bread, tossing scraps of meat to Mackie as he purred and rubbed against her legs. The last luncheon she'd prepared, a couple of weeks back, had been on a Saturday when Jean and Karen visited. She'd done all the same things except she'd made them tunafish. Like so many of these young girls, they wouldn't eat animal flesh, wouldn't smoke or drink. These were things she'd never needed in abundance, living the frequently simple and lonely life she had, but still, without drinking, without smoking, without eating in restaurants, what kind of social life could they have? No wonder they got into so many emotional messes with each other. Their world was so small, filled only by themselves, friends just like them, and an old lady they seemed to think had drifted in from the moon.

Their fascination at meeting a lesbian in her eighties still lingered: "How do you handle this? How did you do that? Did you have a lot of lovers? All at once? Were you ever committed to just one woman?" Questions, questions, questions! As if their lives hadn't been so similar that transplanted to her time, they probably would have lived very much as she had.

There, she said, setting the pink glass plates with their

sandwiches on a shelf in the refrigerator. She supposed she should cover them with waxed paper, but decided they would keep till Nan arrived. She had to economize in small ways or her money disappeared even faster. She clumsily emptied a tray of ice cubes into the tea pitcher and refilled the tray with water, wiping up the spills. She set the table with her best napkins and silverware.

Out back of the house, on a tiny strip of land fenced off from the tracks, she had noticed a smattering of wild-flowers. She went to pick some for the table, but stooping, got dizzy and walked unsteadily, with darkened sight, back towards the door, wildflowers drooping from her left hand, while with her right she felt her way along the cool stones of the house.

"Augusta!" cried Nan on her way from next door. "Are you all right?" She hurried, in that broad-shouldered, long-legged, yet timid way she had, to her.

"Will be in a minute," she growled. "Here, take the blasted flowers. They were too pretty up the table for lunch, but I see now I wasn't meant to pick that particular bunch of flowers."

"How many times have I told you about stooping down? You're just like my husband who would not listen to me till his dying day and would exert himself in every way he could find until he killed himself doing it."

Gussie had never been able to decide if Nan blamed her-self or Mr. Heimer for his death while he was mowing his tiny patch of lawn under a hot sun, or even whether she really minded that she had been finally left completely alone in her home. Nan was taller than most women of her time and bent over like a tree under a constant wind of antici-pated disapproval. Above her body was a plain face, so un-marked by age Gussie had wondered if it had had more character when she was young. Eventually she realized it was this very plainness coupled with her height that had led Nan to a life where she could avoid the pains and re-jections that line faces. Given money and circumstances, she might have been raised "a lady," but she became, instead, a girl forced to find her own protections. And she had found them in a husband who kept her home, though childless, until the war, when she reemerged to work until there were callouses on her hands and a certain courage that kept her from again retreating entirely to her home. Still, the world's early imprint was in that stoop and in a way she had of not looking into Gussie's eyes. But her smile, when it came, was broad and unafraid, as if laughter was something she could easily share. Her hair was still brown, in feathery short curls fluffed up all over her head, and she wore thick glasses to help her cataract-afflicted eyes.

No wonder she hadn't a boarder, Gussie had realized: her shy safe home was sacred to her. "But what will I do if I go blind?" Gussie wouldn't answer her, not wishing to be presumptuous. Someday, she thought, Nan would figure it out, though Gussie would miss her own water wing of a home. Meanwhile, she enjoyed watching that strangely young face soften in her presence.

They walked inside slowly and Gussie sat in her chair. Nan went to the kitchen for a glass of water. Mackie, sensing something wrong, rubbed against Nan. "Scat," she said, preoccupied. He ran to leap heavily again into Gussie's lap, startling her. But the poor old boy looked so concerned she couldn't be angry. Nan found the cat and his friend nuzzling one another.

"Like a couple of old lovebirds, you are," said Nan, handing Gussie her water.

"He's worried."

"How can you tell?"

"By the look in his eyes."

"Hmph," said Nan, a little jealously, thought Gussie. "Are you better?" she asked after a moment.

"Yes. Much better. I'll sit a moment before I get lunch out."

"Why don't you let me? Is it all ready?"

"But—"

"Well, why not? We've done this enough. I know your routine."

"You're my guest—"

"And you've been mine. I already know how good a

hostess you are. It seems to me," Nan said, leaning close towards Gussie and looking her in the eye for once, "that it's about time we treated each other like friends, not like old ladies come visiting."

Gussie's lines all deepened and her smile reddened her face.

Nan reddened too, and looked quickly to the floor, as if someone else entirely had been speaking so frankly.

"Well, then," challenged Gussie, to relieve them both of their embarrassment, "why don't you move yourself on out to the kitchen and bring me my lunch!"

"Yes, ma'am," Nan said, almost saluting.

Gussie knew that Nan had greatly enjoyed her war work. The military atmosphere had replaced many of the more normal social conventions which had made her feel so shy. Not to mention that she worked almost exclusively with women. Gussie herself had been called "Sarge" then. As accountant she'd taken over many of the men's administrative tasks while they fought. This new authority, combined with the walk of a tightly muscled drill sergeant, had earned her the nickname. Now she and Nan fell into their wartime personas easily.

They ate in the cool parlor, Gussie with her feet up, Mackie pleading with his eyes and an occasional flick of his tail for more scraps, and Nan relaxed, listening to Gussie's stories of the morning. "Gussie," Nan said as they finished lunch, "you could make a story of anything, even a walk across the street to the store."

The two friends, meal done, sat in silence for a while. An occasional car speeded annoyingly up the street to one side of them, while silence hung over the railroad tracks. The sound of the present was, for the moment, louder than that of the past. Gussie dwelt on what Nan had said about the stage of their friendship. It made her a little nervous to be getting this close to a woman after all the years of being without a lover or friend of any depth. She had always assumed old people didn't begin new things and she hadn't expected this.

100

But before they could get any further in their relationship, she would have to reveal her past to Nan, and she didn't know how Nan felt about lesbians. She looked at her friend sitting quietly despite all the energy she sensed in that bent body. She wondered if Nan had ever questioned her own life and how she'd lived it. She wondered if she would question Gussie's life.

Despite her concern, there was a pervading air of peace and comfort in the parlor. She was reminded of two old men who'd lived in her town when she was young. Their habit, as a matter of fact, had been to sit together outside the fire station evenings, just inside if it rained. They'd been friends all their lives and though you seldom saw them exchange a word, you knew that the act of sitting together, smoking cigars, was one of great intimacy, respect, and comfort. She imagined the air filled with the foul smelling smoke, could even smell it across the years. She must mention this to Karen and Jean — how when she thought of friendship between old people, she thought of two men.

The little 2:00 p.m. passenger train went quickly north past her windows. Five minutes later the train to the city slowed toward the station half a mile down the road. Mackie was sleeping on the windowsill, his legs hanging over the edge. She began to talk again.

"I've been thinking of trains a lot lately, Nan. Every time I hear one it seems I remember something from my past. Trains meant a lot more then. They were a way of life for the train families, and as for the rest of us, we would become terribly excited when they ran through town on their way to big cities, to the coasts, to anywhere that wasn't familiar. As kids we'd often play along the tracks and could tell a train was coming from the vibrations in the ground. We'd stop whatever we were doing and we'd raise our heads and watch for it to come down the track, then wave as if without our signal the train would never reach its destination.

"Once in a while in my travels around the country from job to job I would settle near a railroad." She laughed. "Who am I kidding? You know me."

101

Nan looked quickly and darkly up, as if afraid of something in Gussie's still strong voice. A little too much intimacy, perhaps?

Gussie explained. "I found a place near them whenever I could, even when I could afford better. And New London, Connecticut, was no different.

"As a matter of fact, I lived closer to the tracks than ever. When I first got there and knew nobody, I'd walk across the street on a Sunday to the big old station and sit on a bench watching, maybe talking to somebody waiting for a train." She paused as if to rest.

"Can I offer you a beer?" she asked finally. "Seems to me two old ladies like us might as well get what we can out of living this hot afternoon."

"Should you . . . ?"

"Of course I should. I had a little faintness from bending over was all. Go ahead and get it. I hope you don't mind a quart bottle of ale. The railroad tracks reminded me of it," she said, not trying to reach Nan in the kitchen with her words. "I bought it the other day, hardly realizing I was, thinking about tracks and New London and Violet."

Nan returned. Gussie smiled to see the bottle. "Hasn't changed much in all the years," she said for Nan to hear. When Nan looked puzzled she explained, "I can remember sitting in a tavern in New London, near the station, drinking ale with Violet."

She took a deep breath as Nan poured the amber stuff. "When I think of New London that's who I remember. I can't even recall what might have made my job different from other jobs, except that Violet's father owned the factory. He'd started the business in his hometown, Providence, Rhode Island, then built a plant in New London. As he got older it got harder for him to travel. Violet was his only child and she was not planning to be a retiring housewife. She wanted to take over the business. To prove her worth to her father she would come down to New London when she was needed, on top of doing the job he'd given her in Providence.

"That's how I met her. She was waiting for the train

back to Providence. The rain was pouring down, but I'd arrived at the station before it started and sat there dry as a bone watching the people come in all bedraggled. Violet sat next to me, dripping, and placed the wet newspaper she'd held over her head between us. She sneezed. When she took out her ticket I saw it was for Providence. The schedule board said her train would be two hours late, and I waited for her to notice it. Meanwhile I noticed her.

"She was tall, like you, thin and elegant looking, in a competent kind of way, if you know what I mean. Well-dressed in the latest fashions, but no frills about her, as if she dressed that way because it was the thing to do and she was going to do it well. Now, of course, she looked as if she could use a change of clothes.

"Suddenly I heard a very unladylike curse under her breath. She'd seen the schedule board. I kind of smiled in sympathy toward her and she shrugged and set off for the phones, leaving her suitcase behind. She stopped and looked at me as if to ask me to watch her suitcase and I made a gesture as if to say of course. Whoever she called, she felt better afterward. Perhaps a young husband? I had no way of knowing at the time she was not married. To a man.

"When she returned I realized it had stopped raining and I rose to go. On impulse, perhaps because she had asked me to watch the suitcase, I turned to her and explained that I lived nearby and was now headed home. Would she like to change into something dry at my apartment?

"At that moment we saw the stationmaster walk casually toward the schedule board. We both tensed watching him. He erased 'Two hours late' and chalked in 'Three hours late.' Violet rose and walked home with me.

"I had started to make tea, but she admitted she'd really like something to drink. All I had then as now was the ale, and that pleased her. I got out glasses while she changed. I remember there was a fresh moist smell of deluged pavement coming in through my windows and I felt moved, sexually, if you don't mind my saying so. The smell of summer rains always has that effect on me. Too, there was something about Violet which was very sensual."

She looked casually toward Nan to see how she was reacting to these words. Nan was sitting, as she had all along, legs stretched before her, ale in hand, a sleepy far-away look on her face as she stared out the window before her. Gussie was not within her view.

"Violet came into the kitchen, all smiles. I wondered why. That she was a truly attractive woman I could see even more now in her dry clothing. 'Might I,' she asked, 'leave my wet things here with you and pick them up on my next trip?'

"Of course I offered to send them, but she explained how often she was in New London, her position, where she stayed, and I agreed to keep them. We drank ale and talked, in a way I hadn't been able to talk since I'd moved there. I enjoyed her immensely and she seemed to enjoy me. I made her a sandwich before she left and we had a jolly little picnic. When she learned I worked for her father's company she seemed pleased. I never thought to say I'd bring her clothes to work with me, so we left it, when I walked her to the station, that she'd stop at my office and tell me when she was next in town.

"She returned sooner than she'd anticipated. The next week. I had thought of her a lot in the meanwhile. Why not? I was lonely and she'd been so pleasing to me, somehow, like slipping into a warm bath when you ache and luxuriating in its smoothness on your skin."

Nan was looking curiously at her.

"She agreed to come to supper and I put on quite a spread. She was, after all, the boss's daughter. My pleasure in her company was almost incidental to the way I would have treated her anyway, knowing that. And you see, I thought I knew why she was all smiles when she emerged from my bedroom that first visit. Never expecting company I'd left certain books, certain photographs lying about the room as I usually did. One photograph in particular may have intrigued her." Gussie fidgeted in her chair a bit, thinking how these things never got any easier with age. She took a long draught of ale. "It was of myself and another woman. We were embracing. Kissing. A friend had taken it because she was so enamored of the way we looked together and wanted to show us why."

Nan said nothing, didn't move. Didn't even breathe differently.

She went on. She had come this far, what else could she do? "So, you see, I thought her smile might mean an acceptance of me. Or more. Perhaps a kinship with me. I hoped to find out which that night.

"Dinner went nicely, the walk was once more wonderful. When it was time for her to go I wanted to tell her to stay with all my heart. But then, she'd given no indication she'd be interested — and she was still the boss's daughter. I wanted so much to touch those long arms, to feel those long legs next to mine. She was, simply, the sexiest woman I'd ever met. 'I must go back to my room,' she said, 'to place a call home. I call Denise every night I'm away.'

"I knew this was my signal. Our kinship was real. 'Oh, there's no need to go all the way back there,' I said innocently. 'My landlady has a phone. She'd be glad to let you use it. I always have privacy when I do.'

"She must have known I was offering more than a telephone because she hesitated, looking pained, a few long minutes before saying yes.

"And this is another reason I've been remembering New London lately. Her pain. You've seen my friends Karen and Jean." Nan nodded very slightly. "Well, half the time they arrive crying about what they're going through. This one wants to be lovers with that one without letting the other go, and the other is tired of being lovers with others and just wants to stay with her own, and then this one is in pain because that one is in love. And on and on about how they must go through this in order not to stifle one another, to grow and change and I don't know what all. They ask me what to do but I know they don't want to hear my answer, so I just listen to them thrash about in their pain and confusion, knowing no one can answer these questions for you.

"Once in a while I'll tell them a bit of my own experience and they listen, oh yes, they listen, as if to some quaint fairy

105

tale that has absolutely nothing to do with them. As if loving in my time was so very different, as if Violet did not hurt as much as they would by deciding yes, she would wrap her lovely long legs around me that night and a great many more nights while her lover off in Providence longed for her. As if I, wanting Violet so badly, being immediately seduced by her elegance, her sexiness, and lost, lost in the most intense desire I have ever felt for anyone, as if I could deny this to myself or proceed from reasons other than those that had grown suddenly and spontaneously in my heart."

She raised her voice as another freight train rolled by, unendingly. "Each time I hear a train I'm reminded of the joy of her arrivals, the sheer bliss to know she was walking down those wet steamy streets toward me, bringing the smell of travel, of railroad cars, of another city, another woman to me, bringing that long smooth body and those hands that did such magic in the night. And, too, I am reminded of the pain of her departures. I knew she would never be mine. I knew her love for Denise was deeper, stronger, longer than her love for me and that ours could only be a brief, intense love. But the sound of her train pulling out, the withdrawal of those hands from me, the exquisite sadness of it all — I cannot tell you.

"And to see these girls belabor it, think they are different with their *reasons* for loving who they do. In time, in time, they will decide which is for them. As Violet decided it was the long slow comfort of what she had with Denise. The rich shared time and the common belongings, memories, friends. The familiar body in the bed. The warmth and comfort of a home. Just as I decided to pursue my heights, keep riding the trains, see all I felt I must. I was thirsty for experience. She was hungry for substance. We both knew and accepted this, though we never talked about it. Whether she told Denise I never knew. That was their business. Sometimes I suspect these girls simply do not want the consequences of their decisions. They want the heights and comforts without having the pain, without having to choose, to lose anything along the way. They must talk it to death, beat one

106

another over the head with their pain. What makes them act like that?"

"Cars," said Nan simply.

They sat quietly, Gussie thinking about her answer, realizing it was hard to grasp what Nan meant — hard even for Nan. It had to do with the new ways, the fast pace, the mobility that cars had brought. The young people had gotten used to getting what they wanted and where they wanted fast. Or perhaps young people always thought they could do things better.

Nan rose and filled Gussie's glass with more ale. She went into the bathroom. When she returned Gussie took a turn, rising with difficulty after sitting so long. She looked at herself in the bathroom mirror. Her round reddened cheeks. Her shaggy white hair and its cowlick. The lines that traveled like tracks to her eyes, her still-full lips, her sensitive ears. She felt numbed by the ale, but good, warm and buzzing, as if her body were a hive of busy little bees cooking up something she couldn't quite cook up for herself. She smiled at the face that showed all the life she still felt inside.

"I hope my story hasn't upset you," she told Nan when she returned to the parlor. No train was passing and there was silence. Mackie had abandoned the window. "I suppose I had to talk with someone my own age about what I see the girls are doing. I don't know how to help them. I suspect they simply must live through it as I did, in their own way. Or perhaps it was wrong of Violet to have hidden her affair from Denise."

Nan looked at her, smiling slightly. "Then again," continued Gussie, "perhaps this is all hogwash. Just an excuse to tell you about myself." They were both silent for a moment and the sunlight faded from the window. The sky darkened quickly and by the time they looked over to the window huge drops of rain began to fall, their sound almost that of sizzling as they hit the hot street. A smell of wet asphalt came up, a smell of wet earth, the steamy smell of a quick summer shower. It slowed soon, getting quieter. Gussie knew she should rise and close some windows, but instead she said, "You know, Nan, I think you're lovely."

107

AT A BAR III
Sally the Bartender Goes on Jury Duty

Afterwards, when anyone would mention jury duty, Sally would shudder, as if reminded of a nightmare. Yet it started well enough.

It had rained all day and the *Cafe Femmes* had been in turn crowded with kids escaping from the weather, and empty because few would venture into such dampness to hang out anywhere. Even Sally had longings, this day, to be home under the covers with Liz. But they had a bar to run and it was Sally's shift; so she served the drenched women who took refuge in her shelter, and did some cleaning, ordering, what have you, when she was alone. She wiped the counter absent-mindedly as she watched the workmen across the street. They kept as far back from the loading docks as possible, filling and emptying trucks with unusual dispatch. The sky was grey, like the warehouses themselves. But the bar had a cheery feel to it, especially when Sally remembered to switch on the pinball machines with their silly bright lights.

Late in the afternoon, Sally saw Liz rush by their plate glass window, her bright yellow slicker streaming. A moment later the cowbells over the door sounded and Liz came in, shaking her short dark hair like a wet dog. As usual, she hadn't worn her hood because she hated the way it looked. Sally peeled the wet coat off her and took the dry mail Liz removed from her pocket.

"What's this?" Sally asked. "Are we in some kind of trouble?"

"With who?" Liz stood on her toes to peer closely at the oversized envelope. She was wiping steam from her glasses. She was nearsighted without them.

"From some court."

"Betcha it's jury duty," Marian said from a barstool. She was from the Bronx and had just recently taken to hanging around the bar. Liz guessed she was hiding out from an ex, as *Cafe Femmes* was pretty out of the way. But Sally thought she was trying to meet somebody to bring her out, because she looked too straight to be in the life yet.

"Oh, no," said Liz.

"I got one of those a couple of years ago. In an envelope just like that," Marian continued.

"Open it, Sal. Let's see what's up."

"Go take care of Gabby then. She probably just wants more ice for her coke."

"How'd you guess?" called Gabby.

" 'Cause it don't cost nothin'!" laughed Sally, opening the envelope.

Liz was back. "So?"

"So it's jury duty."

"That's what I thought," Marian said, a little boastfully.

"What the hell are you going to do?" groaned Liz.

"Go, I guess."

"Go, she says, just like that. What about the cafe?" Liz liked to call it a cafe. She'd been to Europe once, a college graduation present, and had fallen in love with Paris. Especially with the lesbian bars to which she would steal at night when her mother and sister were already in bed. She swore someday she'd open a Parisian bar for lesbians in New York. But first, there had been the years of bracing herself to tell her parents she was gay, then the years it had taken for them to adjust to that. Then the time to get them to lend her the money. She was paying it back, too.

110

"I know it won't be easy, baby, but I got to go," Sally said.

"Why?"

"Well, first off, because it says here I could be fined or put in jail if I don't."

"Tell them you have a business to run."

"What. A gay bar? I bet they'd think we're real essential."

"So? Who cares what they think. Tell them it's how you earn your living."

Sally put the notice down and pulled Liz to a table out of earshot of the others. "Listen, Liz, I feel like I ought to do this. Like it's my responsibility. I mean, I'm a citizen. I have the right to a jury myself if I get in trouble. I ought to be willing to give them some time."

Liz looked at Sally. What a baby she was, at forty, with that long skinny body, that fair, fair skin and hair. All innocence, as if ninety percent of the people who got jury duty notices didn't try to worm out of it. "Okay," she shrugged, "we'll get by." Not only was it useless to try and dissuade Sally of anything once her mind was made up, but Liz respected her determination. And of course loved her. If she believed in this crap, what could she do? She gave her a kiss and, standing, pulled her head against her breasts for a second or two. "Maybe Chickie will take over for you. I don't think she's working."

"Is she still drinking heavy?"

"No more than she was last time she helped out. She's okay behind the bar. It gives her a feeling she belongs somewhere so she doesn't need to drink as much."

"I'll ask her."

On her eighth day of jury duty, as on every other day, Sally sat slumped in a molded plastic chair staring at her very long, very skinny legs stretched full length before her. Liz said they looked like toothpicks with doorknobs for knees, but when Sally offered to keep them out of sight

111

in bed, Liz quickly uncovered them and reached between Sally's legs, stroking her as she said, "Don't you dare."

Suddenly Sally sat up, feeling as self-conscious about her legs, in their floppy old bell bottom cords, as she'd begun to feel about all of herself. Were the other jurors looking at them? Did they think her legs were another weird thing about her?

Jury duty. Such a simple normal thing. She stood and walked to the window, half-glowering at the other jurors in case they should look at her, should whisper and giggle as they had the first days. Most of them had just returned from a case settled out of court at the last minute. At least they'd been chosen. She had acted as respectable as she knew how, saying yes sir and no sir until she felt obsequious, but still they hadn't wanted her. So she'd been sitting in the plastic chairs, looking out the windows, and, when no one was around to make her feel self-conscious, pacing.

The first day, she had even been a little excited. Here she was, wearing the old navy blue pantsuit she'd bought long ago for a funeral, a businesswoman with enough money to live as she wished and a lover she'd been with longer than a lot of straight marriages lasted. The city had deemed her respectable enough to serve on a jury. She had proudly given her name to the clerk of the court and smiled at the prospective jurors around her, all talking nervously among themselves. When they gave instructions she'd wished she had something to take notes on so she would do everything right. They'd gotten out early that first day and Sally, feeling good about doing her civic duty, noticing the rain had let up for the afternoon, had walked all the way to her apartment and woke Liz. The sun was even shining in their window. They'd made love for a long time, until Liz had to go downtown to take over from Chickie.

For the next few days Sally had continued to be nervously excited as she went through the selection process over and over. Finally she got used to being rejected. One by one the other jurors didn't return to the waiting areas. Then, one day, Sally was the only one in the lounge. She was sent home early again.

When the others returned from their various assignments, they seemed to have formed bonds among themselves, even though they scrupulously avoided discussing cases.

"Still not picked, dear?" asked one blue-haired older lady.

Sally smiled. "Not yet," she said brightly.

Old blue-hair looked her up and down as if to determine why she hadn't been chosen, smiled falsely, and moved to sit with a young woman in a dress. Later, Sally saw out of the corner of her eye that they were talking about her. She blushed, and casually left the room.

Another time a man, middle-aged, neatly dressed and always complaining he should be at work, spoke to her. "You work?" he asked brusquely.

"Sure," she said, glad to talk.

"What do you do?"

"I run a bar in the Village."

He drummed his fingers on the arm of the couch. "You must be losing money, being here." It seemed he wanted to lead the conversation to his favorite topic.

"Maybe a little, but somebody's got to be on jury duty," Sally said, knowing she sounded idealistic.

"Whereabouts is your bar?"

Sally told him.

"Maybe I'll stop in sometime. I get down to that end of town quite a bit on business."

Sally was torn between being friendly, in which case she'd have to welcome him to the bar, and warning him that it was a women's bar.

As she hesitated he began to nod, as if to say, I thought so.

"Sure," Sally finally responded weakly, knowing he'd figured it out. She watched him make elaborate preparations to smoke a cigar, and moved away when the first smell of it reached her.

No one else had spoken to her. She was now too self-conscious to try to start conversations with any of them. There was one woman who Sally thought might be a very

113

feminine dyke, the way she stared at her. If she was, though, she was determined to pass because she responded curtly to Sally's overture and never sat in the same room with her again.

On Friday of the first week Sally had been once more summoned for selection, the criminal trial of someone accused of burglarizing several apartments. When they brought the defendant into the courtroom Sally's heart began to pound. She was a very young black woman. And Sally could almost swear she was gay. She walked like a dyke, sat like one when she forgot to sit up straight with her knees together and her hands folded, and looked all wrong in the skirt and blouse the lawyer had probably brought for her to wear.

Sally was determined to get on this jury. Not because she wanted a gay girl to go free if she was guilty (and Sally, familiar as she was with her customers' problems getting and holding jobs, thought the defendant well might be guilty), but to be sure she really did get a fair trial by a jury of at least one peer.

Sally cringed with the selection of each juror. Old blue-hair. The man with the cigar. A black man in a three-piece suit who was never without his briefcase and work from the office. Another man who liked to tell dirty jokes to the ladies who would listen, although he'd never tried with Sally.

When Sally was questioned, she sat up straight, but not so straight she would look too tall, and she looked the questioners in the eyes. Maybe that was her mistake, she thought on her way back to the lounge. Maybe ladies didn't look judges and lawyers in the eye. Or maybe she was marked. It did seem almost as if she wore a sign around her neck: *Not this one, she can't be trusted to think like us.*

Once more, she was dismissed early. The sky was threatening rain, but held on to it. This time she did not walk straight home. She walked first to the East River, then to the Hudson River. It took her hours to get home, the way she criss-crossed the city. When she finally arrived, she was too tired to be angry anymore.

She fixed herself some dinner and watched TV until

she couldn't stand it anymore. Every program was about some dumb straight family or a bunch of straight men who liked to act tough. She was tempted to get drunk on the white wine she kept in the refrigerator, but wine was something she drank when she felt good, as if to celebrate, when everything was just right and she was in tune with the world just as she knew it. She did not feel good this Friday night. Never mind, she told herself, it's the weekend. She didn't have to go to court the next day and would be at the bar working.

She went to bed early so she would be fresh in the morning, but kept thinking of the young black dyke so much like herself, and fell asleep to dream of her: the jury had judged her guilty before her lawyer had had a chance to defend her. He stood objecting meekly while the jury filed smugly out. The black dyke went crazy, attacking the cops, the judge, the witnesses. The judge threatened to increase her sentence. Then she turned to Sally who was tied and gagged on the evidence table, and the black dyke spoke softly to her, touching her gently, untying her ropes. "I know it's not your fault," she said, but Sally woke up mumbling into her pillow that it was, it certainly was because they would've let her on the jury if she'd worn a wedding dress. Then she lay awake, terrified of sleep, until Liz came in and soothed her.

Now she had returned to her molded chair. Old bluehair and the young straight woman were the only ones left in the waiting area with her. She was suddenly furious again. Maybe not everything about running a bar was legal, she thought, but at least the people you dealt with treated you according to the way you did your job, not who you loved. The guys who pushed pinball machines, or delivered beer, at least they didn't drop their teeth when they looked at you.

The clerk of the court told Sally she could go home for the day. She shoved her hands in her pockets and left the building, walking head down, butchy, shouldering out of her way anyone in her path. What the hell good did it do to look respectable? You didn't fool anyone. To them you were only a goddamn queer. Maybe that's what the sign they hung around her neck said: *Queer.*

★ ★ ★ ★ ★

Halfway through the last week, Sally was released for good. By this time her anger fit around her like the molded chair. She shied away from any contact with the others, and of course said goodbye to no one.

She walked into a fine spring day. The rains had been diminishing daily until now the city seemed washed clean after weeks of it. Delicate white and pink flower petals fell silently to the sidewalks as she passed intermittent trees. Again, she was walking, for the last time in a while. As a matter of fact, why go straight back to work? Perhaps she should enjoy the spring outdoors for a few more days, since Chickie was scheduled to work the rest of the week. The separation between jury duty, with all its depression and anger, and her normal life, might do her good. Then she laughed, right out loud on the sidewalk. *Normal!* She wanted nothing to do with normal ever again.

Try as she might, she was not able to veer away from the Village. Soon she stood in front of *Cafe Femmes.* She could taste the white wine she knew sat cold in a bottle under the bar. Should she go in? Begin her life again?

Chickie looked up at the sound of the cowbells. "Hi, stranger," she said cheerily from behind the bar. No one else was there.

"Hi, Chick, what's happening?"

"Dead day. It's too nice to be inside. They'll all be here later."

"Would you rather be outside?"

"Most of the time, no, but I took Marian out last night and I'm itching to finish what I started." She winked. "You know she's never come out?"

Sally congratulated herself on her instincts. She knew her own world well. "Why don't you give her a call? Go pick her up?"

"You mean it? You don't have jury duty?"

"It's over."

"Forever?"

"Jeeze, I hope so."

"So you don't need me no more?" Chickie asked sadly.

"Listen, you can finish out the week if you like, because that was the deal. But if you want to take off, that's okay too."

Chickie was pulling her jacket on slowly. "What if I take today, see how things go, then let you know later about the rest of the week?"

"Fine with me."

On her way out the door Chickie stopped. "Hey, Sal?"

"Yeah?" She was already behind the bar pouring a glass of cold white wine.

"This Marian, did you know she's got kids?"

"I thought she might." Sally wet a bar rag.

"She left her old man a long time ago, but she still has the kids with her."

"You can handle it, Chickie."

"You think so? She makes me feel so . . . wanted. You know what I mean?"

Sally ran the bar rag over the counter absent-mindedly. "Yeah, I know what you mean."

THE MIRROR

The only sound on the placid lake was the murmur of the tiny motor.

Careful not to startle her pensive lover, Connie whispered, "Trudy?"

Trudy jumped anyway, but smiled gently. "Aye aye, captain, you called?" She lifted a hand to her short grey hair in salute.

"Want to go for ice cream now, or stay on the water longer?"

Trudy searched Connie's eyes behind their horn-rimmed glasses to get a sense of her preference. She loved the way the dark eyeglass frames set off Connie's nearly white curls. Connie was only fifty-three, three years younger than herself, but she'd gone straight from blonde to white. Trudy leaned forward to muss the white curls. "What do you think?"

"Trude!" Connie jumped back, making the boat swerve a little as she leaned too hard against the motor.

"Watch it!" Trudy warned.

"Well, don't be scaring me like that in public."

Trudy slumped apologetically. "Nobody can see us out here," she explained. "Besides, all I did was touch your hair."

Connie was back on course. "You're right, dear. I'm just jumpy tonight. We've had such a beautiful, peaceful vacation week, I suppose I'm afraid something will happen to spoil the second week."

Trudy rearranged her skirt where it had bunched under her on the boat cushion. "It's always peaceful up here, Con. I don't know why you worry. No one even suspects what we are to each other."

"Shhh," Connie warned. "Every sound carries across the lake on a night like this. I think we'd better head in before it's dark." She smiled lovingly at Trudy. "How I wish sometimes that we didn't have to go even back to the cabin, but could sleep on one of these little islands all night, with no one else around, in a world all our own."

"And what would we do all night?" Trudy teased as Connie turned the boat toward the ice cream stand's small dock.

"Oh, *I* don't know, my strudel," Connie said shyly.

Trudy leaned forward and caressed Connie's breasts, under a large windbreaker, with her eyes. Connie had always been embarrassed when Trudy looked at her body, but now Trudy was fairly sure that after admiring her for the eighteen years they'd been together, her lover had begun to enjoy it as much as she did.

"You are *awful* tonight," Connie reprimanded her.

"Must be Saturday night. You know how I get on square-dance night up here."

"I wish we could go, too. If we could only dance with each other, instead of those horrid, hairy men."

They were silent as they docked in the twilight. Trudy lifted her heavy body out of the boat and tied up, then held the boat steady while Connie joined her. Their footsteps were muffled on the dock. The noise and light of the ice cream stand, suddenly appearing from behind a row of pines, startled them. They did not look at each other as they joined the lines at the windows. Around them were teenagers and families, some from their own campground, and they greeted them like neighbors. Most, like themselves, had been coming up for years.

They paid separately for their ice cream and started back to the boat. "What did you get?" Trudy asked.

"Chocolate chip, tonight," Connie answered. "How about you?"

They sat at the end of the dock, their feet dangling toward the water. "Peppermint stick."

"Again?"

"I love the little bits of candy in it," Trudy said, licking around the pink ice cream, then nipping a hard piece with her teeth. "Want some?" she offered.

Connie didn't answer, but watched her lover enjoy the cone. Sticky-lipped, Trudy grinned at her, both of them feeling sheltered and relaxed as the darkness began to surround them in this open, yet secluded, spot.

★ ★ ★ ★ ★

They woke the next morning to the sound of a small car crunching the pine needles outside their window.

"Uh-oh," Trudy said, suddenly wide awake and peering out the tiny window over their bed. "New neighbors."

"Get down, they'll see you," Connie whispered to her.

"They don't know we're both in this bed," Trudy reassured her. "Wait, it's two girls!" she added.

"It is? Maybe their husbands are following them."

"Not from the looks of that little tent, Con."

"They're in the tent site out back?"

"Yes, and, oh, Connie, they're so excited. They look like us our first trip up."

"Do you think they're . . . ?"

"Maybe. You look and tell me."

"Can they see in?"

"No, they're too busy anyway."

"Aren't they cute? Look at the little one with the sailor hat."

"I remember wearing one of those when I was a kid."

"Trudy?" Connie said, looking at her in consternation. "I hope they're not *obvious* if they're like us."

"Why? What have they to do with us? I don't think

121

we'll be inviting them over for whist every night."

"No, but with them being right behind us and all. If people see them and then remember us being here too. . . . Don't you think it'll make them wonder?"

"You've got a point. But, honey, we don't even know if they *are* yet, so let's have breakfast and worry about that later."

"You're right. We slept so late we may never make it to church."

"You didn't want to go to sleep, honey," Trudy reminded her, rolling over and reaching under Connie's nightgown to touch inside her thigh.

Connie sighed, slipping a hand under Trudy's pajama top. "Mmm. I wish there was more time," she said.

"We could take the Dodge down to church instead of walking." Trudy admired the mellowing flesh of Connie's breasts and looked up toward her face. "Oh dear," she said in a small voice as something caught her eyes.

"What is it?" Connie asked, alarmed.

"I can see right in their tent and they're doing what we're doing."

Connie rose to look. "How could they? Don't they see our window? You don't suppose the owner told them they were being put in back of a couple of old queers and not to worry?"

"Of course not. I guess they just don't care."

"We'd best get to church," Connie decided, already out of bed and moving toward the bathroom. "You start breakfast and I'll take over as soon as I'm dressed."

As they ate they watched their new neighbors out the kitchen window.

"At least they're not doing it outside," Connie commented.

"Count our blessings. I *love* their little dog."

"What is it, Trude?"

"A mix of something, I'd say. They certainly love her. Don't I wish we had one."

"It would bark and make messes," Connie sighed sadly. "You just can't control an animal. Besides, who wants people to point and say, 'There go those two old ladies and their dog. They're always together, like man and wife.' "

"I know, but it might be worth it. Look how much fun they're having. And being affectionate with the dog makes it seem natural for them to be affectionate with each other."

"Maybe to you. What will the families think?"

"Those girls don't care. I heard the big one's name . . . Sue."

"I heard her call the little one Ally. And they call the dog Mutt."

Trudy laughed. "What a wonderful name."

"Oh, I think it's crass. If we ever had an animal I'd want it to at least have a pedigree that comes with a name."

"Fifi L'Amour," Trudy teased.

"Only pansies have poodles."

"And little old ladies."

"We're not little old ladies yet, thank goodness." Connie laughed, getting up to wash the dishes.

"They certainly are full of energy out there. Makes *me* feel like an old lady."

"Oh, no."

"Well, I do."

"No, Trudy. I'm oh-noing them. They don't care who knows. They just hugged. Right out there with the little dog barking up their shins."

Trudy joined Connie at the window and smiled. "I wish they wouldn't do it here, but it *is* nice to watch. You know I've never seen two women, except for us, hug each other out of love? Of course, family, and I suppose some friends. Oh, and those movies, *Sister George* and *The Fox*, but not in real life."

"But Trudy, we'll never be able to come here again. Don't you think people will guess about *us* when they see *them*?" They stared at each other in frustration and disappointment.

★ ★ ★ ★ ★

That Wednesday, Trudy and Connie rode down to the

town Fair. They had been looking forward to it all year.

"How do you like my Lake Winnepesaukee sweatshirt?" Trudy asked, modeling it for Connie as they walked onto the fairgrounds.

"It looks very soft and snug, Strudel. I'm glad you bought it. It's not masculine after all. Look at all the books here this year. I know *you'll* have a good time."

"They always have more white elephants for you than books for me, hon. Be fair."

"And I'm off to find them. Shall I meet you back here in an hour?"

"How about over at the refreshment stand? I'll buy you lunch," Trudy whispered.

The sun crept to its noon height while the Fair became almost crowded. Children screamed on rides, other middle-aged women jostled Connie at the white elephant tent. She was suddenly aware of being watched and looked up under her straw sunhat to see Sue and Ally. They smiled and moved away. Connie pretended not to notice and argued with a seller over the price of a tiny china poodle.

"But it's chipped," she protested, her hand shaking slightly as she showed the woman the small chip.

"You can have it for a dollar," the woman conceded, smiling pleasantly at Connie.

"I have a dollar here somewhere," Connie said as she nervously searched her purse. "I just know I put money in this morning. Here it is." She paid for the dog, noticing out of the corner of her eye Sue and Ally and their little Mutt. The two women wore matching sweatshirts like Trudy's. Her heart thudded with fear. She checked her watch, but she had twelve more minutes to kill in this interminable hour. She might never find Trudy in the crowd if she went to look for her.

Sweating, Connie carefully put the poodle in her bag and looked for a table she had not yet pored over. She walked up to one and pretended to examine each item closely until she realized she had been at that table before. Startled, she moved on to another, wondering if Sue and Ally had noticed.

124

"Hi," she heard someone say as she was turning an old shaving mirror around in her hands. "What good shape that mirror's in," the voice continued.

"Isn't it," Connie answered, expecting to see a seller next to her. It was Ally.

"Are you thinking of buying it? We collect all kinds of junk and Sue loves small mirrors like that one."

Connie could think of nothing, aware only of her urge to get away from this woman and find Trudy. She felt so hot she suspected her menopause had returned.

"Is anything the matter?" Ally asked. "I thought you might be a collector too."

"No, nothing's wrong. I'm not a collector. Here," Connie said, offering Ally the mirror. "You buy it." She managed a weak smile and hoped it would not encourage the girl to be friendlier.

Ally said regretfully, "I'd love to, but we spent our limit on souvenirs before we saw the Fair was here." Then she let a wide smile cover her face. "You're staying next door to us, aren't you? With your friend?"

Confused, Connie fussed in her pocketbook looking for money again. "I'm not sure," she lied. "Where are you staying?"

"At Pine Vista, up the Lake a few miles."

"Ah, yes. We may be neighbors, then. Excuse me," she said and walked away from Ally to pay for the mirror.

She made her way out of the back of the tent and headed for the outdoor bathroom to hide until she could meet Trudy. Inside the smelly cubicle she breathed only when she had to and wiped sweat from her forehead. Why had the girl sought her out? Or had she? Perhaps the mirror really did interest her. Embarrassed, Connie realized she had bought it. She didn't want it — what had come over her? She stared at her dim self in the mirror where it leaned against the door. Are we so visible? she wondered.

Suddenly she could no longer stand the odor of the bathroom. As she slipped awkwardly out the door, mirror under one arm, purse under the other, she saw Sue going into the bathroom next door. The girl smiled at her. Were they following her? Did they sense she was like them?

All these years they had slipped unnoticed, invisible, in and out of New Hampshire. What had changed? As she propped the mirror against the hot dog stand it caught her face more clearly in the light and she saw her pained eyes and said, aloud, "So what? So what if people know about us?" The face in the mirror relaxed. "So what?" she repeated and watched the face in the mirror smile a bit. Connie stood slowly, pondering what she had said, but she couldn't think more about it because Trudy was there with an armload of books.

"Maybe we should put the books in the car and eat in town," Connie suggested, still seeking, by habit, escape from Sue and Ally.

Trudy looked disappointed. "I was looking forward to eating here."

Connie struggled with her fear. "Okay, then." She smiled, wondering where her courage was coming from. "We'll just sit on the grass under a tree and have a good time."

"In your white slacks? They'll get dirty."

"You only live once!" Connie replied, admiring Trudy's sweatshirt again, still glad she had bought it. "Oh, I bought you a present," she said, finding the little china dog in her pocketbook.

"I love it, hon," Trudy said, taking it with a barely free hand. "And I love you." Connie looked quickly around to see if anyone had heard. "Here," Trudy continued, "your present is on the top of this bag."

Connie pulled out a used paperback of D. H. Lawrence's *The Fox*. "Thank you," she beamed, quickly putting it in her purse, but this time not looking around to see if she had been observed. "I can't wait to read it."

"You can bring it to the beach this afternoon to read. No one will know what it is."

Connie's eyes smiled behind their glasses. "Maybe I will," she said bravely.

★ ★ ★ ★ ★

126

The next night was stormy and Connie and Trudy stayed inside playing whist. As the night wore on Connie could no longer bear to keep her thoughts inside. "Do you think we're missing out on something?"

"What do you mean?" asked Trudy, more interested in the hand she was dealing.

"Something those kids have that we don't have. They seem perfectly happy and no one bothers them, yet they don't hide what they are."

Trudy could see how upset Connie was and stopped dealing. "They may be living more fully this moment, but what about later? When it all catches up with them?"

"Maybe they think they'll suffer later when it comes, instead of suffering through it all their lives."

Trudy was silent. The fireplace seemed jolly with its red and yellow flames, the noise and warmth that kept almost all sign of the storm from them. The whitewashed rough walls and unpainted beams reminded them of how close to the earth they were here. Only the scraping of boughs on their roof and occasional distant thunder reminded them of danger. "I love you, Connie," Trudy finally said to comfort her. "And I think we've lived the way we had to for us, and for our time."

"I keep seeing Sue and Ally frolicking under the pines with their little dog. I don't think I'll ever forget the sight of them or the longing they give me to live like they do." Their eyes looked across the firelight. Very gently and tenderly, they held each other on the hearth. "I'm afraid, Trudy."

"Of what, honey?"

Connie was silent for a while. "The storm makes me afraid. But it makes me feel safe, too, here with you." She turned to look at Trudy fully. "What is it? What makes me so uneasy? What am I trying to say?" Connie turned from her lover's arms and went out to the porch. "I feel like ripping my clothes off and running out there onto the beach," she said when Trudy joined her. "I'd enjoy it so much."

Lightning, the lightning Connie had always feared,

flashed across her face and Trudy marveled at the woman who looked out from her eyes. Her face was changed. Its lines were deeper, but more delicate in the light of the storm; they were rugged, but filled with the stuff that had been her life thus far; Trudy could see pain and joy in them, instead of age and time. She looked naked, open, revealed, and Trudy felt her heart expand with a feeling she had never felt before, so powerful she could only stare and realize something was changing her, too.

The storm threw rain at the porch screens. Its cold mist stirred them to move back inside where they warmed themselves, arms around each other, by the fire.

★ ★ ★ ★ ★

On the morning after the storm, everything was more clear than they had ever seen it before. It was their last full day of vacation and they headed out to their favorite island for a picnic.

"How I hate to leave."

Trudy laughed. "You say that every year."

"I mean it more this year." Connie helped spread the blanket.

"Why?"

"I'm not sure. I just feel it deeper inside me. I feel everything deeper. Maybe it's old age."

"Not yet, honey."

"Is it just me, Trudy?"

"No, I feel it too," Trudy admitted. "Let's take a walk. I need to work on my appetite, you fed me so much breakfast."

"I did overdo it a little, but I wanted to pack a very light lunch. We have to walk back to the camp after we return the boat, remember."

Trudy parted the branches in front of them and they found a path. The island was so tiny they reached its other side in a few minutes. "I feel like Robinson Crusoe," Trudy said.

"Uncharted lands. But it's much too rocky over here.

Let's go back to our side."

They filed back through the woods. "It must have been wonderful to live here before the explorers came," Trudy mused.

"Do you think there were women here like us?"

"Nothing but," Trudy laughed. Their blanket was in sight through the woods. "Want to pretend we're Indian lesbians?" Trudy whispered in Connie's ear.

Connie giggled, guessing what Trudy was suggesting. "You mean right here in the open? They at least had tents like Sue and Ally."

They kissed and hugged and touched one another for a long while, rolling around on their blanket, and Connie, though she kept watch for intruders, enjoyed herself thoroughly. Their appetites finally whetted for lunch, they ate ravenously, without words, grinning at each other, feeling very untamed. When they left, they didn't even use their motor until halfway across the lake, but paddled canoe style, feeling, they told each other later, as if they were vibrating to every sound and sight and feeling of the lake. It was a shock when they reached land and had to talk to the old woman who had rented their boat to them. As she paid, Connie felt Trudy tug on her sleeve. "What?" she asked sadly, missing their silence.

But Trudy didn't say anything, only pointed to a hand lettered sign which read simply, "Free Puppies."

They looked at each other. "Can we see the puppies?" Connie asked the woman.

"You surely can, ladies," she said as she spryly flipped up the old wooden counter and led them into a back storage room. "Got two little girls left and ain't they beauties. The liveliest of the litter. They're old enough to eat dog food and they go outdoors, don't have no house accidents."

She thrust first one, then the other, at Connie and Trudy who took them gingerly in their arms. "I know you girls are from town and need well-behaved dogs, so what you need to do is not even think of separating them and then they'll behave, 'cause they got each other, like you two. You know life's a lot better in twos, no matter what you got to bear."

129

She rushed on as Connie and Trudy looked uncertainly at each other. "Now you go on down to the general store and tell Mrs. Wilner these are my pups and she'll give you a break on the collars." She stood back and looked approvingly at her work, wiping her hands on her apron, watching the women shrug at each other in embarrassed, but pleased resignation. "I got business to tend to, so I'll wish you ladies luck. What are you going to name them?" she asked as she led them out the door and to the road.

"Sue," said Trudy without thinking.

"Ally LaMutt," said Connie.

They looked at each other and laughed all the way to the general store, their puppies full of life in their arms.

THE ABRUPT EDGE

I sit on the floor in the rich circle of light cast by a study lamp. The rest of my new apartment is very dark around me. I am alone as usual, feeling empty, needing I know not what. My first job after college graduation will begin tomorrow and I am nervously avoiding thoughts of it, rifling through mementos in a dark wooden chest before me. I pick up three ragged photographs.

In the first, two young women on wooden swings are poised to leave the ground, hands clenched around the thick ropes. I am on the left, the white girl whose birthmark, grayish in the photograph, wraps itself halfway around my face. How I had wished it had stolen all the way around me so that I could be all dark. As Dawn was.

She sits on the right hand swing, my best friend and the only black at camp. We'd had to plead with another counselor to photograph our friendship: the odd ones. She later gave us both print and negative, not wishing to keep our images. In the picture you can see us trying to look small, to be invisible to the staff and campers who shrank almost imperceptibly away when we were near. I had this sad commonality with Dawn to thank for the friendship that flared immediately between us, fanned by our isolations.

But I describe more than is in the picture. It only shows,

in the harsh noon light, two young women, stiff and smiling almost bitterly at the reluctant photographer. We are hard to look at.

Lifting my eyes, I peer into the darkness of my apartment. Dawn seems to shimmer there like a vision, still near me, agonizingly touchable, as terrified as I was of touch . . . I look down to the next photograph, a sunlit one that floods me with light.

Someone had caught us from the beach as we, on the lake, led a convoy of girls on a canoe trip. In the shining aluminum canoe my back shows first, upright, lifted paddle dripping water. The straight line of her tiny back proves Dawn's new mastery of canoeing. Her paddle thrusts back and back and back at me. In the picture I am poised to follow her stroke with my own. The current we create flows between us. Her stroke has become my stroke.

She cared as fiercely for me as I did for her. "Here come the saddle shoes," the kids would chant, for we were always together. There, on the dark and glistening lake water, the camera reflected us, shining in white camp shirts, as we called our fantasies to each other across the bowed opening of our canoe. The camera exposed our dazzling visions, suspected our dazzled hearts.

The brightness closes my eyes now in this memory-heated room. I feel. My heart begins to thud in excitement as it had when we taught the little girls to dance, by dancing before them. Slowly I open my eyes, losing a film of brightness to the dark around me.

I tingle now as I examine the last image, bringing it close under the lamp. It is dark, taken at night from the bottom of a steeply rising cliff by a camper experimenting with her new camera. All I can make out is the sand of the cliff, some dangling roots and patches of dark bushes. Perched atop the cliff's abrupt edge are the shadows of a tent luminous from a lantern within. We are not in sight.

But it was there, in the darkness, on an overnight camping trip, that we faced each other finally.

My need to touch her raged. My words strangled me, caught with emotions thick in my throat. Her almost black eyes seemed swollen as I lay one all white hand lightly against her dark cheek, and she trembled — but whether from desire or fear I could not tell. She gave no other sign.

I took my hand away and collapsed in disappointment into the shadows of the tent, full still of my own tense need. Slowly, Dawn submerged the lantern wick, then faded into her sleeping bag.

"Oh," I cry aloud to myself as if in pain, "how could I have stopped?"

It is as if now, in my own first home, I have finally stepped from the edge of that cliff. As if I am suddenly ready to redeem myself from the failure of that dark night and plunge into a blinding knowledge of who and what I am. I hug myself to soothe the white-hot pain of revelation that sears through me, thus spilling the photographs around me. The pictures catch the light, shine up at me, their various images engraved on my eyes, my mind, my heart. My need is suddenly so clear.

I will love a woman. If one will have me I will see, be seen; touch, be touched; love, be loved, by one as womanly as Dawn, as womanly as myself. Searching through the chest I find some tacks and pin the images of my life solidly to my new wall, lighting as well several candles before them in celebration. The wavering images glow at me and I glow through my mottled face back at them.

THAT OLD STUDEBAKER

Andy was redheaded and scowled a lot. She was probably the most unsociable person in the universe. She'd as soon spit as look at you and sometimes she did spit, if a man made remarks at her.

Almost the only thing Andy loved in the world was that old Studebaker her father thought he had run into the ground. He'd sold it to her for fifteen dollars without a second thought. Andy took a free night school course in auto mechanics and learned how to make the old car run. Then she got herself a job down at the auto wash to pay for good parts and for gas.

But one thing always leads to another. Shining those fancy cars up at work made Andy realize how dull and unloved the body of her Studebaker looked, so she washed and polished it regularly and began to replace the chrome bit by bit. The boss from the auto painting shop, who sometimes brought them jobs to do, noticed Andy's brilliantly polished Studebaker and offered her a painting job which would give her more hours. When she hesitated, hating to make yet another change in her life, he told her she could have a free coat of black paint for her car, and she followed him to his shop.

Andy still didn't talk to anybody, but one day when

she'd been at the auto painting shop a couple of weeks she met this girl. She was the prettiest girl Andy ever saw, maybe because she'd never been interested enough to look before. The girl was admiring her Studebaker when Andy first noticed her.

This pretty girl, whose name was Regina, was girlfriend to one of the other painters, named Roy. She had an old Chevy which he'd souped up for drag racing. It was a pretty impressive car, Andy thought, and much faster than the Studebaker. She wondered which car the pretty girl Regina liked better. Not that she cared.

Regina began hanging around outside the painting shop a lot, leaning up against the cars. Roy's mostly, but sometimes Andy's.

Besides the Studebaker, the only other thing in the world Andy loved was rock'n'roll music. She'd fixed up the Studebaker with a working radio and played it so you could hear it out the windows on long rides in the country. One reason the auto painting shop was a better place to work than the car wash, even though it stank, was because the guys always played the radio on the best rock'n'roll station and they played it real loud.

Andy had never danced, but sometimes, painting cars, especially when she caught sight of Regina leaning against the Studebaker, she found herself doing funny little steps and hops to the good songs.

While all these new things were going on in Andy's life — the Studebaker, the pretty girl, her job and rock'n'roll — Roy and the boys were always talking about drag racing. Andy became so fascinated by it, she listened more and more closely to their talk. Since she couldn't seem to ask questions, or for help, she began to study the car magazines on the drugstore shelf. She'd stay there reading them so long the counter clerks would remind her she wasn't at a library and kick her out.

Then she'd go straight home to tinker with the Studebaker, making it roar in ways she thought sounded like Roy's car. When she left the painting shop nowadays, she'd roar away, hoping Regina would be impressed.

One day Regina came over to Andy as she was about to rev up her engine and began to talk to her, hanging over the car window chewing gum, just like she did with Roy. Andy got one whiff of her perfume, her Marlboro breath, her juicy fruit gum, all exaggerated by hot girl sweat, and thought her heart would pump right out of her mouth.

Regina talked about this and that, seeming to understand Andy wouldn't give her much in the way of answers. After a while Regina led her conversation around to dancing.

"I seen you like to dance some."

"Who, me?"

"Well, you got good rhythm."

Andy couldn't very well say who, me, again, so she blushed into the roots of her red hair.

"You mean you don't know how to dance?" Regina asked.

Andy shook her head no, ashamed.

"Want me to teach you?"

And so they began to meet in the evenings, at Regina's house, where they would dance until Roy revved his engine outside and Regina had to go.

Every evening it got a little harder to let Regina go, so to prevent that, Andy found herself talking. She would talk a blue streak until she was too embarrassed to go on. She never guessed she had so much to say to one person before.

One night there was something in the air. Andy wondered, was this what they called spring fever. She got to Regina's in an excited state after eating hardly any dinner at all, but taking two showers. Regina, too, seemed different. She kept forgetting to teach Andy steps, so they ended up just dancing to a lot of slow songs. Andy realized it had been weeks since Regina had last predicted Andy would be a fine dancer someday and would catch herself a boyfriend.

On this night Roy revved so long Andy was scared he'd run out of gas. Still they danced and danced and danced, Andy weaving words she didn't know she had in and out of their rhythm together, as if to make a chain to bind Regina to her.

All at once Regina pushed Andy away and ran outside.

Sighing, Andy tucked in her good shirt and got ready to leave. But Regina rushed back in, all smiles.

"I told him I got the curse," she explained.

Andy looked puzzled, then blushed when she figured out what the curse was, then heard Roy roar away, and smiled too.

Regina went to Andy and they danced long into the night, until they were so tired they lay down together and even then they didn't really stop dancing. Andy felt this creeping warmth that made her shake, made her sweat, made her, finally, cry as she touched the soft places on Regina's body and watched the girl move in ways that were like dancing she hadn't learned to do yet.

After that, Regina began to lean on Andy's Studebaker at the auto painting shop a whole lot more than she leaned on Roy's Chevy. She didn't see much of Roy evenings anymore, either.

Roy started looking at the two of them strangely. One night he barged into the room where Regina and Andy did their dancing, and he began to shout, to call them names. Then he said to Andy, "You want a woman? You prove you're man enough first. I'll meet you on the country road tonight at eleven and race you for the woman. If you don't show or if you lose, either one, I get her. Looks like I just got to show her who's the real man around here."

When he slammed out of the room Regina cried, as if suddenly seeing how it would be if she gave up Roy for a girl.

Andy hadn't said a word the whole time Roy was there, but she rose to the challenge now, full of words like, "I'll beat the pants off that boy." She spent the rest of the evening in her Studebaker, waiting for the old church clock downtown to strike half past ten. Secretly, she was quaking. Of course she couldn't win. She hadn't known enough about cars to make her Studebaker as fast as Roy's Chevy. But maybe, with a little luck. . . . She looked toward the heavens. The stars were twinkling up there like they did in her head when Regina did those things to her that felt so good.

She could hear Regina crying through the window of

the room where they'd danced. When it came time to go, Regina came running out to the Studebaker and got in. She took one look at Andy's miserable face and started to cry, saying, "I can't lose you."

What could she say? It looked to her like Regina was too scared to choose her. Maybe the race *was* the best way to decide.

When they got to the country road it looked like the whole town had heard about this race between the man and the girl who thought she was a man. But out of all those kids, Andy didn't have one damn person rooting for her. At least now she knew what made her so unsociable. She didn't have anything to say to those people at all.

She dropped Regina at the end of the strip and came back to the start line.

The kids lined the route, making ugly threats at Andy. She wished she could spit.

Instead, she stroked that old Studebaker, admitting to herself and the car it would do fine now on long distances, the shape she'd got it in, but it wasn't cut out for racing. Maybe she just ought to ride out of town and clear across the country before she made a fool of herself. But to leave Regina behind without even trying?

Roy revved. Andy answered. "I'm counting on you," she told the Studebaker hopefully. The stars were still twinkling through the windshield, like they knew a secret and were teasing her.

Next thing she knew the starter signaled, Roy was off, and she was on his tail, trying the best she could to keep up with him.

She couldn't. Not only that, but she felt so bad for the old Studebaker, whose engine she'd so lovingly restored, that rather than hurt her car she slowed down, letting Roy win by a whole lot more than he should have.

When she saw Regina, though, she felt just like dying. Maybe she had saved the car she loved, maybe she couldn't have won the race anyway, but she'd lost the only girl she'd ever loved.

Roy swaggered over to Regina. Andy could see him

puckering his big lips for a victory kiss. He was the man, the natural winner, and maybe Regina would be better off with him anyway.

Looking at Regina one last time, Andy admired the body that had made her shake and sweat so, the lips that brought stars into her head, the hands that made her dance even when she wasn't dancing. But as she looked, she realized Regina wasn't giving Roy his kiss, wasn't even looking at him. Was she staring at Andy as an abomination, shocked she could have let such a loser ever touch her?

Andy started up the Studebaker as Regina began to run toward it. When it started as sweet as a brand new Cadillac, Andy patted it quickly, certain it was thanking her for being kind during the race. As soon as Regina had slammed the door behind her, and settled as close to Andy as she could get, they were off.

That old Studebaker was anxious to prove that, yes, she was meant for a good long trip clear across the country.

Andy allowed herself one last look in the rearview mirror at the astounded and diminishing Roy.

FRUITSTAND II
Honeydew Moon

You know that song about the moon hitting your eye
like a big pizza pie — how that's amore? Well, that's what
the moon was like on our honeymoon, only it wasn't a pizza
pie, it was a honeydew. A fat juicy honeydew, perfect, like
I sometimes get for my fruitstand, almost white, but with
the tiniest bit of yellow in it to remind you about the sun
that grew it, hanging loud in that night sky, looking like it
would fall right into our laps. And if it did, it'd pop right
open, split clean in half: half for her, half for me. We'd roll
back on the cool night grass on the edge of that sand cliff
like we were the only people in the world, lay back for a
while on the edge of our lives together, and we'd be sucking
sugar from that honeydew moon.

Now what got me started on that? Right, you want to
take your girl away for the weekend. You should, you
definitely should. New York might be the greatest city in
the world, and Queens the greatest borough in the city, but
fresh air and the ocean are something you remember all your
life, am I right, Beanpole? Okay, okay, I'll tell you the whole
story of my honeymoon, but first, look, it's late already,
we got to start cleaning up. Hand me the broom. You start
weeding out the fruit that's too manhandled to sell full price

141

like I showed you. Here, ouch — stooping's not as easy as it was back when we took our honeymoon, Kathy and me — here's a crate to put the bad stuff in.

Yeah, those berries are too far gone to save. Would you look at this light? I swear, if they made syrup out of gold this is what it'd look like, the way the sunrays look coming in these little windows in the late afternoon. Did you ever see anything so pretty? Gold-syrup. That's why I like to keep the windows so clean, it makes everything look prettier, more open, with all the little panes clear as air for the gold-syrup to pour through the fruit. My dad had this all closed in, all wood, but I put in plenty of windows, maybe from that taste of open air markets I got on our honeymoon. I wanted something that looked more like the country, more like where fruit deserves to be sold. Not food factories like the supermarkets.

You said you're thinking about Atlantic City? I wouldn't. I mean, I hear the beach is okay down there, but it's too crowded. No place you can go to cuddle in some lonely spot. No place to get away from it all. Am I right? How about the Cape? Or out on the Island? No, I hear they got a lot of good restaurants on the Cape, and you need them. Never mind you want to do *that* with your girl all weekend. You take her to some of those good restaurants and feed yourself. Skinny as a rail. I don't know how you lift these crates, except you have to if you want to keep your job. Little dykes like you are a dime a dozen, Beanpole. You get some weight on your bones or you'll keel over someday and I'll sweep you out with the old straw.

Yeah, me and Kathy went to Long Island for our honeymoon. Way out near Montauk, the Hamptons. What do you mean? Of course they let us in, there's working people out there too. Who do you think makes life so easy for the rich people? We stayed with friends — but stop asking questions, I'm not telling you another story until we get this place cleaned up. Look — look how the light's shining on those red apples, like they're going to catch on fire any minute. What a sight.

I'll tell you what, why don't you come over tonight,

142

Beanpole. Come have supper with us and I'll tell you the story of the honeymoon — maybe Kathy will fill in what I leave out — and we'll feed you. No, don't worry, we eat so little meat we're practically vegetarians too. No, I'll make you something nice, and fattening, right out of this store, what do you think of that?

★ ★ ★ ★ ★

Okay, Beanpole, how does this dinner look to you? Has Kathy been chewing your ear off while I fixed supper? Oh, the picture albums, did she bore you with those already? No, we didn't have a camera on our honeymoon. They weren't as easy to come by back then. Now I have two. Wait, let me get the Polaroid, take your picture with Kathy here and the fruit salad. I'll call it Fattening the Beanpole. You don't like me calling you that? Too bad. Let the kids call you whatever cool nicknames you think up, you're the Beanpole to me. There, it's starting to develop already. The salad came out better than you! See, I made strawberries in gold-syrup — or the closest I could get with the sun already down — they're soaked in honey instead of sugar water. The rest here is chunks of watermelon, cantaloupe, some pieces of fresh coconut, pineapple rings, banana slices. And here in the middle, I cheated, this isn't from my store, some sherbet. Now that ought to fatten you up a little. Let's eat before it melts!

So she wants to hear all about our honeymoon, Kath, you want to help me tell it? That's a long story to tell all by myself, you just butt in when I leave something out. Wish we had some May wine with this. Kathy makes good May wine, learned how from Monica, one of the women we stayed with on our honeymoon. She died real soon after Johnnie did, her lover. They had a good long life, though, don't you worry, Beanpole. Am I right, Kath? They didn't die till their eighties. That made them, what, sixty-something when we stayed there.

This wasn't long after my folks died and left me with the fruitstand. It was harder to find little baby butches like you

143

back then, so I had to close the stand for a week. But I never took a vacation before. Figured I deserved it. And Kathy was determined on a honeymoon. Said she was tired of falling in love and breaking up in a month or a year. She had this idea that when she found the girl she wanted to spend her life with, if we did some of the things straight people do to tie the knot, maybe ours would have a chance of staying tied longer than most gay people. You know, since the religions won't bless us or anything, she thought up other ways to make what we were promising each other more important so we'd take it serious when things got rough.

You bet it worked. This year will be our twenty-fifth anniversary! Good, I'm glad you're impressed. Some of these little dykes today think it's not such a hot idea to stay together, to have a rock in your life you can lean on. As far as I'm concerned, except for my stand and my girl, life wouldn't be worth living. I couldn't enjoy it and I'd probably be drinking myself to death. It's rough out there. Didn't you find that out yet? Wait, you'll see what I mean.

Me, I wanted to really do it right and go to Niagara Falls. But Kath was right, as usual. Hey! What are you giving me a dirty look about, can't I pinch my girl?

Maybe Long Island wasn't the perfect honeymoon spot, but at least we weren't stuck in the middle of thousands of straight people showing off how straight they can be and staring at us because we weren't like them. Besides, we had a lot of time alone there at first.

See, Monica and Johnnie lived right on the beach. How can I explain this to you? In the old days, queers didn't have it so easy as now. For some reason the world hated us even more. Johnnie had a really bad time of it, so she had to do things different.

You ever hear about women who dressed like men, pretended they were men? No, it's not disgusting. Sometimes that was the only way you could be queer and get along. Our friend Johnnie did it when she couldn't get a job any other way. The story she told, through Monica, was that between looking so much like a man — she was almost as tall as me, but I guess you'd call her burly, and she had these real rough features. She'd be called ugly if she dressed like a girl, but in the kinds of clothes she wore she was just mean looking. Had a scar on her chin that healed all red and ugly because she didn't have the money for a doctor. She hated doctors, anyway, from listening to their comments when she had to strip to get examined. Professional? No, there's something about a woman who looks like a man that makes even doctors get nasty. On top of all that she had a beard. Really, she had to shave. Dressed as a woman she'd shave every day to hide it, but pretending she was a man, she didn't have to worry about it.

Oh, and the worst thing for her — she was mute. Could hear, but didn't talk. So she couldn't explain herself. You see why she had a hard time? Yes, she really was a woman. It was only the world said she wasn't. Monica told us the older Johnnie got, the gladder she was to be a woman. Acting like a man she saw a lot of the stuff men do that women wouldn't usually see. She hated them. Wanted to start a woman's army and someday take over the world.

But meantime, she had to earn a living. She kind of fell into gardening. She was from a city, some place upstate, so she grew up without knowing much about growing things. Still, when she was looking for any kind of work at all, getting knocked around by the men who found out she was a woman, laughed at by the women who found out she wasn't a man, Johnnie heard about a job as a gardener. It didn't pay much, but it didn't need any talking neither and the guy let her use his garage to sleep in till she made some money.

He was the only man I ever saw her smile about. He thought she was a mute boy, and Johnnie let him as he took a liking to her. She learned everything he had to teach that summer and would have worked with him forever except it turned out he was gay. He was married, see, and toward the end of the summer Johnnie began to figure out why he went downtown one night a week. When he started coming on to her on his night out she knew she'd better take off before he found out he really did love a woman.

So she hit the road again, spent a bad winter cleaning johns, whatever she could find to do, and ended up on Long

Island, washing dishes in this mansion. It was spring, and having no one she could be friends with, Johnnie used to wander around the grounds a lot taking care of them out of love. Her luck changed again when the gardener quit. The rich people who lived in the mansion had noticed her work and gave her the job. To make sure she would stay, they let her have an unused cottage on the beach. She wouldn't make a salary off-season, but she wouldn't have rent either. All around the cottage she grew her own garden, and she learned from the cook at the house how to preserve the fruits and vegetables the rich people didn't want. This was the second happy season of her life. She had a job, a home, and so far nobody bothered the strange mute gardener who lived all by himself in the cottage on the beach.

Hey, Beanpole, eat up, your sherbet's melting. No, you didn't have enough. What's the matter? The story's upsetting you? Hey, this is the way it was, count your blessings.

Anyways, to make a long story short, here's Johnnie living on the beach in back of this mansion, happy as a peach pit about to grow a tree, when she starts to get real lonely. She remembers the few friends she's had in her life, and, being young and healthy, remembers in particular this girl back home who used to walk with her in the woods. And kiss her.

Then, on a trip to town, she notices the new girl at the hardware store. They always had a man before, but all the sons were off fighting the war, so the daughter got the job. It was a welcome change for Johnnie since the sons never had the patience to listen to what she needed. Instead of dreading going into town once a month, she began to go weekly. There was something about this girl.

Next thing Johnnie knows, she's sitting outside her cottage one night after dinner, watching the birds fish, when the girl comes walking up the beach. She's in pants, like Johnnie, and that was unusual then. Johnnie pulls her other chair out of the cabin and they sit together awhile, the girl chattering enough for the two of them and making Johnnie laugh. The next night the girl comes back and Johnnie pulls the chair out again. By the third week Johnnie's bought another chair at the junkshop in town, and she's suffering. She's wondering if this girl is like the one back home. By the flush on her cheeks when she looks Johnnie's way she might be. But of course Johnnie knows she hasn't got a chance with a girl who thinks she's a man. Except there's the pants, which the girl wears every night, like she might be trying to tell Johnnie something.

One day the girl shows up early, when Johnnie's still washing her dishes inside. Wandering around the cabin she picks up an old picture of Johnnie as a young girl, holding her mother's hand. Johnnie figures it's now or never and points first to the little girl in the picture, then to herself. The girl from town smiles, puts the picture down carefully and walks over to Johnnie. Without saying a word she reaches up to put her arms around Johnnie's neck and presses herself to her. "I know," the girl says, kissing Johnnie. The girl's name was Monica.

Will you look at this table? Picked clean. Looks like Beanpole could do with a good feeding once in a while, am I right, Kathy? Let's clear it off and put up coffee. You want tea? Herb tea? No, we don't have any of that stuff. What's the matter with you, Beanpole, you got to be different? Yeah, I heard caffeine's bad for you, but I got to have my fix. Wait, I know what we'll do. How about tea made with fresh mint leaves? Think that'll work? I'll try it too. Sit, sit. This kitchen's not big enough for the three of us to work in. And yes, I'm getting to the honeymoon. You had to know the whole story.

No, Monica's folks weren't upset. Johnnie and her ran off to New York City and came back saying they'd gotten married. Nobody even asked to see the certificate. I guess Monica's folks might have been disappointed she didn't marry a man with money and looks, instead of a mute gardener, but Monica was so happy. She said she suspected her mother envied her, living such a simple life right on the water, instead of having five sons and an ambitious husband to take care of.

They never did find out Johnnie was a girl, or bother the young couple much. Monica kept working at the hardware store till the war was over. Then, because she still needed money when the brothers who were left came home and took her job, she began housekeeping for the rich couple. They were pretty nice, for rich people, and years later, when Johnnie and Monica were getting too old to work like they had, they gave them a small pension and told them the cottage was theirs for life. What more could they ask?

Give me the dishtowel, Kath, I'll dry. Your coffee's almost ready. I don't know, Beanpole, this tea's pretty weak stuff, no wonder it's so good for you.

How we got to honeymoon out there, Kathy met Johnnie and Monica through some friends of hers. It seems Monica was not exactly innocent when she put her arms around Johnnie that night. She'd known a couple of women like her from the school where she went. Those women knew a couple more and on like that till there were a little circle of them, and that's how Kathy met them. Johnnie and Monica never had parties or anything because of being afraid Johnnie would be found out, but once in a while some of their friends would visit them, quietly. They loved Kath, of course, how could they resist her? And she had a standing invitation to bring a friend and stay in the unused cabin down the beach.

Umm. Mint-water. I think I'll start a company. Sell mint-water and gold-syrup. Mix them and bottle Henny's Golden Mint-Syrup. Healthy, refreshing, dull as an unripe watermelon. You don't think it'll catch on?

By this time, when she met me, Kathy was visiting the old folks a couple times a year, and she hadn't seen them for months, so that's where we decided to honeymoon. Besides, I guess you kind of thought of them as your own people by then, am I right, Kath? Wanted them to approve of me or something. Goodness knows I was nervous enough to need their approval to marry you. I closed up the stand that Saturday night and we drove out there, pulling in real late. We didn't want to wake them, so we slept in the old panel truck I hauled the fruit in. I kept a couple of old blankets in the back and Kathy brought pillows, so we were all set.

Yes, that's where we spent our first honeymoon night,

locked in the dark old truck, lying on the ridged metal floor, covered by smells like cantaloupe rind, strawberry juice, lemons and limes and bananas, all gone a little musty, like in a dream. I called it my cornucopia. Kathy was my new treat and I had a feast. Oh, stop blushing, Kath, I didn't mean *that*. Besides, Beanpole knows the facts of life.

In the morning I met two of the finest human beings on earth. I thought Kathy was a magician to have found those two. Monica was this little grandmother type in a faded bib apron with flour up to her elbows and hairpins sticking out of her grey hair. Johnnie was still pretty burly, but bent from gardening so many years. She had a kind of rough way about her like some people get when they have a hard time being understood, but once you caught on to how she talked, with her hands, with Monica's help, with scraps of paper and a shaky, old-fashioned handwriting, she was just as shy and gentle as could be. Birds would pick crumbs off her big palm, am I right, Kath?

The grounds around their cottage, even with the sandy soil and the salt water, were like a picture book. She had flowering vines trailing all up and around their porch, rose trellises, fruit trees. You could see why the rich people were letting her live out her life in that cottage: she'd planted so much of herself in it.

And the way they were together! Their eyes still shone when they looked at each other. They were so patient and appreciative you would have thought they were the ones on a honeymoon. I mean, who ever thought of two old ladies like that loving each other? All of a sudden I could see me and Kathy twenty, fifty years down the road. Being gay had always meant being young, fooling around, going out. Now I was looking at the happiest people I ever met and they didn't fit any of that. We had a future!

That week, what a week it was. The pretty little cottage we stayed in was all open to the wind and sun. It was painted white outside, but inside was rough wood that smelled just cut under the sunlight. One whole side of the beach ran into the monastery next door, so we had that whole stretch all to ourselves and we would get up in the morning and run

149

along the water's edge as far as our breath lasted, holding hands and hugging. There were little sand-cliffs above the beach with short trees and tall grasses on top of them and we'd lie there making love carefully, always alert, because we would've killed ourselves if we gave Johnnie away like that.

They didn't have a car, so we made a big shopping trip into town to save them the bus ride. Johnnie put on a tie and Monica her best hat and dress. It was a small shady town, after all that white beach, and we carried their packages as they visited every store. Here and there along the road were produce stands. I had to stop at all of them. That's where I got some of the ideas for my place: the straw on the floor, all the light coming in, the bushel baskets I use. Little tricks like that make people feel they're in the country, think my fruit is fresher. Even the supermarkets are catching on now, prettying things up.

In the town I saw for myself what Johnnie had gained by playing a man. I guess I was like you, because even though I liked her a lot, it really bothered me: the shaving, the haircut, men's clothes even down to the boxer shorts Monica hung on the line. It seemed perverted. And I suspected Johnnie liked playing a man, Monica didn't really want a woman. But when I saw everybody Johnnie met on the street stop and say hello to her, smiling and passing the time of day . . .

I mean, twenty-five years ago Kathy and me were still being careful not to be seen together on the street too much, afraid people would put two and two together and stop shopping at the fruit's fruitstand. And here was little old Monica leaning on her lover's arm like she'd been doing for years, wearing a matching wedding band, and doing this in a small, stuffy rich town.

So don't put Johnnie down, Beanpole. If she had looked like you they might have killed her, wouldn't have given her work for sure. Her life, even if somehow she stayed, wouldn't have been as full as it was. What choice did she have, anyway, being queer and looking the way she did? You compromised then. Even now, maybe you're not afraid, Beanpole, with

150

your marches and your bookstores, but I am sometimes. There may even be some Johnnies left.

But that day, the four of us were happy as bananas grinning on a tree: us two on our honeymoon, even if we couldn't act like it in town, those two enjoying the fruit of their long years of hard work and caution.

We got back to the cottage exhausted, and sat around talking. You'd think me and Kathy would have wanted to get off by ourselves for a while, but we knew we had a whole lifetime to do that and every minute with those old people was too precious to waste. They gave our honeymoon something nobody who goes to Niagara Falls will ever get. We even talked about setting up a farmers' market and lunch counter out there — Kathy was waitressing back then too. Now and then Johnnie's eyes would brighten and she'd put in her two cents, her hands going a mile a minute in her own kind of sign language, and Monica trying to keep up with her.

After a while when the ideas were flying fast and it really seemed like me and Kathy might move out of the city, this big silver car pulled up in the driveway. Monica threw her hands up. "It never rains, but it pours," she said like she knew it was trouble. She hadn't mentioned any problems to us, but we felt their fear. While Johnnie sat tight and tense the lawyer talked at Monica. I had trouble following, he talked so smooth and polite and slimy. He said he represented the monastery.

What Monica hadn't wanted to worry us with, was that the rich people from the estate died, and their kids sold everything to the monastery next door. Now Monica and Johnnie, they said they signed papers when the rich people gave them the cottage, papers saying the house was theirs to live in all their lives, rent free. But they never got copies of the papers, the church people claimed there never *were* any such papers, and the lawyer was there to tell them they had to leave.

Me and Kathy sat there speechless while the lawyer said he'd be back with the final papers ordering them out. The brothers had offered to put them in a senior citizen project, but Johnnie's pension didn't include rent because she'd gotten the cottage. They wouldn't be able to pay rent and they wouldn't be able to grow their own food to stretch the money they had if they moved. Until this afternoon, they hadn't been too worried. One of the things pretending to be straight had done for them was to make their church respect them like the townspeople did. They figured ministers were just too ignorant to look past what the world thought and see their love was a good thing. They'd been praying up a storm, sure they'd be saved in the end. It was beginning to look to them like their religion wasn't all they thought.

Didn't they have a lawyer, we asked? No, they said, they didn't want to make a scene with the church. Besides, lawyer talk was over their heads, they weren't the kind to hire lawyers. How would they pay him? And what if, somehow, in all this, Johnnie got found out?

Kathy and me spent the rest of the day trying to figure something out with them. "That's okay, girls," Monica told us, "all we ever had was each other. And the good will of the people on the hill." Nothing we came up with worked, or suited them. The threat of the monastery was over us all night, like evil. After the lies and the pretending, the hard work and the fear, it could wipe out all Johnnie and Monica had. They might just as well have been themselves from the start as go through all they had to prove they deserved a decent life.

By the next day, when the damn lawyer came again, I was mad as hell.

"What's the matter with the Brothers?" I shouted at him as he tried to get out of his slimy silver car. Somebody had to speak up for these women. "Are they afraid of the real world? Let *them* come down here and throw the old people out." Monica and Johnnie watched me, Monica frightened, Johnnie's sensitive eyes worried.

"Why can't your so-called Christians let these old people stay? What do they need the damn cottages for?" I asked. He claimed they'd love to let them stay, but their insurance made it impossible.

"What you mean," Kathy says, "is you don't want to

spend the money insuring two old people who have always lived on the water and now might all of a sudden fall in?" Even Monica laughed.

Silverslime didn't like our tone at all. He finished getting out of the car and pulled himself up. He was prepared to make them one final offer, he said.

"We're listening," I answered.

He wanted to move them up to the caretaker cottage on the monastery grounds. If they were employees, and not as close to the water, the problem would be solved. The old people looked interested, but not at all happy. Seeing that, I couldn't help myself, I risked everything because I knew they were right and even if their church wasn't on their side in the crunch, somebody had to be. Besides, except for the sin of being queer, they lived a godlier life than anyone I knew. Their world was full of peace and love and kindness and even, with the little they had, charity. The god of flowers and fruit and sea and sun had claimed this little piece of land for them and big old Henny was suddenly their appointed priestess. I couldn't help it.

"No, they're not going to settle for changing their whole lives this late, mister. Johnnie paid for this place with all the years of his labor. It's not much reward. You know how little pension he gets. But he and Monica feel they own something here. You can keep them from selling it, from passing it on, but it just isn't right to pull it out from under them. I own my own business back in the city and I know a bit more about your games, unfortunately, than they do. They've got me in their corner now. So get yourself and your papers back in that car and get out of here. Their lawyer will contact you."

Old Silverslime huffed up, looked like he was either going to give me a speech or have a heart attack, and I didn't much care which, but at the last minute he slid back into the slimemobile and roared off.

Maybe I was being hasty, and getting involved where I didn't belong. Maybe I was bluffing a little to prove to these people that I'd be a good mate for their adopted daughter. Maybe it was just my sense of fair play that was offended.

And what did I have to offer them if we lost? My parents' old apartment where Kathy and I already lived? Damn it, I wanted that home for them. For all those years they'd had to swallow their pride and their own natural ways, for all the things they did without to get what they had, for all the queers who had to live half-lives to get any peace at all, I wanted that home.

So our honeymoon took a different turn. We didn't run along the beach that day, or make love that night. We waited and thought, and I'm sure the old people prayed. I wanted to call my lawyer, but Monica said she'd call the one in town, the old one the rich people had used. I said I'd pay him and she accepted gratefully, despite Johnnie's gruff shake no. But she kept putting off calling, like she was still waiting for that church to fix things up.

When two of the Brothers from the monastery came to the front door that night, just as Johnnie was building a fire in the fireplace, I wondered if the old peoples' faith was paying off. How could they order such frail good people out of their home, now that they saw them in person? But an hour later they were gone, whining at not getting their way.

"Faggots," Kathy decided, and we all laughed out loud except Johnnie, whose eyes laughed for her.

In the morning we found a formal letter in the mailbox. In two days the sheriff would begin eviction.

Kathy persuaded Monica to call the lawyer immediately. I paced around outside watching to see if any busybody sheriff dared stick his nose into our business. Kathy called me in. Another setback. The old lawyer had died. His daughter had taken over his practice. Great, a woman, she'd care. But Monica and Johnnie were old-fashioned. They were dead-set against using a "lady lawyer."

Things were at a standstill again. Hell, I decided, I'd gotten them that far against their obstinate wills. I picked up the phone and dialed the lady lawyer's number. Once she heard who was involved she got very interested. The rich peoples' daughter had been her best childhood friend, and she remembered how happy she'd been that the old couple

154

got their home. She would check in her father's files.

We sat down to a cold supper of homegrown vegetables and cold sliced meat, each with the thought this might be the last dinner on the beach, these the last homegrown vegetables ever. Would it kill Monica and Johnnie to move up to the monastery, I wondered, take on some light tasks? It would be better than wandering around Queens, living a new life among strangers.

After the old ones went to bed we sat staring, Kathy and me, long into the night on the front porch of their cottage. Near midnight we were startled – there was a sound in the cabin. It was like a child's cry, or the whimpering of a hurt animal. Kathy put her hand on my arm.

"Johnnie, are you crying?" we heard then. The bedroom was right behind the porch and its window suddenly threw light out the side of the house. Their small sounds carried to us over the sounds of the water.

"I don't want to leave this place," said a sad, raspy, high voice. I felt the blood fall out of my face. It was Johnnie talking.

"Something will happen," Monica comforted her. "And if we do have to move to the city with the kids, why then you can be yourself for these last years. No one will know us. No one cares anymore about the way we are."

"Maybe we *have* been wrong to live like this, though. Maybe we *are* being punished. If only I could use my voice." She cried again. We could barely make out her next words. "I'm so ashamed, Henny having to do this for me. If anyone has to fight for our home, it should be me."

"Johnnie." Monica sounded as if she was whispering a prayer. "Don't you forget, whatever happens, we still have each other."

We could hear Johnnie sigh as she turned over on the bed. There was a smile in the little voice. "That's most important, I know," she answered her lover.

Kathy and I stared at each other in the dark. The voices went on for a while, Johnnie's breathy, unused. It gave me the chills because it was so female in a body I didn't think of that way, and because we never guessed she did have a

155

voice. We waited about an hour after the voices faded away and then very carefully snuck off the porch and over to our cottage. We were still too stunned to talk, but held each other while we cried over Johnnie's girlish sobs, her few rusty words. By the time we went to sleep, I'd realized completely how terrible it had been for Johnnie, how she'd given up her voice so it wouldn't hurt so much to live in her body. I was bowled over thinking how awfully, awfully strong she'd had to be all those years, how she'd stayed as true to herself as she could, and kept loving women, living the whole time like a tomato plant without a stake, holding herself up by sheer will. And now, if she lost everything she'd earned by giving up her voice . . .

By eight o'clock that morning I was at the lady lawyer's office. When she showed up I insisted on helping in some way. The sheriff might come anytime, I told her.

She was a pretty lady, very straight, and looked at me like I was a beetle about to attack her rose garden. "No need," she said, waving a folder at me. I followed her upstairs as she explained. "I found this in Dad's personal files at home with a few closed cases that never made it to the office files." Once in the office she handed me a sheet of paper. It was a notarized statement giving Johnnie and Monica the cottage. I was so happy *I* almost prayed in thanks.

Then the lawyer pulled out two more copies of the same sheet. "He was sick at the end," she said, "and never made it back to the office. If he had, these would have been mailed out."

She thanked me for calling her, both for the old couple and her father's reputation. Then she offered to deliver a copy to the monastery lawyer. She thought the Brothers might still fight it, since the cottage wasn't mentioned in the sale of the property to them, but felt something could be worked out.

Before she knew what hit her, I grabbed her and gave her an enormous hug. I'd swear she was almost smiling despite herself when I ran off to show Monica and Johnnie that beautiful piece of paper. They cried with joy, Monica loudly,

Johnnie silently, though Kathy and I listened hard for a familiar whimper. Kathy treated me like the conquering hero when, later that day, the lady lawyer called to say our problems were over.

Out of respect for their father's wishes, out of a sense of responsibility because her father's office had been at fault, the children of the rich people and the lady lawyer would make a donation to the monastery. But it could only be used to pay the insurance on the beach cottage.

Hey, Kathy, will you look at the grin on Beanpole's face. What's the matter, you were worried? With friends like me and Kathy, you needed to worry?

Our honeymoon? Oh sure, we got back in the mood, what with all the celebrating we did that night. But we were so exhausted from being scared and from fighting we collapsed the last two days.

I kept hoping Johnnie would thank us by breaking her silence, but she never did in words. It was okay, she didn't need to. They gave us so much. Just being themselves, staying together, going though what they did. It was like having parents to look up to. We wanted to live like them, to be decent as they were in spite of what they went through. And we wanted to stay together forever, like they had, because we could see how happy they were.

Yeah, Beanpole, like me and Kath are now. Like maybe you're going to be someday.

Don't get me all misty about it, though. I see you two looking for the tissues. Here, it's late anyway. Take these pastries and get home to your girlfriend. But don't stay up so late looking for honeymoon dew you can't keep your eyes open at work tomorrow!

What's honeymoon dew? Look at Kathy winking at me over there. It's just something we discovered on our honeymoon. You'll figure it out.

157

AT A BAR IV
White Wine

Once, when Sally the bartender was least expecting it, and certainly didn't want it, she fell in love.

Never mind the details of the long, silent courtship. Roxanne came into the *Cafe Femmes*, caught Sally's eye, and Sally, try as she might, could not succeed in looking away.

It was during those early spring nights that have a cold edge to them, when the darkness still seems to belong to winter, when people scurry from one circle of lamplight to the next, in a hurry to get to some light. Just as Sally, sensing a hint of warmth in the air, felt impelled toward spring, felt her whole being pointed toward it, waiting.

She stood behind the bar and, even more often than usual, ran her bar rag over the countertop. She and her partner and lover, Liz, had installed new overhead lights. Half of the old ones had been beyond replacement, and for a few years now, *Cafe Femmes* had been so dim it took the two pinball machines and the jukebox to brighten it up a bit. Now the lights shone on the counter exposing every stain, shone in a new and revealing way on the gay kids that hung out there so that sometimes Sally felt as if she had just seen them for the first time. As for her, she too felt exposed

159

by all this new light, felt flushed out of the pleasant daze in which she usually worked.

It was about this time when Roxy first began to frequent *Cafe Femmes*. What was it about her? Sally couldn't quite put her finger on it, on what made her heart flutter when that woman first ordered a white wine in her southern accent. Of course, the accent made her different, more noticeable — but she had never felt drawn to a southern woman before. It was more her knowing smile, which seemed to confide in Sally from the very start a wonderful secret, a connection.

Roxy was tall, but not as tall as Sally; thin, but not as thin as Sally. She was graceful, unlike Sally, in the way she flung her arms out toward the women in the bar, so that she seemed to want to embrace them all; and in the way she walked, as if with every step she might sink down beside you on a bed.

Her hair was light, but not blonde like Sally's, and much longer. Her eyes had a light to them that flared now and then like the streetlights when they come on in darkness. A dimple would form just above Roxy's lips as she gave Sally that wise smile and said something in her slow deep voice like, "Come on home with me, sweet Sal," when Sally was running a lemon around the rim of a glass, when anyone could have heard. Sally's hand, retrieving the lemon wedge, would shake and she'd stand staring at Roxy's hands, wondering how they'd feel if she did go home with her.

Gabby, one of the regulars, teased her about her crush. Sally was panic-stricken because it was so strong she couldn't stop her feelings, couldn't hold them in, and wasn't at all sure, if the opportunity presented itself, that she could keep from falling on Roxy, from devouring her with her hands as well as with her eyes.

Sally had been thirty-eight then. She drank only beer, but when Roxy came into her life, she quickly switched to mineral water. Each time Roxy was near, she would drink bottle after bottle of the stuff, trying to douse the fire inside rather than inflame it with liquor.

As for Liz, their shifts overlapped only a little. Besides,

Roxy came into the bar at all different times, and flirted with many different girls. At home, Sally pushed Roxy out of her mind. At *Cafe Femmes* no one, knowing Sally and Liz' devotion to each other, took Sally's infatuation seriously. How could Liz know?

One night about three weeks after Roxy had first appeared, Sally stepped out of the bright bar after her shift was over. It was still spring/not spring. Earlier it was too warm to put on a winter jacket, and now she felt chilly.

The warehouses that lined the street stood bulky and dark, blocking the sounds of the city. Sally walked from pool of light to pool of light. She stopped beneath one, suddenly realizing this was one of those rare moments when the city was absolutely silent. Standing still, she could feel the silence like a vibration in her flesh, as if she were a bell still tingling after its audible sounds had faded.

A lone car turned onto the street. Its rattling echoed between the warehouses. When it slowed Sally began to walk again — afraid it might be a queer-basher or any man. But inside her body the vibration continued despite the car, despite her motion, until she knew it was silence no longer, but excitement. Roxy had mentioned that she drove up from the south. Could it be Roxy's car? Could it be Roxy? And if it was — what then?

★ ★ ★ ★ ★

"Damn this traffic," said Roxy, inching her old light blue Comet forward. It was rush hour on the Brooklyn Bridge. Two or three times a week for the last few weeks, Roxy had picked Sally up around the corner from *Cafe Femmes* to hurriedly drive with her into Brooklyn, where Roxy had settled.

"The bastards don't care how little time we have," Sally said, putting her hand on Roxy's thigh.

"Umm," Roxy said, moving as sensuously as she could on the ripped vinyl seat.

Sally withdrew her hand and covered her eyes.

"What's the matter, sweet Sal?" Roxy asked.

161

"I can't stand it, wanting you like this." Her clitoris felt twice its normal size and was becoming irritated as it throbbed against the seam of her pants. Even when they got to Brooklyn, they couldn't go to Roxy's place. She had a lover too. Luckily, Roxy had a lot of friends with apartments they could use. They were headed toward one now, under the darkening exhaust-filled sky, suspended over the water. The bridge lights came on.

Roxy was able to advance a few feet. The breeze as they moved felt good against Sally's flushed face. "Talk to me," commanded Roxy. "It'll make the waiting easier."

"Roxy, Roxy." Her slightest look was intoxicating to Sally.

"Talk to me, sweet Sal."

"How's your cat?" Sally croaked.

"Ol' Orange Blossom? She's as sweet as you. When I can't be with you, she curls up against me under the covers and purrs your name all night."

Oh my God, Sally thought. This woman can't be for real. Does she really feel this much for me? If she does, why aren't we talking about leaving our lovers?

"How about Spot?" Roxy asked, moving a little further toward the end of the bridge.

Sally couldn't for the life of her think of anything romantic to say about her dog. "He doesn't understand why I don't come home as early nights."

Roxy laid her hand on Sally's thigh. The car was moving steadily, but slowly. "Where *are* you going nights, sweet Sal?" she asked provocatively.

Sally's heart pounded even harder and she noticed her mouth was dry, totally dry. She licked her lips.

Roxy pointedly watched her tongue.

"To you," Sally managed to say.

Roxy put the brakes on quickly and the Comet stalled. She started it again with difficulty. Traffic had stopped once more. Silently, Sally panicked. What if the old bomb overheated and they never got to the apartment? What if she was stuck atop the Brooklyn Bridge for hours, hungry for

162

Roxy, inches from her, and never got to make love with her? She wouldn't be able to stand it.

But they began to move again. And soon they reached the friend's extra bedroom. Sally was relieved both of her frustration and of her fear that she and Roxy would run out of things to say, that Roxy might find Sally's penchant for silence, her habit of few words, boring, and drop her.

Another time, they had only an hour at Roxy's own apartment. She'd found nowhere else to go, and risked her lover's unexpected arrival. Sally peered around as they entered, trying to catch glimpses of Roxy's life. But what did she expect to see, anyway? Some revealing southern memento of the life Roxy had left behind? A clue to the nature of her relationship with her lover? Closing the curtains, Roxy led her firmly to the bed, turning on only a small night light, as usual. Sally often felt almost trapped in whatever pool of light Roxy chose, usually one which lit only the bed they were on. Nothing was real but themselves, their touches in the silence of a strange place, and the unknown darkness around them. It made their time together even more intense.

They finished — if they would ever feel finished, thought Sally — and hurriedly left. Roxy drove out of her neighborhood fast, and stopped in front of a park. Still wanting one another they embraced, kissed, in a fever of tongues and the smells left from their hour of privacy. They often would do just this, pull over and make inadequate love, unable to wait until they were alone together, or unable to bear parting on their way to Sally's apartment.

A police car drove slowly by. Roxy pulled back, allowing her fingers to linger on the crotch of Sally's pants, lightly. When the cop was out of sight Sally reached under Roxy's shirt to play with one breast beneath its bra. They stared at each other, watching their eyes turn muddy, brighten, finally smile. "I'm hungry," said Roxy.

"Me, too," replied Sally.

It was still early, and because it was almost daylight saving time, the dark sky held a little light. Roxy started the

Comet and tore up and down a few streets, finally struggling into a parking space on Flatbush Avenue. They walked across the wide street without touching, to a brightly lit restaurant.

"Ever been to Juniors'?" Roxy asked.

"What is it, a hamburger place?" Sally had seldom ventured into Brooklyn.

Roxy laughed. "More. Much more."

They entered a flood of light and noise and motion. The place looked like an enormous luncheonette to Sally. Her hunger increased with the pungent smell of pickles set out on each table in a dish, and grilling pastrami.

Sally would remember the experience all her life. More vividly even than all of their lovemaking, she remembered this hour in Juniors' tasting things together, surrounded, for once, by ordinary people, as if they were ordinary lovers. Their color already heightened by their lovemaking, their eyes still shadowed and brightened alternately by what they felt and had felt, they were as excited as if on a holiday.

They wolfed down the food the shuffling waiter rudely presented to them. "They're like that here," Roxy explained, her mouth full of pickle. Afterward, they ordered cheescake. They savored it slowly, now and then feeding a piece of pineapple, a cherry, to each other, making animal-like sounds of appreciation, and laughing, something they seldom did, so intent were they in their passion.

Around them the shouts of the waiters continued, punctuating the rising and falling drone of the customers, as if to provide for them a love song of sorts. Sally felt as if she'd entered the heart of Brooklyn, her lover's adoptive land, and she watched everything that went on around them while Roxy smoked a long, elegant cigarette. When they left, darkness had completely fallen. The low roar of the city might have been silence, they felt as if they'd walked out of the world. The Brooklyn Bridge glowed beyond them, an intricate pathway back. Their arms went around one another; they didn't want to go back. Roxy pulled Sally into a doorway and ran her hands down her body, pulling her buttocks closer, then kneading them rhythmically as they kissed.

Wet-lipped, they stopped and looked at one another,

then broke away and crossed toward the car. They had not said a word. No one had passed. The silence felt thick as fog as they pushed their way through it. The light blue of the Comet shone like a beacon toward them.

All this time Sally was more, rather than less, attentive to Liz. Not to cover up what she was doing, which she couldn't seem to deny herself, and which seemed to have nothing to do with their life together, but because her passion was always at such a height. It didn't matter that Liz wasn't Roxy. Liz was familiar and soothing, and quieted for a moment, with her gentle knowing hands and mouth, Sally's fire. This was real and long and utterly good, what she had with Liz.

But that same afternoon Roxy would enter the *Cafe Femmes* and they would plan their next meeting.

Could it be Roxy's very unfamiliarity that Sally found so exciting? Did she trail her uncommon, southern origins like a scent behind her? Too, unlike Liz, she looked femme, but she often acted butch. Her come-hither eyes were a screen for her demanding sexual presence. And Sally at times longed to meet Roxy's every demand, forever.

In bed, Roxy seemed to start out each time all submissive female grace. Until Sally would suddenly find herself uprooted, on her back, submitting to touches she'd be too shy to bring home to Liz. Touches so stirring the very thought of them turned her on. Touches so intimate Sally at times felt Roxy touched her soul. And it was not like down-to-earth Sally to think something like that.

So again and again, in a pattern that varied slightly from one time to another, and that variation was mostly in the ways they found to touch, Sally would find herself driven as fast as possible to Brooklyn, then faster back into Manhattan, rattling past street lights in the blue Comet. Often she would be thinking Johnny Mathis songs to herself, too embarrassed to sing them aloud. The breeze through the car windows always felt like an extension of Roxy's last caress, more so as they went deeper into spring and the breezes grew warmer.

Stopping at Sally's apartment building, they would sit

165

looking at one another full of the tragedy of a future of partings. Sally would step out of the car, watching and listening as Roxy accelerated into the night.

She wondered where Roxy went. Home? To *Cafe Femmes*? Another bar? Perhaps she had still another, late night, lover. Perhaps, Sally would fear helplessly as she let her go, Roxy was accustomed to this double life.

But really, when she was alone, Sally didn't care. She would shiver in pleasure, remembering yet another sensation Roxy had given her just an hour before.

And another time, the lovers fled to an old Italian neighborhood in Brooklyn whose traditions had never died. Young men milled about the stoops where neatly dressed girls sat and giggled. The small high-ceilinged apartment had white-framed windows floor to ceiling and textured red wallpaper. The beds were mattresses on the floor, covered in satin quilted comforters. Plush low modern furniture was arranged around a woven straw rug. It was only one room, and a tiny kitchenette, but Sally loved its opulence. Undressing Roxy, she couldn't help but pose her on the furniture, move her from place to place to feel all the textures on their naked bodies. Consequently, when they heard music out the windows, they were not too carried away to wrap themselves in a cool silky comforter and see what was outside.

It was dark. The buildings on both sides of the street were brownstones, their stoops filled now with whole families. Solemnly, slowly, down the middle of the street, marched a procession in white. A priest came first, in his robes, scattering blessings at the onlookers. Many small children marched among women in virginal white gowns. Boys in white suits played the few instruments. Every free hand held a candle, so that the whole procession, which was not long, looked almost like a moving island of lights, except when they passed streetlamps and you could see the set, devoted faces. Toward the end of the walkers, four older boys carried a statue of the Virgin Mary on a platform. Votive candles were arranged around her.

Sally and Roxy stared in wonder at this almost primitive march through the Brooklyn street. How mysterious were the ways of people who clung to such pomp, how different from themselves. Yet it should be Sally and Roxy worshipping the virgin female! They celebrated themselves differently, stepping away from the window, letting the comforter fall, so that they stood looking at each other naked a long while before they lay on a mattress and made love almost ferociously.

She couldn't have said why, but the procession had disturbed Sally. She felt compelled to reassert her own reality, to exaggerate their own celebration, over and over and over.

At some point as they made love, Roxy whispered, "Look!" A full moon shone its light through the huge windows. Roxy switched off the lamp over the bed and they looked at each other for the first time in moonlight. Sally's uneasiness disappeared. She felt somehow blessed, purified. Still, it was one of their last times together.

★ ★ ★ ★ ★

Sally, behind the bar, opened a bottle of mineral water, but didn't feel much like drinking it. She looked over toward the jukebox and the pinball machines, knowing she should have plugged them in long ago. Instead, since no one was around just then, she went around the bar to wipe down the tables with her bar rag. Outside she could see the workmen getting ready to knock off. It was daylight saving time, but just newly, so that she was not yet used to the sky being so bright so late. And in such contrast with the darkness of the bar, since Sally also had not yet switched on the new ceiling lights. She didn't want to surrender her dark silence.

It had been a very slow day. Not even Roxy had come in, as her mother was here from the South for a few days of visiting and shopping. Or so Roxy had said. Sally felt a twinge of doubt, thinking Roxy might simply have found a new passion; but at the same time she felt guilty for suspecting her. Still, these few days off hadn't been as bad as she'd thought they'd be and, to tell the truth, she felt relaxed for the first time in months.

167

There went the workmen. She really had to turn the lights on now. But as she moved to do so, she caught sight of a cab stopping outside the bar. Liz emerged. Something had to be wrong. Not only was Liz early, but she always took the subway.

"Liz?"

"Oh, I just couldn't stand it any longer," Liz said, running her fingers through her dark bangs as she rushed inside.

Sally had a moment of fear. Could she have found out about Roxy?

"I wanted to get here early to install it," Liz said, pulling objects out of her pockets, not noticing Sally's concern. "Every night I come in here and wince, just wince, under these lights. They give me headaches, Sal! I mean, it's one thing to work during the day like you do, when you can keep them off, but at night I can't see to mix a drink without something. So I had a brainstorm today. I think I can install one of these dimmer gadgets, since the lights all work off one switch, and then we can adjust them exactly the way we want. Okay?"

Sally was so relieved she didn't give a thought to the solution of the light problem. She pulled Liz to her and rocked her, saying, "I'm sorry, I'm sorry."

"About what?" Liz asked, pulling back.

Sally looked down into her distracted face and felt a surge of warmth, and more relief. "That I didn't tell you how much I hate them too. Every day I wait longer and longer to put them on. If I'd mentioned it I might have spared you some of those headaches. But I thought you were so attached to these new lights."

"They were your idea!"

"Because you complained how dark it was at night!"

They stopped and laughed at themselves. Then Liz went to work.

A few kids trickled in on their way home from work, Gabby among them. They laughed and talked, and Sally even played pinball with them.

At one point, when Liz was downstairs fooling around with the electric panel, Gabby said in a low voice across the bar to Sally, "It's good to see you laughing and happy for a change."

"Haven't I been?"

"Not hardly," replied Gabby, pushing her glass forward for another beer. "I was beginning to think the rumors might be true."

"What rumors?"

"About you and Roxanne."

Sally slopped the foam from Gabby's beer on the counter. She hoped Gabby would think her red face came from stooping to get her bar rag. "Me and Roxanne what?"

"You know, that you been seeing each other."

Sally got a little hostile. "No, I didn't know."

"Hey, I'm just telling you so you'll know. Listen, you tell me there's nothing to it and I'll beat the shit out of anybody who says I'm wrong."

Sally didn't know what to say. She couldn't lie to her friend. Luckily, some kids had come in and were calling her to serve them. While she worked, the lights came on, and she squinted against their glare. Then Liz came running upstairs, wonderful Liz, and grabbed the knob she'd installed on the wall. If that rumor had gone any farther, wondered Sally, would Liz have heard? Was it worth all the hurt she would have caused her? The lights got dimmer and dimmer as Liz stood turning the knob, a big grin on her face. Maybe Sally should confess to her. Maybe Liz wouldn't think it was so bad and she could still see Roxy once in a while. The lights were down as low as they could go, so that almost the only light was the blue glow of twilight outside the window. Everyone in the bar applauded and Liz bowed, giving the knob its final setting so that the bar was almost back to its old dim self.

The cowbells sounded over the door and Sally saw Roxy come in. Funny, even after three days her heart didn't do its usual flip. Hell, hadn't she known things were slowing down anyway? Why hurt Liz? Why not call it quits while they were still ahead, still felt good about what they'd had, her and Roxy?

Sally felt free. Liz came behind the bar to work with her

for a while. Gabby got up and Sally caught her before she left. "You tell them," she said, "tell them there's nothing going on."

Gabby looked relieved. You could always count on Sal and Liz to stick it out, even when everybody else was breaking up. It kind of gave you hope for yourself.

"What was all that about?" Roxy asked, taking Gabby's seat. She looked tired. Not from the strain of a visiting mother, either, Sally suspected.

"There's a rumor going around about you and me."

"Shit," said Roxy. "And we were so careful."

Sally noticed her use of the past tense. Liz came by and bumped into Sally affectionately.

"Hi, Roxanne!" she said, still feeling cheery from her triumph over the lights.

Roxy seemed subdued by Liz' proximity. As a matter of fact, Sally realized, Roxy had never come in when both she and Liz were on. Was this another hint that things were changing? "Maybe we ought to lie low for a while," Sally suggested in a mutter.

"Just what I was thinking," agreed Roxy.

Their eyes met. It was over. It seemed too simple. Where were the teary scenes? Where was the passion that still burned even a few days ago?

Never mind, it felt good to Sally and she dared to smile at Roxy. "A white wine?" she asked.

"If you please," Roxy smiled back.

Sally poured it, then started to reach for another mineral water for herself. No, she decided, and poured more white wine. She'd been keeping a bottle chilled, as that was how Roxy liked it, and it tasted good. She opened a beer for another customer and went back to her wine. As she sipped, watching Roxy talk with someone, she felt as if she were sipping the essence of Roxy, so often had she tasted white wine on her lips. But no, it was more the essence of what she *felt* for Roxy. It was exciting, this cool stuff, but delicate, graceful going down. Yet it made her hot when it reached her depths. And it made her want more. But not too much more. She drank just enough before she went home at the end of her shift.

COOKIE AND TONI

My real name's Carmelina, but all my friends call me Cookie. You can too.

They're supposed to be here, my friends, but they're late. Seems like no matter how long I take to put on make-up, to pick the right clothes — hey, you like this, the pink boatneck with the black ski pants? — I'm always the first one here.

So I'm sitting here and this lady with the tape recorder asks me to tell you a story. About my life now, in 1962, and about being femme. She says she'll put the tape away and play it in twenty years. How am I supposed to know what you want to hear twenty years from now? I don't even know what you'll be like. Will you look like us? Will you tease your hair like I do? I know you butches will still have short hair — that'll never change in a million years. And I bet you're cute. And freer. You'll hold hands going down the street and tell your moms you turned gay. You won't stick around when your dads slap you for going out with girls — you'll take off. Right? Or is that just my wishful thinking?

I guess I can do this as good as anyone — only where should I start? What do you want to hear? A sad story about what it's like? Boy, I could tell you a few that would

171

get you going. An adventure story? How about some swa-vay butch carries me off to a desert island? Never happen. Would you believe Fire Island? Or a love story. Are you changed so much you wouldn't want to hear a love story? Want to hear about Toni and me? Yeah, I like that one. Besides, it's true. You mind if I chew gum? Oh, not into the mike. Okay, I'll just smoke.

Like I said, I'm femme. I was butch, too, before this, but I think I'll stay femme from now on. Something in the way I love women makes me want to be femme. The ways I like to take care of them. Homey stuff, you know? I can make a meatball and spaghetti dinner would melt any butch's heart. Maybe one of you wants to try my meatballs and spaghetti. . . ?

But Toni, she was from my town, Hicksville. Don't laugh. People really live there. Me and my family thought it was the greatest place going. We moved out from the city, from East New York. It was heaven. I was about eight. We had a back-yard and my school had a girls' gym — boy could I tell you girls' gym stories! Everybody had cars. It was the greatest. Some day I'm going to marry a woman with money and we'll buy a place on the Island together. Do you kids have more money than us?

Say now, here's a girl with money. How'd you know I'd like a Tom Collins? Mixed drinks are too steep for me. What a treat, I even get an orange slice.

My Toni didn't have money. We lived the both of us in little houses with muddy backyards. We both had dads whose stomachs were out to here, who drank beer and thought our mothers should worship them. The difference was, though, Toni didn't see how it was, how her dad was a phony slob.

Toni just graduated high school the year before and was still dreaming of moving to the city. I'd been out of school a couple of years and had my fill of the city for a while so I moved home. My mother loved to have me there. She didn't really care if I was gay. Oh, she'd moan and groan now and then about how she wished I'd get married, the house next door was for sale and me and my husband could move in — like being gay was a temporary thing — but she wasn't real

172

pushy about it, you know? I stayed out of Dad's way. He'd been growling at me for years. I'd come out of the bathroom to go to work in the morning and he'd growl at me. Really. Can you imagine this hairy, foul-breathed pregnant-looking man waking you up like that? What a jerk.

Anyways, it was that last time I lived in Hicksville I met Toni. Her folks were on the other side of Bethpage Road from me and I couldn't believe I never saw her before. She was gorgeous! We met the only place I know of on the Island, the Hayloft. A bar with nothing special except it was closer than the bars in the city. I drove Dad's car down to the Loft one night and walked in all by my lonesome.

I sat at the bar. I didn't like it much, being alone, but I'd been out long enough to be able to do it when I had to. So I'm sitting there, like this, making the beer last 'cause I don't make much at this aircraft place where I work putting together tiny pieces of the planes. And in walks Toni who's just so *butch*. She looked like this − here, let me stand up − real tough with her legs bent almost bowlegged, thumbs hooked in her jeans, cigarette in her mouth, her collar up, and a look on her face that would scare the marines.

In this low sexy voice she asks, "Hi, doll, what're you drinking?"

Holy shit, I think. I mean it's early, I'm the only one in the place and I'm no dog, but nobody ever came on to me that strong and fast before. I guess I looked shocked, like my mouth dropped open or something, so she explains, shy all of a sudden, "It feels like I know you. I mean, we practically grew up together. If I'd known you was gay I'd of been over your place long ago."

I felt really dumb and didn't know what to say. Here's this perfect-looking butch standing there in these pegged black pants, a white shirt and jean jacket and boots, coming on to me when I never even tried to get her. You know how it is with butches − half the time they're so shy they stand at the bar all night talking to other butches and you got to practically throw yourself at them to get them to dance with you.

Not Toni. I'd be sorry about that come-on style of hers

later, but that night she just swept me off my feet. No
questions asked.

"We went to the same school together," she says, leaning
against the bar. "Only you were always two grades in front
of me. Hope you don't hold my age against me," she winks.

So we talked till I had to get the car home. She walks me
to it and wants to know when we're going out. We make a
date for the next night — you expected me to resist? — and
then she kisses me. I felt like rubber. It was one of those long
hot kisses that seeps into your heart. Not a soul kiss, just a
real light long kiss without even touching me with her hands.
I was done for. She made herself so easy to love.

And I did. I loved her for three months. All that time we
still lived with our parents. She'd pick me up in her dad's car
and we'd go to the Loft or the movies or parking. Mostly
parking. Did I ever wish I had my place back in the city. But
then I never would have met her.

She could get the car a lot because her parents had no
idea she was queer. We even used to make out down in their
rec room while we pretended to watch *Route 66* or something. We sure loved that couch. I don't know how her
parents never guessed about her, though, the way she dressed.
Maybe it was her beauty that saved her. Those dreamy green
eyes in a face that even without makeup could've won a
contest. Her hair was long, real unusual for such a butch
chick, but she wore it on top of her head so you couldn't
tell it was there most of the time. And a perfect body,
though I never saw it under her clothes. She was stone butch.
I wanted so much to touch her, especially when she hurt bad,
but she wouldn't let me.

Yeah, this *is* a love story, but it's a sad story too. Maybe
I don't know any altogether happy ones. Maybe nobody
does.

This time it was Toni's dad who ruined things. She always
wanted to be just like him. Used to tell me how strong he
was, how smart and handsome. He was a mechanic so she
fooled around with cars since she was a kid. He played base-
ball on a local team so she was always throwing a ball around.
She wished she was a son, not a daughter. That's why she was

gay, she said, because she wanted to love women like her dad did. And that's why she was so different from most of the butches I went with — she used her dad's style of meeting women.

Then one day her dad just didn't come home. Turned out he'd been cozying up to this real tramp over in Mineola where he worked. Her mom's brother tracked him down and beat him up pretty bad, so Toni's dad went down to Florida with the chick.

She was crushed. This all happened about the third month we were going together. We still saw each other for a while, but everything had left her. Her style, I mean. Something about loving me reminded her I guess of him loving the tramp. She'd be making out with me and start crying. And you know butches: they do not cry. Pretty soon she couldn't even face me no more. Her pride, you know? She couldn't keep up the butch pride. Even the collar on her jacket seemed wilted, like my plants when I don't water them.

I know what it was — she didn't want to be like him no more. But she never knew who she was in herself — who the woman was, you know what I mean? It changed everything for her. She didn't even kiss the same. She wasn't strong, in charge anymore. I guess it wasn't *her* strength, but *his* all along. And when she didn't have that she lost who she used to be — her personality, her style.

So there I was, home night after night, thinking how I'd loved a real dummy, a fake with nothing of her own inside. I didn't go out with nobody for a real long time because I started to wonder if all the butches were like that, empty inside, fake men, you know? There used to be magic for me in that swagger they had, the way they posed so tough. And then I started thinking: if Toni was such a fake, and if all the butches were fake, then what about me? Who was I really? I'm sitting in these bars looking sexy, my face painted, waiting for the butches to light my cigarettes for me, but what was I really like? Was I a copy of my mother? Was I trying to be like some movie star? It started to drive me crazy too, like I think it did Toni.

Little by little, though, I got back on my feet. Started to be interested in love again. Went back to the Loft.

And when I got back, it was with a vengeance. I was so hungry for the gay life I wouldn't bring the car home till closing. Couldn't stop dancing, being with the gay kids and enjoying the hell out of them. My dad got so fed up he wouldn't give me the car no more. Growled at me everytime I asked. So screw him, I decided. I moved back to the city. Got a new job and really started doing the town. Butches had their magic back for me.

But it was different. There was more to it. Wait – I'll explain.

All this time I hadn't seen Toni at all. Then one night at the Swingalong on MacDougal Street I saw her walk in. She was talking and laughing, with a new kind of confidence. It wasn't empty swagger anymore. We said hello and danced a couple of times, but she was going with somebody so I didn't push it. Besides, I felt like we'd been through so much since we were together we were almost new people. But I didn't forget about her and I thought a lot about her. And the magic of the gay life. I don't know if I can explain it exactly. You got to try and feel it with me.

See, I don't think we do just copy the straights. Some of our ways come from them, some of the ways we dress and act, but that's only because they suit us. What I mean is, we choose our ways.

So when I say I like to make spaghetti and meatballs for my lovers, that comes from way inside me. It's *me*. Not because I want to act like a woman's mother, or it's the way I think a wife should act. It's 'cause I love to see a satisfied woman's eyes light up. Like Toni's were at the Swingalong that night. I love to be the one who turns that light on in a woman's eyes. And probably it's the same for butches. When a woman opens the door for you or makes love to you I don't think she's doing it 'cause she's supposed to. I think she's looking for that light, too, that look of feeling loved and special.

And that was the difference in Toni. She wasn't doing it to be like her Dad no more. She learned that being *him* was

176

a bad way to be, but there was stuff *from* him she could use to be Toni. She must have found that part of herself that does its own talking.

Even though that didn't happen to me, but to Toni, I found out how I talked, too . . .

I know what I want now and I have certain ways of my own to get it. And someday I'm going to find the one woman who I please the most and who pleases me the most and we're going to be pleased as hell together.

I'll be sitting here for a while, you know. Maybe in twenty years when she plays this tape to you I'll still be sitting here.

I hope not, but I wouldn't want to miss you if I am.

Come on and buy me a drink. Let me tell you another story. If we like each other maybe you'll come over.

I'll make — you guessed it — spaghetti and meatballs for you.

NATURAL FOOD

Lucy was so tied to the earth it seemed to pull her down from every prominence: chin, breasts, lap, all pointed downward to give the appearance her big body was sagging. The long dim-colored skirts she wore did not offset that impression, but made her heavier-looking, as if she had to carry them around with her too. I half-expected her to complain of the weight of it all, but she never did. As a matter of fact, behind the drooping lines of her face there was a lightness, perhaps a vision of another way she had been or could be, that made her glow. Lonely single women, restless married women, all followed her home from work after their first invitation to supper at her apartment. After three months working in the same department with her I joined them.

It wasn't that she was a gourmet cook or that she put on sophisticated entertainments. She offered pure comfort to the women in the office who were on their feet or rumps all day long. The ritual was simple. You walked in, got pushed affectionately onto the couch, had a cat settled on your lap, a glass of wine or a mug of tea put into your hand and the TV flipped on. Maybe there were other women there, with whom you talked quietly about little of import, or maybe you were alone with Lucy. If alone, all you heard was the sound of Lucy's slippers flipflopping up and down the kitchen floor and scuffing onto the rug where the kitchen opened out to a dining room. The dining room table, which was inordinately large for the apartment, was made of dark, thick wood, and heavy-looking, like Lucy. She had re-covered each chair with red velvet and made a warm-looking unit out of the oddly assorted chairs and table.

Too busy to join her guests before dinner, she seemed to communicate through the smells that she sent out of the kitchen. What she cooked was, as the smells suggested, simple, natural food that never cloyed or titilated, but satisfied.

As I dutifully scratched Cobweb — a cat, not a spider — I would make note of the stories on the six o'clock news. Table talk was subdued and secondary to eating, but Lucy liked to hear other versions of the news because, she said, it was so much more digestible second hand. I've since sat and watched the news with Lucy and understand now why she said it: she gets too upset. I don't think she has ever missed a peace march in our city. Whenever she can, she goes to national marches. Every time the newscasters speak of weapons or warfare she gets all red, as if she were going to cry. Environmental stories affect her as deeply. She is one of those people who won't pick a flower out of respect for its right to live. We need to remember that the earth is our mother, she says, and treat it accordingly.

Dinner for me, then, was a summary of the day's news and a hope that nothing would upset this woman who made me feel so good. After dinner, she would pull out a game or play records. My favorite evenings, she had a certain group of us over who appreciated her collection of rock-and-roll oldies, the only loudness I ever heard in that apartment. The phonograph would be turned up almost as high as it could go, the bass pounding, and *Sally Go Round the Roses* on the turntable. Or Timi Yuro's *Make the World Go Away*. We'd laugh at the absurdity of the songs — but not Lucy. I liked that side of her. It was a less *serious*, but somehow deeper side which was truly moved by the facile lyrics and simple rhythms. Her eyes showed a different spirit, then, one livelier than we were used to — as if they danced. This seemed to come from far inside her, as if stirred up to float to the surface of her mind, to both enliven and disturb.

It was hard, then, to visualize her walking the halls at work, slow and very solid under the fluorescent lights, a hard-working woman who was an institution in that office. Listening to her music she was like a little girl skipping. It made me wonder about her past. Who had been in it? Had she looked the same? When had it gotten to be like it was now? I resolved to find out one day, but kept putting it off, fearing to stir up more than I perhaps wanted to hear.

The others seemed seldom to wonder about Lucy. She had earned their respect as a worker and friend. If she filled them with as much peace as she did me, I can understand why they left her alone and did not subject her to the usual office scrutiny. They were more likely to describe her one bedroom apartment and its comforts than her. When someone new asked who Lucy was they were told: "Oh, she's just Lucy." Newcomers seemed to understand and accept that that was all they would get. Once in a while I heard how it was a shame Lucy had never married because she would be such a good wife, but they knew no man would want this treasure of a woman, with her heavy body and quiet ways. It took us women to see the glow around her.

As for myself, I was a scrawny kid with a lot of crazy curly hair. I liked to think I looked like Bob Dylan. I was working with Lucy and planned to stay there until I went on to the bigger and better things I thought I deserved. Either a better job or hitching to California. Speed was my best friend and I used it at any excuse. I'm trying to live calmer and slower now, but you should have seen me with speed in me.

Anyway, this is not about me, but about Lucy. I was drawn to her, like the other women, because she offered comfort and shelter, even though I was different from the other women. I'm a lesbian and the raw, painful side of my life was full of women, not men. But I treated myself and the women I thought I loved as if we were all men.

It was the time of the women's movement. I was always busy going to this and that meeting, or to demonstrations.

My love life was just an extension of all that. I never had less than two lovers — just on principle — and often three or four. Sometimes we all slept together at once. I was so divided, so torn, I needed speed just to keep up with myself. We talked about women being gentle and deep and how we made love more slowly and caringly than men, but I cannot remember one relationship I would call intimate. We may have had our clothes off and we may have spent a lot of time dealing with parts of ourselves we saw as faulty, but we seldom touched each other inside. I guess the proof of that is the many women from that period in my life who now see themselves as bisexual or straight. They're still living the same kind of lives, sleeping around, totally committed to every cause in the world but themselves. Or they've settled with men in some kind of living group that precludes all but the most superficial privacy or intimacy.

But some of us are still out. Still committed to finding our sources and resources as women in this city or around the country. Some are alone and celibate. Some, like me, are in couples. Some are still trying to have a lot of relationships, to find satisfaction in that.

Back then we were really going to set the world on fire. Smash monogamy and all. Our intentions were good, but we were so self-destructive. So unable to see which of our struggles were important and which meaningless rationalizations for avoiding the real issues.

I went to Lucy's differently from the way I went anywhere else. My visits were probably what kept me alive and sane enough to maintain my pace, though I couldn't see that then. I was poor and used that as a reason: a free meal. But sometimes I went because of what I thought was curiosity, to find out what made Lucy tick.

The last time I went to see her I was alone. Everyone else had had to cancel, or perhaps Lucy wanted me to come alone. While I scratched Cobweb and watched the figures run around on TV, I determined to make Lucy open up to me and tell me about herself. I wanted to be special to her, the only one she talked to as well as fed.

"Listen," I said after dinner, "I'm tired of you communicating only through your food." I was so arrogant. "Tell me more about yourself. I want to get to know you."

Poor Lucy just sat there with the corners of her mouth lifted out of their usual droop, smiling at me. Maybe she was amused. I deserved it if she was.

"Curly," she said, with a nervous little intake of breath, "I'm gay."

It was my turn to smile. Of course, I thought, surprised at the happy feeling her announcement gave me.

"I'm telling you this because I believe you are too," she said and when I nodded vigorously she went on. "I've been living without a lover or any contact with lesbians for a few years now. It's just too painful for me. When I'm with lesbians I can't forget what happened to me. So I've built up this strange kind of social life. I get to show my love for women by cooking, but never have to get involved with any of you. I don't mind you knowing about me because I've kept you in the distant circle of my friends and I think you'll be just as happy to stay there."

"Can you tell me what happened?" I encouraged her.

Her first response was to again lift those corners of her lips. "Of course," she assured me gently, sitting beside me on the couch and tucking her legs under her.

That close to me I felt the full force of her size. She was overwhelmingly present. I moved back a little and refocused my eyes as she gathered her thoughts. It was the first time I had attached any significance to the pinky ring she wore.

"Yes," she said quietly with her slight lisp, "I wear it because I'm a lesbian. I came out when one still did that, wore pinky rings. I was femme."

I must have looked surprised because she explained, "I didn't know how not to be. That was how it was. If you were a lesbian, you chose a role. I had no idea how to be aggressive, so I settled for the passive role. And I enjoyed it. I went out with two or three different butches, teased my hair, dressed sexy, cooked for them, let them make love to me. It was beautiful to feel so attractive and comfortable, finally

183

finding a world where I belonged. It didn't even matter that I was so big, and I wasn't as fat as I am now," she said, pinching the soft flesh on her upper arm. "Though the gay world closely followed the straight one, a woman didn't have to conform to the same rigid norms straight women do. A big woman could be attractive, could be loved," she sighed.

"Then I met Gerry. She was a precursor of the women's movement and wasn't into roles. Of course that suited me fine. We fell in love and moved in together. I'd never lived with a lover before. I was blissfully happy. Not only was I a lesbian, I was a whole person too, not having to fit into categories. In our sixth year Gerry became more involved in the women's movement. I followed her, but didn't throw myself into it as she did. I was very contented with my life and already involved in the peace movement up to my ears."

I could tell it was getting harder for Lucy to tell the story because her eyes kept clouding so that I couldn't see any life in them. They had changed almost to black in the depth of their pain. I reached to her soft arm and lay my skinny fingers on it, wondering what the hell kind of comfort I thought *I* could give this incredible source of comfort.

"Gerry started bringing women home. Our place had always been open to friends, but these women . . . crashed. Sometimes for a week or two. And Gerry seemed to have this fire in her I'd never seen before. She was in love half the time, plain and simple. She wanted to sleep with them. It took her a long time to tell me and I might have taken it better if she'd just said it, if she'd admitted to me and herself that she was very turned on to the movement and the women in it and it made her love them and want to make love to them all. But she didn't."

Lucy shifted away from me in her seat. "She trailed home this elaborate reasoning about being what she called non-monogamous and how it would be good for our relationship if we slept with other women. That was the last good laugh I had."

We both sat silent, mourning the lack of laughter in Lucy's life.

"I told her I didn't want to sleep with all the lost children she brought home, that I understood how she felt, but I didn't share in it. I told her we had a very close, warm, secure relationship I cherished and found satisfying. That I thought she was getting her enthusiasm for the movement mixed up with her love life and responding inappropriately to how she felt. She said I was old-fashioned and she didn't want to separate her feelings like that."

Of course, Lucy could have been talking to me, quoting me, and I hoped I had never caused anyone such pain with my politics. "It went on," she said, "this argument went on. And still goes on in my head even now."

She turned back to me. The pain had receded from her eyes. "I believe the intimacy two people can achieve is a very special thing that's diluted when you try to share it with others. I hope you won't take this as criticism if you're trying to have a lot of relationships yourself, but for me, that's just a waste of time. After all, if every woman could have one relationship, one close, satisfying sexual-love relationship that's healthy, just think of the energy we could derive from it to give to our causes. The human beast is such that when you start sharing those kinds of nurturing, sustaining, absolutely life-giving feelings with whomever excites you, you really disturb something in yourself, some balance you need, and you go away drained instead of replenished. As if you'd gotten drunk instead of having a drink of water when you were only thirsty!"

I didn't let on that I was feeling criticized. This was her night and I didn't want to talk about myself. But it wrung my heart to hear her voice falter when she said, "We broke up. She went her wild way, as she called it, and I moved out here so I didn't have to feel it every time she took a new lover. It didn't last long, though." She laughed, but bitterly. I was surprised Lucy could be bitter. "Gerry decided she didn't like living that way after all and I heard she settled down in a new couple relationship. I suppose I should feel vindicated, but all I feel is loss."

"Didn't you try to meet someone else?"

She thought for a moment, stooping to pick up Cobweb.

185

When he was settled in her roomy lap she explained. "For a long time I didn't want to meet anyone. I thought it was pretty useless. I couldn't win. Either I was promiscuous like everyone else and wasn't satisfied, or I committed myself to a woman who couldn't be satisfied because she wanted other lovers." Lucy threw up her arms in exasperation, startling Cobweb, who had to then settle himself again.

She went on, "When I got more rational I saw I was oversimplifying things and began to think it would be good for me to meet women, but then I didn't know where to go. I'd gained this weight and felt self-conscious in the bars. Although I knew I would be accepted, somehow the thought of going out and being seductive in that atmosphere made me feel foolish. I knew I'd be a fat old femme to many of them. And going to women's movement functions meant putting up with all that dealing and struggling around those issues when I wanted to put my political energy into peace. I just didn't bother."

"You were caught between two worlds," I said dramatically.

Lucy leaned over, upsetting Cobweb, to muss my curls. "You've got great hair," she said with a real smile. It captivated me; it was a part of Lucy I'd never seen, that warm, charming smile. It reminded me of the delectable smells that came from her kitchen. "So here I am. Sergeant Lonelyhearts herself, pouring my heart out to you. Thanks for listening."

I still felt funny about her smile, funny about the things she'd said about the way I was living my life. It seemed as if she'd stirred some stuff up in me as well as in herself.

Soon afterward I left, edgy, perhaps scared that she would want to make love. And I was certain I wasn't attracted to her. She was slow and heavy and depressed. I had a life to live, a world to subdue, a revolution to win, women to love. She'd made her decision, I told myself as I returned that night to the collective I lived in. I talked about her at my next house meeting because she was on my mind. The women voiced sorrow for poor Lucy. Not long afterwards I moved to Denver and never found the time to say goodbye to her.

In all those months after I moved, what stood out most in my mind was the way she said she had felt when we women came to visit her. How she would sit in her living room after dinner, playing the evening's game or talking quietly, how she'd wallow in the waves of sensuality she felt rolling over her from the comfort and security the women were feeling. As if her home, her cooking and her body were an oasis women could come to and get a little of what they needed, what their men friends and husbands couldn't give.

That literally turned me on. Making love with women whose politics excited me or whose difference from myself led me to want to be in an intimate relationship with them, I wouldn't be able to have an orgasm unless I fantasized being back in Lucy's living room with her telling me about warmth and comfort and having a place to rebuild oneself. I thought it was pretty weird. I even went to the bars and picked up women a couple of times, to see if being a femme was what made Lucy stick in my head. That didn't work either. And I couldn't talk about it to any of the women I knew. How could I admit I felt as if I'd fallen in love with comfort and security and I was scared to death my need would sap energy from my politics? I told myself, You can't have it, stop thinking about it.

But everything became less and less meaningful. I knew I'd had it when I was in San Francisco and Harvey Milk got shot. The rioting felt like madness to me. A lot of craziness which had been inevitable because there was no core, no anchor for us all. We were energy run wild, like hurt animals running in circles as new wounds opened. Maybe nothing was wrong with the women's and gay movements as a whole, but *I* was mad with pain and frustration and loneliness. I lived with lesbians, worked with them, planned with them, slept with them, but I was empty and alone. I had nothing, not even the self I'd been so carefully developing. I needed something else.

When I realized suddenly, one day, sitting looking at the Pacific, what a gold mine Lucy was, I couldn't get back to her soon enough.

"Lucy," I said at the door, falling on my knees before

she could even ask me in, "Lucy, can we get to know each other so I can ask you to marry me?"

She had been waiting for me, she confessed later. She'd told me her story, she said, because she sensed it would have relevance for my life. It was only in telling it that she realized she wanted me to stay that night. She said she'd only hoped she'd tied her story around my ankle, like a homing pigeon's message, and I'd remember the way back.

As I knelt at her door that night she laughed that great big belly laugh she'd thought she lost after Gerry. I had a twinge of anxiety she'd learned to laugh since I went away, but when she got on her knees too and bear-hugged me right there in the hallway, I knew it was me who'd brought her laughter back.

AT A BAR V
Summer Storm

At the height of that summer, when Sally the bartender looked out the plate glass window of the *Cafe Femmes*, even the afternoon shadows cast by the warehouses looked part-bleached and didn't cool the street at all.

Sally had stepped outside earlier to escape the air conditioning. Sometimes it made her feel trapped to breathe all that air filtered through a machine, and she needed to breathe the sooty but real air of the city. As she stood on the hot sidewalk, tall and blonde and skinny as a bar rail, she began to feel the heat even through the rubber soles of her sneakers. The cobblestones in the street, after a few minutes, looked like bubbling lava. She went back inside, and *Cafe Femmes* was a dark, cold relief. Through the plate glass window she watched the workmen wipe their brows as they loaded and unloaded trucks across the street.

When the gay kids began to come in for lunch they looked wrung out. Their slicked back d.a.'s, their short-sleeved shirts or halter tops, were all damp. More often than not they paid Sally with soggy dollar bills carefully pried from damp pockets.

That was the first day the five black dykes made their boisterous entrance. So spirited were they that as they

189

swung open the door Sally missed the sound of the cow-bells and she had to look up to make sure they were still there.

"Woo-ee!" said a woman in glasses, whose name, Sally found out later, was Mae. "This place feels like the North Pole!"

"About time some place did," grumbled a woman with a thick Afro who seemed to just about make it to the table where she collapsed.

"Even the packing line's cooler than that street," said another of the group.

"How you doing, sister?" asked Mae, who ordered drafts for all of them.

"I'm doing fine," Sally replied as she wiped the bar with her bar rag and started to draw the beer. She liked seeing new faces in the bar. "I'm lucky. I work in here all day."

"Sure do wish I could fix it so's it was me instead of you!" laughed Mae.

Sally explained to Mae how, if they were going to be in the neighborhood, they were welcome to bring their lunches in and she'd serve beer or soda, whatever they wanted.

"Sounds good," Mae said, after delivering four of the beers to her table. "We ate down the street already, but it'd sure be cheaper for us to bag it. Rate they pay over at the hair-spray prison, we just about making our subway fare here. But when we start piecework, it'll get better."

"You just start there?"

"Last week. One of the white girls told us about this place. She don't come in here days, she says, afraid some-one'll see her, but if the someones who see us don't already know by looking at us, they too dumb to figure us out no other way!" she finished, laughing again.

Sally saw what she meant. Four of the five she would peg as butches, the one with the Afro and the two, like Mae, with short straightened hair. Three were hefty and even the butch who wasn't hefty walked like she meant business. The femme had longer straightened hair, but was so obviously in love with her butch no one could miss it.

190

"What a sweatshop that place is. But you know how it is, you work where you can get it. When Randa got her job there — that's Willie's girl —" Sally nodded her understanding that Mae was referring to the femme, "— she right away brought Willie down the next day. When they didn't bat an eye at Willie, the rest of us applied. They have a lot of girls quitting, 'specially in the summer. Most factories shut down two weeks come summer. Not this one. These bosses going to squeeze every penny out of our asses they can. Then they'll hang us up to dry and catch the drippings. And there's plenty of them in this heat!"

Sally found Mae's laughter infectious. Though usually straight-faced behind the bar, she found herself chuckling and smiling.

Mae leaned over on her elbows and lowered her voice. "I can see you play okay, but you think we're gonna get hassled by the trade?" she asked, indicating with a nod of her head the white kids who were getting ready to go back to work.

Sally looked around the room. These were all kids who'd been coming to *Cafe Femmes* for years. She liked most of them. They seldom caused trouble unless they were very upset, and then the fight was usually taken outside. Her eyes traveled back to Betty Marie and she worried about her for a moment, but shrugged. What could one bitter drunk do by herself? "It's hard to say," she told Mae. "We never had any trouble like that. We even have a couple of black kids who come in pretty regular. They live around here, or go with white girls. Most of these kids are pretty nice."

Mae was looking hopefully at her. "Reason I ask," she said, "this job is bad, real bad. I don't know if we can stick it out without some kind of nice thing to happen in our days. This *Femmes* bar is that kind of thing."

Sally understood. After all, she hadn't always been half-owner of a gay bar. Before she and Liz got the place she'd worked in an office surrounded by straights. She remembered how hard it had been to go in there every day and to stay there without punching somebody in the mouth. "I'll tell you," she answered, "I'll do what I can."

"You're a pal," said Mae. Laughingly she added, "For a honky."

Sally laughed back, and shook hands over the counter. Mae soon gave up trying to get Sally to follow the complex handshake she attempted, and laughed again as they did a simple "honkeyshake," she called it.

The bar was eerily quiet after the lunch crowd left. More so after the five black dykes who, because Sally wasn't used to them, had seemed bigger than life. The only one in the bar with her was Betty Marie, steadily sipping at her second or third gin and tonic of the day. But she was over by the window, still, watching the activity on the street. Sally poured herself a chilled white wine and tipped it a little as she brought it to her lips, toasting the Five, as she was already thinking of them. Mae had made her feel good, had given something a little extra to an otherwise dull day and she appreciated that. She hoped they'd come back.

Later Betty Marie came over to the bar for another drink. Sally drained the last of her wine and wiped the countertop, knowing she was in for a long afternoon.

Betty Marie had just returned to the *Cafe Femmes.* She seemed to move in cycles, from one bar to the next, wearing out her welcome wherever she went, disappearing unerringly just before she got kicked out for good. A few months later she'd slink back in, more full of rancor and sarcasm than ever after her new series of bannings. And every gin and tonic seemed to fuel her anger.

Sally, being the softy she was, felt sorry for her. She let her come back even though Liz declared she couldn't stand the woman. Liz happened to be a Jew, and that subject, along with blacks, illegal aliens, liberals and atheists, were some of Betty Marie's favorite targets. However, Betty Marie had quickly learned not to talk in front of Liz. Sally tuned her out, knowing she should shut her up instead, but what could she do? The woman had to go somewhere and what she spouted was what she believed. It didn't seem to hurt anyone. Everybody knew about her drinking.

Today's topic was to be expected: the Five and how they were going to take over *Cafe Femmes*, New York City and anything else Betty Marie felt was worth saving.

As she went around the bar to sweep, Sally looked at Betty Marie. She was a small woman, only about thirty-five, with large dark circles under her eyes, chewed fingernails, and frizzy dark hair she straightened now and then, when she had the money. This was not one of those times and her hair had begun to grow out. Smooth it down as she might, out it would spring. Often, after a long day of drinking, Betty Marie's hair would resemble something like an electrified halo.

As Betty Marie spewed her hatred, Sally couldn't help but remember other long afternoons like this when Betty Marie had revealed more than she meant to.

"Maybe I do have a chip on my shoulder," Betty Marie had said one day, "but I have my reasons." She seemed to dip into her glass like one of those trick plastic birds Sally had seen in novelty shops: dipping and filling, back and then forward, moved by nothing but the weight of the liquor. "I went to parochial school, see, but I had to pass the public school to get home. The colored girls went to public school, but they lived in the projects on the other side of my school." She closed her eyes and a faint shudder seemed to run down her frail body.

"I had to fight my way to and from school almost every day. 'Girlie,' they'd call at us, 'Hey, gir-lee!' We'd be in uniform and there they'd be in their bright colors. Your black folks have their taste in their toenails," she spat, using the word Sally usually insisted on. Betty Marie would be thrown out for using anything really offensive, and she knew it. "Then they'd say something about our uniforms, or about Catholics, the heathens. Or they'd make fun of how we looked or of our families. Pretty soon they'd get one of us going and we'd go at them, tearing their hair, pushing them down, you know how girls fight. Somehow, though, it was always us white girls who looked worse afterwards. And me that got into trouble."

"You mean you didn't do anything to provoke them?" Sally asked skeptically.

Betty Marie ignored her at first. "If it was on the way to

school, the Sisters would yell at me in front of the whole class, then slap me around and put me in a corner. And they never believed it was all the colored girls' fault. Sure we called them names too. Wouldn't you?" she asked, looking blurrily up. "No, maybe you wouldn't. You're such a goody-goody. They looked funny, though, and they talked so nasty you just had to. But it was always them came across the street to start something with us, I swear."

As Betty Marie kept muttering, Sally shook her head and moved away. Perhaps someone else would come in and she could escape by talking to her. There'd been times she'd even taken the paper and read it by the window, pretending the light was better there. What could she do? Betty Marie needed some place to go, maybe even more than a lot of the kids, so she let her be.

The Five came in every noon for the rest of the week. There were some stares, some elbow nudgings, but for the most part, the kids were cool. When the Five didn't come Saturday, Sally assumed she'd seen the last of them that week, but Sunday morning, when Liz came home and slipped under the sheets with her, she told Sally three had come with their girls.

"How'd it go?"

"The kids can get used to them, I think. No one really hassled them. You could tell they weren't really welcome, though. I tried to make up for it without looking con-spicuous."

"I know what you mean," Sally said sleepily. "You don't want to treat them different, but you want them to know you like them coming in. Was Betty Marie around?"

"Oh shit, don't tell me she's back."

Sally yawned. "No question about it. Wonder why she wasn't there?"

"I don't know, but she doesn't have to explain her absence to me as long as she stays away. Do you think she hates blacks as much as Jews?"

"At least," Sally said, pulling Liz toward her, intending to show her how much she herself liked a certain Jew right there in her own bed. But the next thing she knew the sun

194

was shining in the window and she had to get dressed to go open the bar. Before she left she watched Liz sleep, golden-colored in the sunlight, looking vulnerable without her glasses. She wondered if she would have loved her if she'd been black, but that was silly — Liz would have been a different person altogether.

The sun was as strong as it had been all week, but somehow, perhaps because it was Sunday and the street was deserted, the heat felt softer, more merciful. Sally even sat outside on a barstool for a while, sipping white wine and soaking up the rays before the kids began to drift in, discussing cures for their hangovers. She had the perfect cure: a glass of white wine, chilled, whenever you wanted it, up to two times a day; but they told her she was a teetotaler and ordered shots of whiskey or Bloody Marys.

Betty Marie came by soon enough, and even before she ordered her first gin and tonic she said, "I hear you were recruiting for the N.A.A.C.P. again last night."

Her tone, like the day's heat, was fairly light so Sally kidded her along. "That might not be a bad idea. A gay chapter of N.A.A.C.P."

"You two would be full-fledged members, that's for sure. Give me a g and t, will you?"

Sally felt like saying, "Only if you behave yourself," but what was the sense?

Betty Marie leaned over the bar to watch Sally make the drink. She asked speculatively, "Liz did wash the glasses last night . . . ?"

"Of course, why?"

"You never know who's been there before you."

Suddenly Sally realized what it was Betty Marie was saying. Was she just being mean? She couldn't believe Betty Marie might be serious, and she eyed her as she put the drink down and took her money. "What's the matter, you afraid being black's contagious?"

But she didn't really listen to Betty Marie's answer. She was remembering, as the woman went on and on, another long afternoon of her reminiscences and complaints.

"If it wasn't the Sisters or my mother yelling at me it

was my father," Betty Marie had whined. "Before I went to school I used to play down at the playground. I made a new friend one day, named Wayne. He had a bike and let me ride it a lot. When it was time for lunch I invited him. I was always dragging kids home with me, my mother was used to it. We rode double all the way there and I was having the time of my life.

"My Dad was laid off at the time so he was home, eating. When I walked in that kitchen with Wayne — he acted crazy! 'Course I know why now. Didn't mean nothing to me then that Wayne was black. Dad bellowed for Wayne to get out of his house, then started hitting on me for bringing him home." She took a long draught from her glass.

"I mean I didn't know. Nobody ever explained it to me, what they were like. I didn't understand it was people like Wayne my father and his friends talked about so much. When Dad calmed down he explained to me how Wayne's father took his job because he worked cheaper. Said you didn't need as much money to live like those people did. And he told me there were other ways they could hurt us, asked me if Wayne touched me at all . . .."

Sally listened to Betty Marie drone on again today. "I'd rather be a queer than black any day," she was saying and Sally, feeling sick to hear her, wondered if she hated queers, too.

She had to say something. Maybe no one had ever tried to reason with her. "Black people don't get poor by choice you know," she started.

"Don't give me that bullshit about them being so down we have to make exceptions for them."

"That wasn't what —"

"Just call me Archie Bunker," Betty Marie said proudly.

How could you argue with someone like that?

Sally left Betty Marie to herself and watched out of the corner of her eye as various of the kids now and then talked to her. A few even seemed to agree with her. Sickened, Sally thought it was bad enough that Betty Marie was such a waste of a good lesbian, riddled with hate as she was. Still, she could accept her as long as she didn't hurt anyone else.

196

But she was beginning to wonder if she *was* hurting someone . . .

At the beginning of the next week, the heat relented a
bit. Everyone's mood was better, including Betty Marie's.
She didn't come by at all Wednesday, and Sally hoped *Cafe
Femmes'* turn to host her had ended sooner than she'd
anticipated. But it was strange — without Betty Marie's
obvious, even exaggerated prejudice around, the other kids
began to get a little out of hand.

"I don't care about Rosa coming in here," Gabby, a
regular, said on Wednesday night. "After all, she lives right
around the corner. And I think Dolores is real nice. I'm even
kind of tight with Almeda. But Sal, don't it kind of scare
you — a bunch of them moving in like that? I mean, they
have their own bars."

Sally argued with Gabby, and thought she'd brought
her around. Then she had to contend with everyone else's
comments. She couldn't ignore the situation anymore, but
as long as the Five didn't come in on weeknights, and Betty
Marie wasn't around, at least she didn't have to upset Liz
by talking to her about it.

By Thursday, though, both the heat and Betty Marie
were back. At lunch, Sally watched Betty Marie, to see how
she acted and to avert any confrontations. But she was only
one or two gin and tonics into the day, and did nothing more
than cast hateful glances when none of the Five were looking.

Sally could remember her words of another day.
Actually, it had been a night, during a bad snowstorm, when
almost no one had come into the bar. Betty Marie had started
on bombs and how sending men into outer space had upset
the weather, and before long she was fully launched into
blaming everything on blacks.

"Once I had a chance to run in a city race," Betty Marie
said. "I belonged to the Police Athletic League."

Sally looked at the small woman. She was light, and at
one time might well have been very swift and agile, but
certainly too small to have had much of a future running.

Betty Marie went on, "The PSAL was going to have this
field day and since I won so many races at school I figured I

197

had no problem. I didn't count on so many of your black friends being there. It would of been my big chance. I could be a real champion, maybe of the city, probably at least of Queens. But I forgot how fast the black girls ran. I mean, it isn't fair to let them run against white girls. It comes natural to them and we have to work real hard to beat them. I was knocked out in the first race. And if I couldn't beat them that day, I knew I'd never be able to — they were getting taller and taller and I was staying the same. It was the one damn thing I did good."

Sally thought Betty Marie might begin to cry just talking about it, but she ordered another gin and tonic and toasted her lost career. "Come on," Sally couldn't help saying, "aren't you making kind of a big thing of this?"

Betty Marie had perfected the evil eye, and Sally backed down; but not before deciding she could close early. No one else was going to come in with all that snow. The bitter, self-defeated woman at the bar had drained her drink and left mumbling that she knew when she wasn't wanted.

Today, too, Sally wished she could close early. Instead, she walked out to stand in the blazing heat, to burn off the despondent mood Betty Marie had put her in. Across the street, the workmen were red-faced with exertion and heat, slick with sweat.

"Wish I had your job today," called one to Sally.

She laughed, shading her eyes against the glare from the sky. "No you don't!" she shouted back, shaking her head. She turned and walked back inside, not wanting to get too friendly with them. It wouldn't do at all for them to get comfortable about coming into the bar now and then for a beer. Then she'd have another eviction problem.

Inside, Betty Marie was holding court at a window table with two kids who worked nights. Good, thought Sally. Their voices were low enough not to bother her. She lounged behind the bar, enjoying the chill of the drying sweat under her white shirt. After a while, she wiped down the bar, feeling the familiar rhythm of an afternoon at *Cafe Femmes*.

Friday was the same, unbearably hot, with the black dykes — only three that day — coming in at noon, Betty

Marie grumbling the rest of the day, the other kids eyeing the black women like their presence was some kind of threat.

Sally and Liz talked about it finally, and decided it would be best if Sally hung around Saturday night. What with the heat, the continued presence of the Five, and the growing hostility of the regulars as Betty Marie egged them on, anything could happen. Besides, Sally liked to stay nights once in a while both to enjoy the bar and to spend a little more time with Liz. Usually on those nights she would treat herself to dinner out.

That night she walked over to little Italy and her favorite restaurant, tiny and unimpressive except for the rich red sauce and perfectly cooked linguine. She wanted to ask where they got their delicate pastries, but at the last minute felt too shy. The girl who served her appeared to be the family's eldest daughter, and she, too, was shy. As usual, they smiled obliquely at one another when Sally left. On her way back to *Cafe Femmes*, Sally carried with her the acceptance behind the young girl's smile as well as a takeout order of linguine for Liz. Why couldn't life always be so good, she wondered. People always so nice. Sally was obviously queer, but the girl had treated her with respect. If Mae had walked in would she have been treated as well?

Despite her leisurely walk Sally was sweating when she returned to the bar. It was just one of those hot city nights when the day's air never left. It fit over the city and over *Cafe Femmes* as snugly as noon light.

Most of the kids had arrived early to enjoy the air conditioning, and it was noisy inside as well as cold. The juke-box was roaring, the two pinball machines clamoring. Betty Marie was talking with a group at the same table under the window.

It was pretty late when four of the Five, with their girlfriends and a couple of other friends, came in. Sally could tell from their partying mood, as well as their unsteadiness, that *Cafe Femmes* was not their first stop.

It had been easy to forget how hot it was outside until they opened the door. Their group was so big that what felt like a streetful of sticky, breezeless old air came in with them. Sally felt sweat on her upper lip and looked at Liz, wondering if it was from the brief heat or anxiety. They both looked over at Betty Marie who sat at the same table as she had all night, only now she was scowling bitterly toward the black dykes. She turned suddenly toward Sally and Liz as if to say, "I told you so. I told you they'd take over."

Ignoring Betty Marie, Sally helped Liz meet the haphazard and high-spirited orders. Sally found herself smiling and laughing again with Mae, glad the women didn't seem to have noticed the relative silence their entrance had produced in the bar. But then, she thought, maybe they were used to it.

It was the dance floor that proved to be the undoing of the evening. It was small, too small for even the regular crowd, some of whom would sit out a dance to make space for others. At one point a particularly fast song with complicated rhythms began to play, one the kids normally sat through. The black women cheered it and got up to dance.

The air conditioner noisily pushed icy air into the bar, the kids talked and laughed, admiring two of the dancers who were particularly good. The lights were dim, everyone was served for the moment, and Sally wiped the bar with her rag, enjoying the dancers, considering having an unheard of third glass of wine because things were going so well. But Liz leaned worriedly on her elbows across the bar.

Betty Marie never danced. Nor did she get up when the rest of the women at her table did. The same usually unpopular song played frenziedly on as the four whites pushed their way onto the dance floor, looking somehow menacing. They began to dance in a stiff and jerky way — obviously not for the fun of it. Sally looked at Liz and, almost unconsciously, began to roll up her sleeves. Gabby came to the bar and stood near Sally. Betty Marie watched the dancers, smiling.

On the dance floor, a white couple seemed to stumble in the path of a black couple, then apologized in an exaggerated way. It happened again. The black women began to frown. Mae looked toward Sally, saw she was watching, and went on dancing, but less eagerly.

The record stopped, but instead of returning to their tables, everyone on the floor stood her ground, obviously thinking that to yield it at this point would be some sort of defeat. When a slow song came on, Sally relaxed a little. Perhaps this would cool things down and the tension would pass. A story ran through Sally's thoughts as she watched the dancers for any sign of abuse, as she looked again at Betty Marie. Did any of these women remind Betty Marie of her 'lover' in prison? Is that why she was feeling particularly vindictive tonight?

"I'd never done time before," Betty Marie had told Sally, rambling through an afternoon; Sally couldn't remember what had started her on the subject. "I was in for passing bad checks one too many times and though I was new at this, I'd heard enough on the street to know I better watch my p's and q's around everybody, even the other prisoners.

"So what happens? What's the worst thing can happen to me inside? This *black* girl in for manslaughter and tough as nails, falls for me. Even the idea gave me the creeps. I was scared to death she'd kill me if I let on I didn't want her. So I played hard to get, flirted, pretended I wasn't out yet. All this time she's gentle as a lamb, patient as a saint with me. If she was white I bet I would of loved her, she was so good to me.

"So it went on like that for a while and pretty soon she's getting a little mad. But to tell you the truth, by that time I was enjoying it some. Knowing she liked me, knowing I wasn't going to give in to her, knowing how hard it was for her to be wanting me and not getting me.

"Then one day in the yard one of her friends comes up to me. 'Listen,' she says, 'you're really getting to her. I don't like to see her hurting like this.' 'What do you want from me?' I says. 'Don't lead her on. Leave her alone. If you don't want her let her down easy. Just stop torturing her.' 'Why, you got a soft spot?' 'Could be,' the girl says and I'm thinking this is getting more interesting all the time. Now there's two of them hung up because I won't give in and I won't let go. I pulled out my trump. 'If I tell her I don't want her, she might hurt me bad.' The black girl shakes her head. 'No way she'd hurt you or anybody she loves. She's in here for going after a guy who tried to rape her, not someone she ever cared about. Not only that, but nothing she could do to you would hurt you as much as what you're doing to her. And I can guarantee she won't touch you.' 'How?' 'Me and my friends, we'll watch out for you.' I thought about it, trying to figure which I'd enjoy more, leading my 'lover' down the garden path a while longer, or dropping her so hard she'd never forget it."

Sally's stomach churned to hear the cruelty in her voice. Betty Marie went on. "So I told her okay, thinking I was getting bored by the whole thing and might as well get out now when I had protection. The next day out in the yard, in front of all her friends, making sure they were there for me in case I needed them, I told her. And boy did I tell her. I didn't hold nothing back. I felt like I was telling off the little girls who beat on me and Wayne who got me in trouble, and all those runners. She went creeping away from me like I broke her in two.

"And then you know what her friends did? The ones who were supposed to be protecting me? They turned on me. Got me behind this wall and hit me over and over till I got sick to my stomach I was so hurt. Just turned on me, the bastards, when I trusted them."

In a way that was Sally's favorite story, because of the ending. All she had to do was remember, and it decreased her own desire to hit Betty Marie. She wondered again, as she watched her stare at the dance floor, what made Betty Marie tick. What kind of life she lived with all this hatred inside her, how she got so twisted.

The funny thing was, what happened next was really an accident. While they were dancing all jammed together, Mae's femme stepped on a white femme's toe. Both jumped as if a shot had rung out. Gabby moved to Sally's side.

Now, as well as a matter of territory, it was a personal matter of pride for the two butches, each of whom felt she must protect her girl. The white butch cursed the black femme's clumsiness, using a racial epithet. You could see Mae was in conflict. She knew, first of all, that by throwing the first punch she risked getting kicked out of the bar. After all, that would be the easiest way for Sally and Liz to react. And since her friends would back her up, none of them would be able to return either. On the other hand, if she did nothing, she would lose face with her girl and her friends and probably still get hassled out of the bar. It would just take longer. She had to decide quickly what mattered more to her, her black friends or some white women's hangout.

Mae started yelling. Betty Marie's cohorts were ready for her. The other whites weren't about to see their own pushed around; the other blacks felt the same.

While it was still in the stage of shouts, threats, and some shoving, Sally knew where to go. She ordered Betty Marie out of the bar.

Stumbling and laughing, knowing she'd win in the end by driving the blacks out, Betty Marie left.

This had the effect of distracting everyone from the fight so that when Sally politely asked the white dancers to follow their friend out, no one moved except Sally and the two couples. Without their leader to egg them on, they went willingly enough, stomping, threatening to meet the blacks outside, vowing never to return.

Things went back to normal. The Five, as if to prove their courage, danced. Mae nodded her thanks to Sally. The white kids went back to their conversations, but none of them got up to dance as long as the blacks were on the floor. Mae and her friends weren't comfortable either and got ready to leave. Sally followed them into the muggy still night, shaking hands with Mae on the way, telling her to come back another time, apologizing for what happened.

Outside there was no sign of the two white couples, but Betty Marie was leaning against a lamppost across the street, swaying and watching from under the electrified halo of her hair. In full view she taunted the black women as they made their subdued way past the hulking, sleeping warehouses, up the uneven pavement toward the subway. They saw her, heard her, ignored her — perhaps the most courageous thing they could do as they filed past her, hand in hand, stoic and silent as the night.

Betty Marie's cries echoed off the buildings and bounced back at her. Was she disappointed when they didn't beat her up? Were their blows the only way she could convince herself of her own worth? If they'd abused her she could feel wronged, deterred, kept from being all she could be. Ignoring her, whose fault was any of it but her own? What ending could she give this story to cast herself in a sorrowful light? Who would take pity on such a bully?

Sally was so sad when she locked the door behind the last of the women that she wanted nothing but to get out of there and go home.

"Come on, Liz, I'll clean up in the morning."

Liz stopped sweeping. She leaned on her broom, looking back at Sally.

"Come on," repeated Sally, switching off the air conditioner, turning off all the lights. The streetlight shone in the window. Liz stood under the shadow cast by the words:

C A F E
F E M M E S

Tears ran down the shadows on her face, glimmered behind her glasses.

"Someone like that," Liz said as Sally put her arms around her, "ruins everything."

"I know." The machine-cooled air had begun to seep out of the bar already. Sally felt like she was trapped in a warm ice box.

"She's so full of hatred. The same hatred that led half my family into the camps." Liz raised her voice, crying into the empty bar, "Why does she have to bring it here?"

"She knows we can't turn a dyke out into a world that hates her," Sally answered sorrowfully.

Liz lay her head on Sally's shoulder. "That's what paralyzed me," she explained with a sigh. "What if someone ordered me out? Where would I go? But then, will Mae and her friends ever come back?"

"I could think of better ways for them to spend their Saturday nights."

"Then I think we have to turn that monster out for good."

"You think that'll keep hate out of our little bar? Banishing her? It's in all of us."

"You're right, you're right. It wouldn't have happened if it was just Betty Marie." Liz held onto Sally. "What are we going to do?"

"Talk to the kids maybe, one by one. That's what Betty Marie was doing. If we really show them we like the black women to be here . . ."

Sally and Liz found they were smiling as they left the bar.

Thunder was rumbling in the distance when they emerged from the subway and they cheered quietly to hear it. Perhaps a summer storm was what they needed to break the heat wave. Even a little rain might help.

A few of the publications of
THE NAIAD PRESS, INC.
P.O. Box 10543 ● Tallahassee, Florida 32302
Phone (904) 539-9322
Mail orders welcome. Please include 15% postage.

CHERISHED LOVE by Evelyn Kennedy. 192 pp. Erotic
Lesbian love story.   ISBN 0-941483-08-8 $8.95

LAST SEPTEMBER by Helen R. Hull. 208 pp. Six stories & a
glorious novella.   ISBN 0-941483-09-6   8.95

THE SECRET IN THE BIRD by Camarin Grae. 312 pp. Striking,
psychological suspense novel.   ISBN 0-941483-05-3   8.95

TO THE LIGHTNING by Catherine Ennis. 208 pp. Romantic
Lesbian 'Robinson Crusoe' adventure.   ISBN 0-941483-06-1   8.95

THE OTHER SIDE OF VENUS by Shirley Verel. 224 pp.
Luminous, romantic love story.   ISBN 0-941483-07-X   8.95

DREAMS AND SWORDS by Katherine V. Forrest. 192 pp.
Romantic, erotic, imaginative stories. ISBN 0-941483-03-7   8.95

MEMORY BOARD by Jane Rule. 336 pp. Memorable novel
about an aging Lesbian couple.   ISBN 0-941483-02-9   8.95

THE ALWAYS ANONYMOUS BEAST by Lauren Wright
Douglas. 224 pp. A Caitlin Reese mystery. First in a series.
                                        ISBN 0-941483-04-5   8.95

SEARCHING FOR SPRING by Patricia A. Murphy. 224 pp.
Novel about the recovery of love.   ISBN 0-941483-00-2   8.95

DUSTY'S QUEEN OF HEARTS DINER by Lee Lynch. 240 pp.
Romantic blue-collar novel.   ISBN 0-941483-01-0   8.95

PARENTS MATTER by Ann Muller. 240 pp. Parents'
relationships with Lesbian daughters and gay sons.
                                        ISBN 0-930044-91-6   9.95

THE PEARLS by Shelley Smith. 176 pp. Passion and fun in
the Caribbean sun.   ISBN 0-930044-93-2   7.95

MAGDALENA by Sarah Aldridge. 352 pp. Epic Lesbian novel
set on three continents.   ISBN 0-930044-99-1   8.95

THE BLACK AND WHITE OF IT by Ann Allen Shockley.
144 pp. Short stories.   ISBN 0-930044-96-7   7.95

SAY JESUS AND COME TO ME by Ann Allen Shockley. 288
pp. Contemporary romance.   ISBN 0-930044-98-3   8.95

LOVING HER by Ann Allen Shockley. 192 pp. Romantic love
story.   ISBN 0-930044-97-5   7.95

MURDER AT THE NIGHTWOOD BAR by Katherine V. Forrest. 240 pp. A Kate Delafield mystery. Second in a series.
ISBN 0-930044-92-4   8.95

ZOE'S BOOK by Gail Pass. 224 pp. Passionate, obsessive love story.   ISBN 0-930044-95-9   7.95

WINGED DANCER by Camarin Grae. 228 pp. Erotic Lesbian adventure story.   ISBN 0-930044-88-6   8.95

PAZ by Camarin Grae. 336 pp. Romantic Lesbian adventurer with the power to change the world.   ISBN 0-930044-89-4   8.95

SOUL SNATCHER by Camarin Grae. 224 pp. A puzzle, an adventure, a mystery — Lesbian romance.   ISBN 0-930044-90-8   8.95

THE LOVE OF GOOD WOMEN by Isabel Miller. 224 pp. Long-awaited new novel by the author of the beloved *Patience and Sarah*.   ISBN 0-930044-81-9   8.95

THE HOUSE AT PELHAM FALLS by Brenda Weathers. 240 pp. Suspenseful Lesbian ghost story.   ISBN 0-930044-79-7   7.95

HOME IN YOUR HANDS by Lee Lynch. 240 pp. More stories from the author of *Old Dyke Tales*.   ISBN 0-930044-80-0   7.95

EACH HAND A MAP by Anita Skeen. 112 pp. Real-life poems that touch us all.   ISBN 0-930044-82-7   6.95

SURPLUS by Sylvia Stevenson. 342 pp. A classic early Lesbian novel.   ISBN 0-930044-78-9   6.95

PEMBROKE PARK by Michelle Martin. 256 pp. Derring-do and daring romance in Regency England.   ISBN 0-930044-77-0   7.95

THE LONG TRAIL by Penny Hayes. 248 pp. Vivid adventures of two women in love in the old west.   ISBN 0-930044-76-2   8.95

HORIZON OF THE HEART by Shelley Smith. 192 pp. Hot romance in summertime New England.   ISBN 0-930044-75-4   7.95

AN EMERGENCE OF GREEN by Katherine V. Forrest. 288 pp. Powerful novel of sexual discovery.   ISBN 0-930044-69-X   8.95

THE LESBIAN PERIODICALS INDEX edited by Claire Potter. 432 pp. Author & subject index.   ISBN 0-930044-74-6   29.95

DESERT OF THE HEART by Jane Rule. 224 pp. A classic; basis for the movie *Desert Hearts*.   ISBN 0-930044-73-8   7.95

SPRING FORWARD/FALL BACK by Sheila Ortiz Taylor. 288 pp. Literary novel of timeless love.   ISBN 0-930044-70-3   7.95

FOR KEEPS by Elisabeth Nonas. 144 pp. Contemporary novel about losing and finding love.   ISBN 0-930044-71-1   7.95

TORCHLIGHT TO VALHALLA by Gale Wilhelm. 128 pp. Classic novel by a great Lesbian writer.   ISBN 0-930044-68-1   7.95

LESBIAN NUNS: BREAKING SILENCE edited by Rosemary Curb and Nancy Manahan. 432 pp. Unprecedented autobiographies of religious life.   ISBN 0-930044-62-2   9.95

YANTRAS OF WOMANLOVE by Tee A. Corinne. 64 pp.
Photos by noted Lesbian photographer. ISBN 0-930044-30-4 6.95

MRS. PORTER'S LETTER by Vicki P. McConnell. 224 pp.
The first Nyla Wade mystery. ISBN 0-930044-29-0 7.95

TO THE CLEVELAND STATION by Carol Anne Douglas.
192 pp. Interracial Lesbian love story. ISBN 0-930044-27-4 6.95

THE NESTING PLACE by Sarah Aldridge. 224 pp. A
three-woman triangle—love conquers all! ISBN 0-930044-26-6 7.95

THIS IS NOT FOR YOU by Jane Rule. 284 pp. A letter to a
beloved is also an intricate novel. ISBN 0-930044-25-8 8.95

FAULTLINE by Sheila Ortiz Taylor. 140 pp. Warm, funny,
literate story of a startling family. ISBN 0-930044-24-X 6.95

THE LESBIAN IN LITERATURE by Barbara Grier. 3d ed.
Foreword by Maida Tilchen. 240 pp. Comprehensive bibliography.
Literary ratings; rare photos. ISBN 0-930044-23-1 7.95

ANNA'S COUNTRY by Elizabeth Lang. 208 pp. A woman
finds her Lesbian identity. ISBN 0-930044-19-3 6.95

PRISM by Valerie Taylor. 158 pp. A love affair between two
women in their sixties. ISBN 0-930044-18-5 6.95

BLACK LESBIANS: AN ANNOTATED BIBLIOGRAPHY
compiled by J. R. Roberts. Foreword by Barbara Smith. 112 pp.
Award-winning bibliography. ISBN 0-930044-21-5 5.95

THE MARQUISE AND THE NOVICE by Victoria Ramstetter.
108 pp. A Lesbian Gothic novel. ISBN 0-930044-16-9 4.95

OUTLANDER by Jane Rule. 207 pp. Short stories and essays
by one of our finest writers. ISBN 0-930044-17-7 6.95

SAPPHISTRY: THE BOOK OF LESBIAN SEXUALITY by
Pat Califia. 2d edition, revised. 195 pp. ISBN 0-9330044-47-9 7.95

ALL TRUE LOVERS by Sarah Aldridge. 292 pp. Romantic
novel set in the 1930s and 1940s. ISBN 0-930044-10-X 7.95

A WOMAN APPEARED TO ME by Renee Vivien. 65 pp. A
classic; translated by Jeannette H. Foster. ISBN 0-930044-06-1 5.00

CYTHEREA'S BREATH by Sarah Aldridge. 240 pp. Romantic
novel about women's entrance into medicine.
 ISBN 0-930044-02-9 6.95

TOTTIE by Sarah Aldridge. 181 pp. Lesbian romance in the
turmoil of the sixties. ISBN 0-930044-01-0 6.95

THE LATECOMER by Sarah Aldridge. 107 pp. A delicate love
story. ISBN 0-930044-00-2 5.00